CEMETERY OF DREAMS

CEMETERY OF DREAMS

A NOVEL

S. MOSTOFI

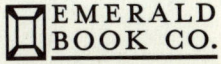
EMERALD BOOK CO.

This book is a work of fiction. Names, characters, businesses, organizations, places, events, and incidents are either a product of the author's imagination or are used fictitiously. Any resemblance to actual persons, living or dead, events, or locales is entirely coincidental.

Published by Emerald Book Company
Austin, TX
www.emeraldbookcompany.com

Copyright ©2011 Sasha Mostofi

All rights reserved.

No part of this book may be reproduced, stored in a retrieval system, or transmitted by any means, electronic, mechanical, photocopying, recording, or otherwise, without written permission from the publisher.

Distributed by Emerald Book Company

For ordering information or special discounts for bulk purchases, please contact Emerald Book Company at PO Box 91869, Austin, TX 78709, 512.891.6100.

Design and composition by Greenleaf Book Group LLC and Publications Development Company
Cover design by Greenleaf Book Group LLC and Cooley Design Lab

Publisher's Cataloging-In-Publication Data
(Prepared by The Donohue Group, Inc.)

Mostofi, S.
   Cemetery of dreams : a novel / S. Mostofi. -- 1st ed.
   p. ; cm.
   ISBN: 978-1-934572-51-1
   1. Extortion--Fiction. 2. Iran Hostage Crisis, 1979–1981--Fiction. 3. Iran--History--1979–1997--Fiction. 4. Americans--Iran--Fiction. 5. Man-woman relationships--Fiction. 6. Historical fiction. 7. War stories. I. Title.
PS3613.O786 C46 2010
813/.6   2010930287

Part of the Tree Neutral® program, which offsets the number of trees consumed in the production and printing of this book by taking proactive steps, such as planting trees in direct proportion to the number of trees used: www.treeneutral.com

Printed in the United States of America on acid-free paper

10 11 12 13 14 15   10 9 8 7 6 5 4 3 2 1

First Edition

To my parents &
To my husband James,
with all my love

PROLOGUE

"**KHODAYA. KHODAYA,**" **HAMID CALLED** out God's name and squeezed his eyes shut.

The door flung open and the prison guard, the one they called Haji, a broad shouldered man with no neck, who had repeatedly kicked him in his ribs and punched him in the face, stepped into his solitary cell. Hamid crawled back until he hit the wall and then he braced himself for the inevitable.

But the inevitable never came.

Haji threw him a warning glance and stepped to the side, showing a young man into his cell. The stranger was tall, in his late twenties, wearing a dark brown suit but no tie. This was the style of dress for government functionaries, a way to look formal while avoiding a symbol of westernization: the prohibited tie. It occurred to Hamid that Haji was worried that he'd say something to make himself look bad in front of this stranger. The thought that vicious Haji might be concerned about his reputation seemed so ridiculous to Hamid, that he chuckled like a mad man.

"General Rahimi?" the stranger asked.

"Yes?"

"Do you recognize me, General?"

He searched his mind frantically. After more than a month in this graveyard of a prison, this place called Evin, the Bastille of Iran in northern Tehran, you'd slowly forget your own name. "No."

"My name is Doctor Reza Ketabi. I'm a lawyer. We met at the Mayor's house a few months ago." Reza turned to Haji. "Please leave us alone."

"Should I bring you a chair, Doctor?" Haji smiled politely and Hamid cringed. He couldn't bear to look at Haji's insane calm smile. "This floor is filthy."

Reza looked at the floor, one hand in his jacket pocket. "If it's good enough for the general, it's good enough for me." He looked over his shoulder. "Now please go."

Haji threw a hostile glare at Hamid and walked out, locking them inside.

"Khatami's associate asked me to come here." Reza glanced around as if doubting his noble decision to refuse Haji's offer, because for once Haji was telling the truth. Hamid's new home was filthy and only had a stinky carpet on the corner of the cement floor, which Hamid was sitting on. He moved to the side, making room for Reza.

Reza nodded but then threw a quick uncomfortable glance at Hamid's feet. Hamid let him have a good long look. They were covered with blisters from the routine flogging. The pain would've been unbearable but all he could think of was the bone-chilling cold.

"You're cold?" Reza asked.

"It's damn freezing here."

Reza took off his jacket and put it around Hamid's shoulders.

"Thanks," Hamid said. Reza's jacket smelled of cologne and he breathed in the fresh scent, suddenly conscious of his own embarrassing appearance and body odor.

Reza rolled up the sleeves of his black shirt. "Now. Let's discuss the allegations against you."

"What's the point?" He chuckled. "They're hanging me the day after tomorrow."

"The reformists managed to make a deal with the judiciary today. If we provide proof within twenty-four hours, they'll delay your execution and reconsider the case."

Hamid didn't dare say a word because he was afraid he was dreaming. He took in a deep breath.

"This case is an excuse, of course." Reza finally sat cross-legged on the floor and opened his briefcase. "You're here because you told the press the Revolutionary Guard Corps is planning to establish a military dictatorship. And you've made a lot of enemies in the government by being an outspoken member of the reformist party. The conservatives needed an excuse to hang you and they found one."

"Murder." Hamid shrugged.

"Correct. But you have a lot going for you. Your record is spotless. You were a firm supporter of the revolution, one of the bravest commanders during the Iran-Iraq War, and a member of the Revolutionary Guard Corps for fifteen years." Reza put his wrists on his knees. "I've researched the case but there are some gaps that I'm hoping you can help me fill. I'd like to start from the beginning. What happened in April of 1980?"

"That was years ago. I don't remember."

Reza frowned. "Thirteen days ago you confessed to the murder of Commander Shirazi. Now you don't remember?"

"After weeks of torture, you'd confess to slaughtering your own mother. I said what they wanted me to say."

"General, he was your commander and you were with him that April. You were conducting an investigation into a coup by military officers who were working with the CIA to overthrow the republic. Your investigation reportedly led to the failure of the American hostage rescue mission, code name *Eagle Claw*. Isn't this true?"

"Yes."

"And when Commander Shirazi's body was found, in his uniform jacket pocket, they found identification papers belonging to a navy officer who we believe was involved in the rescue mission."

Hamid's ears perked up. He hadn't known this. "And?"

"Why did Commander Shirazi have Lieutenant Arman Pakran's information on him?"

Hamid felt danger closing in on him. It wasn't only his life at stake here and he had to be careful. He looked down at his cold white feet. How haggard he must look, his head shaved, his body emaciated and weak.

Reza leaned forward. "Is it true that your father worked for General Pakran and that the general was also murdered in April of 1980?"

Hamid didn't respond.

Reza shrugged. "It's your choice to tell me the truth. But we know General Pakran had a son, half American, raised in Iran to become an officer of the Shah's navy before moving to California in September 1977. His name was Arman Pakran." Reza lowered his voice. "He was a close friend of yours, wasn't he?"

Hamid pulled the jacket tighter, feeling colder than before. "My parents worked for the Pakrans. My mother was Arman's nanny. I left early on to attend the University of Tehran. I'm an old man now. It seems like centuries ago."

"Arman was somehow involved in the coup and in the American rescue mission." Reza held up the folder in his hand. "Our reports indicate that he was a CIA agent. So was his father, who helped overthrow Prime Minister Mossadegh in 1953. Not only that, but Arman disappeared on the eve of the American rescue attempt after Commander Shirazi's death."

He put the folder back on the floor and pulled out a paper. "The commander was reportedly respectable, straight and honest, a hard worker, a brave man. His death was a great loss to the revolution." He threw a quick glance behind him as if afraid someone might hear and then turned back to Hamid. "My theory is that Arman killed the commander but I have no proof of this. I need your help."

Hamid eyed him for a few long seconds. "You really think you can get me out of here?"

"If you tell me the truth, yes."

"Why should I trust you?"

"What have you got to lose?"

Reza had a point. Hamid took a deep breath; that flicker of hope, that scrappy part of him they'd trampled on but not crushed, urged him to make one more attempt. He pressed his lips firmly together, which must've looked like he was refusing to speak because Reza slammed the folder shut. "Why don't you trust me? I can save your life. I have a tremendous amount of respect for all you've done for this country. If you tell me the truth—"

"The truth will condemn me more."

"Leave that up to me." Reza scratched his upper lip. "Now, let's start from the beginning. My report indicates that in 1978 you were accepted to the University of Tehran and there you joined the revolutionaries."

"Your report is right."

"It was about that time that you got into a fight with Arman. What happened?"

"I didn't get into a fight with Arman. I had an argument with his father, General Pakran. But what has that got to do with anything?" Hamid's eyes rested on the bloodstained wall. Memories of last night's horror came back to him. Haji and the other guard, the deaf-mute man with a limp, had taken turns beating his head against that wall. But that had been better than what happened in the other cells to the young ones who got raped night after night. He would give anything to get out of this place.

"Tell me about Zia Mohseni."

"What about him?" He was aware that his voice trembled slightly.

"He was in the Shah's intelligence (SAVAK) before the revolution. Was he also a friend of Arman's?"

"Absolutely not." Hamid rubbed his bald head. "SAVAK was keeping an eye on Arman's family. It was because of some disagreement Arman's father had with the Shah. Zia was their enforcer. He was an awful human being. Not as horrifying as Haji, the guard here, and his buddies, but still pretty awful."

Reza chose not to acknowledge the last statement. He scribbled on his notepad. "What was Arman like?"

"Outgoing, pleasant, had this casual American thing about him that we all found appealing."

"He also spoke four languages. Seems like a great fit for the CIA." Reza's pen moved down the page. "Why did you hate the Pakrans so much?"

"Hate them?" Hamid looked up in surprise and then he laughed and was shocked by the sound of his own laughter. "Yes, maybe. Maybe I hated them because I owed them so much."

"Owed?"

"Yes owed, Doctor. I was raised in the general's house on equal terms with Arman. The general paid for my college expenses. Without him I wouldn't have been able to make it—"

"Then why the argument?" Reza asked.

Hamid sighed. The truth was that he had thought he didn't care anymore, that he had accepted his fate. But Reza had awakened a glimmer of hope in him and suddenly he could imagine walking freely outside. He cleared his throat. "Arman had left the navy and moved to California. He came home one spring and mentioned his feelings for a girl he wanted to marry. Melody Zandi. Her father had forced her to marry someone else, a richer man, from royal blood. I told him that with the revolution these sorts of class divisions would soon disappear. The general heard me and got furious. He called me an ignorant fool following a bunch of religious morons who fed us nonsense. He was so mad that he threw me off the estate." He hadn't spoken this much in days and it was gradually wearing him down. Besides every single part of his body hurt and he had a hard time focusing. "My parents heard everything and were naturally upset. They liked the Pakrans but also liked the new revolutionary movement, which promised them equality. So they packed and came with me to Tehran."

"What did Arman do?"

"Took his father's side." Hamid shrugged. "I didn't expect anything else."

"And then?"

"After the revolution, I heard from Arman again."

"How?" Reza asked.

"The general had high blood pressure. When the military surrendered, he had a heart attack. Arman came back and stayed with him until . . ."

"Until?" Reza leaned forward.

"This'll take awhile . . ."

"I have all night." Reza lowered his voice. "Please go on. Until when?"

"Until the night everything changed."

ONE

A HEAVY NORTHERN WIND shook the thick branches of the ancient maple trees and a sudden fierce rain drenched the scrambling pedestrians. Arman paid the driver and slammed the yellow taxicab door shut.

If he could go back home.

He'd never thought of America as home but now it was all he could think of; the way the Pacific Ocean sparkled on a sunny day when he ran barefoot on the beach in his shorts, his flat only a block away. Why had he refused to recognize this before? After all, his mother was American, though she'd chosen to live most of her life in this country, this world full of chaos and unpredictability. Why had she done it? A desire for the exotic to make up for the unbearable routine she'd experienced as a child in Idaho?

Arman pulled the woolen ski scarf tucked into his black winter coat up around his chin. In his left hand he held a folder containing pages of his father's medical report. With his right hand he held a newspaper over his head as shelter from the rain. He'd just left the hospital where his father had been recently admitted for another heart attack.

The dim streetlights guided him. He was glad the electricity was on tonight. Tehran had experienced a power outage every other night since the eve of the revolution, something that never happened in San Diego. What was he going to do about Julia, his girlfriend, probably his future wife? She'd followed him to Tehran despite his protests. She had claimed she wanted to see her father again—Frank Hutchinson, the Economic and Commercial Officer, third in command at the American embassy in Tehran—but he had known better. She'd come here because of him.

He should be flattered, but he wasn't. He was merely worried. Who would've known that three days after her arrival revolutionary students who called themselves the followers of Ayatollah Khomeini would occupy the American embassy in Tehran and take more than sixty American diplomats—including Frank—hostage? Who would've thought such a thing was possible in this modern day and age?

Despite the dim glow of the street lamps, he barely found his way home. Nowadays the streets of Tehran were not safe: if you had a nice car, or played loud music, or were obviously associated with the previous regime, the revolutionaries would stop you in the street, sometimes break your windshield, and harass you. It was much safer to walk.

He hurried into Babak Avenue, a dead end alley, and stopped at the second house to his right. He turned the key in the front entrance door and walked in. Before he could find the light switch in the hall, the living room light came on.

"Hello, Arman. It's been a long time."

Arman turned to face the voice. On the brown sofa sat a middle-aged white haired man with a scar on the right cheek of his clean-shaven face. He had crossed his legs and his left arm rested on the sofa.

SAVAK agent. Zia Mohseni.

"What are you doing here, Zia?" Arman asked.

"I want to talk to you."

Arman took off his gloves. "I sure as hell don't want to talk to you."

"Is this a way to treat an old friend?"

He shook his head. A friend? Had Zia forgotten the way he'd harassed Arman's family for the last five years? Had he seen Julia?

"How did you get in?" he asked, sounding calmer than he felt.

Zia caressed the edges of the sofa fabric with elegant fingers, almost as long as a pianist's, each nail carefully manicured. "One of the requirements of my old job, remember?"

The irony in his voice made Arman throw him a sharp glance. Did the man actually think it was a joke, the way he had treated innocent civilians while working for the Shah's Intelligence Agency? "They taught you to pick locks at the good old SAVAK? Nice. In case you've forgotten there's no SAVAK anymore. The Shah fled, the military surrendered, and your boss was shot. You're lucky to be alive—"

"Hey, calm down, Arman." He raised the hand resting on the back of the sofa. "Can we talk?"

Arman took off his wet coat and glanced in the mirror, his hair plastered to his head. "No."

"I'm here because I need your help."

"You need what? Pardon me while I finish laughing." Arman ran an impatient hand through his curly wet hair. "Now if you're done entertaining me, leave."

Arman didn't expect him to leave. Zia wouldn't be here unless he had some kind of leverage. So he poured himself a drink without offering Zia one. Tomorrow he'd change the locks. Thank God he had warned Julia to stay in the bedroom if she heard anything suspicious. She must be locked inside there now, curled up under the sheets covering her face like a child, the way she always did when she was scared. Because if she couldn't see anyone, then no one could see her.

"Hear me out, Arman," Zia said in his almost-feminine voice, like a boy going through puberty. "Things aren't looking good. The economy's collapsed. The regime has gotten off to a bad start, especially since the hostage negotiations are dragging on. We need America for trade purposes and they're upset. They're also furious about Russia's invasion of Afghanistan so close to the hostage crisis. Their National Security Advisor seems to think Iran may be—"

Arman leaned against the bar and sighed. "What is it you want, Zia?"

Zia observed him for a few long seconds and then leaned forward, resting his hand in front of him, as if Arman had been any nearer he would've patted him on the wrist. "You okay? How's your father?"

Before he could stop himself, Arman said, "He suffered another heart attack. One more and the doctors say he'll be gone, no thanks to you and your SAVAK friends and all those idiot advisors, not to mention the Shah himself who was nothing more than a coward."

He was bitter, and that surprised even him. For eight months he hadn't been able to return to his job in San Diego, for two months had considered himself unemployed, and in the last month hadn't had a good night's sleep. He was even more worried about Julia who since the hostage crisis couldn't leave the house comfortably during the day. They had an argument almost daily, which was unusual for them. They got along well in San Diego.

"The CIA contacted me a week ago, Arman."

Arman looked up as the words slowly sunk in. "What are you talking about?"

"They are frustrated with the hostage negotiations. They want to try a different route."

"What?"

"Military." Zia took a pack of cigarettes from his pocket, his slender finger pulling one out. "Not a full-scale war, but maybe a coup. They have information that there are a few hundred officers who'd be in favor of it. So, they're thinking of killing two birds with one stone."

"A coup and the hostages?"

"Exactly." He lit a cigarette.

"How do they think they can pull this off?"

"They're a superpower, Arman. They can pull off whatever they want."

"They can't pull off another Mossadegh. In 1953, the CIA wasn't alone. Eisenhower's administration had put aside one million dollars for the operation against Prime Minister Mossadegh and ended up using only seventy thousand of it to bring the Shah back. The people wanted the Shah back then. Now the people want the Ayatollah."

"America is very strong, Arman. They've got the weapons, the intelligence, and the special ops forces. They can do magic, and you just said yourself that you blame the revolution for what's happened to your father. Don't you want to do something about it?"

Arman sank into the brown leather chair by the fireplace, waving away Zia's cigarette smoke. "What do you want from me?"

"We need the assistance of at least three hundred officers loyal to the Shah to pull off a coup and the rescue mission. I need your help to gather those officers."

"You're kidding, right?"

"I'm very serious."

"Well, there aren't three hundred officers left to recruit." Arman took a deep breath and, suddenly realizing how tired he really was, stretched his legs in front of him. Seeing his father so ill drained his soul to the point that sometimes he wished he could fall asleep and never wake up again. He pushed the thought aside. "Besides all weapons were confiscated by the Islamic government."

"The U.S. Marines will bring weapons. That's easy."

"And how are the marines getting in?"

"Helicopters."

"Landing where?"

"The vicinity of Tabas."

Arman took a sip of his drink and frowned. "Why there?"

"I can't explain that right now. The important thing is I need help with a lot of things, and you're the best man for the job."

"Me? Why me?"

"You were one of the best navy officers." He leaned toward Arman, his wrists on his knees, cigarette in one hand, his eyebrows raised, like a friendly weasel. "You're a great shot, you have a lot of friends, you're fast, and I need things to happen fast."

"I left the navy long ago. Why not somebody else? One of the other officers?"

"You're the best."

"Don't flatter me, Zia." Arman gave out a short laugh. "If they're really planning on this crazy rescue mission, when are they going to do it?"

Zia leaned back. "April 24."

"That's in less than three weeks."

"I know. Like I said, I need things to happen fast."

"Your problem, not mine." Maybe if he was unyielding enough, Zia would give up. "Besides, I don't see how I can help."

"Oh believe me, Arman, you can."

"What's in it for you?"

Zia smiled. "The good of the country."

"Uh-huh. How much is the CIA paying you?"

Zia sighed. "They've promised to give me American citizenship if this works out."

"You're risking your life for a U.S. passport?"

Zia sucked on his cigarette and blew out the smoke. "I agree that awhile back it would've meant nothing. But now my wife and children are in the States illegally. An American passport means the world to me."

Arman knew there was money changing hands as well, but did it matter? His eyes were becoming heavy as he watched the firelight flicker across the scar on Zia's face.

"So, will you help me?" Zia asked.

"I still can't see how."

"I'll give you the details once you agree. But first I need you to talk to your officer friends. They won't trust me."

Arman chuckled. "No, really? Have you forgotten how you and your buddies scrutinized the military? The Shah was so paranoid he had to check his officers monthly to make sure they were on his side." He paused. "I shouldn't trust you either."

"I don't give a shit what you think, Arman." The old Zia was back. "This is about Iran, not you or me. I know you didn't like the SAVAK, but even you've got to admit it was nothing like this new regime. They're killing non-stop. Before you know it, it'll be you and me next."

"I wish you a painful death," Arman said in a voice hardly above a whisper.

"Listen to me. This regime will take Iran back hundreds of years. They're primitive. They're terrorists. If we don't stop this regime, it'll be the end of the Iranian civilization as we know it."

Arman had to recognize the truth in this. The executions, the mismanagement, the cutting of dialogue with the outside world, the closing down of airports were all indications of an irrational government. He hated Zia, he hated the SAVAK even more, but he loathed this new regime. At least he had this in common with Zia.

He sat upright in his seat and rubbed his eyes with his thumb and forefinger. "Why you? Why did the CIA contact you?"

"They tried to get a hold of Nasiri. As the head of SAVAK, he was well known by the CIA, since SAVAK was a product of CIA and Mossad's collaborative work. They trained the agents and—"

"I know the history."

"Anyway, the CIA realized Nasiri was shot a few days after the revolution, so they contacted me. They knew I was a close friend of Nasiri's. Did you hear how Nasiri died?" Zia's jagged lips pulled back into a smirk. "In the end he got so weak he caved in like a coward."

"Nice thing to say about your old boss."

Zia shrugged. "He deserved it. As soon as he took over the agency, he ordered his people to work with brutal force. If we didn't, we'd lose our jobs. We had no choice."

"If you're trying to excuse your behavior, don't bother." Arman pointed his finger at him. "I still remember how you beat our poor gardener to the point where he passed out because my father wasn't home and you thought he was planning a coup and our gardener was his right hand man." He shook his head.

"Those days are gone. We have to learn to forgive and forget."

"I don't," Arman said. "I'm not getting involved."

"Then you leave me no choice, Arman."

Arman saw the nasty look on Zia's face and knew disaster was heading his way. "What do you mean?"

"I mean that I asked you nicely and you didn't agree and I understand your preference."

"And . . . ?"

Zia crushed his cigarette in the ashtray on the side table. "Let's talk about your old man, Arman. I know that your father was one of the generals involved in the 1953 coup against Prime Minister Mossadegh. He had close contacts with the CIA and MI6. Sure, he fell out of the favor of the court after that but—"

"The old man has been out of it for years. He hasn't even gone to the palace or attended any court functions since the 1960s. He's a forgotten legend. Even this regime won't kill him for something that happened thirty years ago."

"Maybe, but there's something more. He was involved in the arrest of Safavi, the leader of Fadayan-e Islam. After they assassinated your father's close friend Prime Minister Razmara in the 50s, your father took revenge by personally hunting down Safavi and having him shot."

"Safavi was an insane fanatic." Arman was aware that his voice trembled slightly. "Besides, what has that got to do with now?"

"Did you know that Safavi's nephew, Mehdi, is one of the prominent members of the revolutionary council? A man like him would never forgive the murderer of his uncle. He's been on the lookout for the person responsible for his uncle's death for years and he's as insane as Safavi. I'm sure he wouldn't mind a tip from an old SAVAK agent."

Arman glared. "You son of a bitch!"

Zia pulled out his pistol. "I need your help for a noble cause, Arman. Your father was a respected man. You, as his son, have a lot of pull."

Arman threw a quick glance at the gun and focused on breathing evenly. "You're wrong. My father retired years back. I left the navy in '77. We've lost contact with our old colleagues."

"Officer Kami Brujerdi is a close friend of yours. So is Colonel Moradi. They were here just last week. They kept you company when your father was taken to the hospital. They've both got major connections."

Arman sighed. "If you know so much why don't you talk to them directly?"

"It won't do any good."

"Why? Don't you have any dirt on them?"

"That's right." Zia gave a little shrug. "I don't have access to that sort of information anymore. I did my research on your family in my SAVAK years. That's why I picked you."

"So I'm the easy target. Sorry. Even if you give me to the authorities, I won't agree to follow your little scheme and sure won't risk my friends' lives for it."

"Let's not get sentimental, Arman." Zia chuckled, placing his pistol on the side table. "After all, you can be a very calculating man. You were one of the best naval officers the military ever had, though rumor had it that you didn't like it too much. But when you set your mind on something, you got it done. That's what I need."

"No."

"What you don't get is that it's not your life that's in jeopardy; it's your father's. You wouldn't want the poor old man to be torn to pieces, would you? And I'm speaking literally. Mehdi and his buddies aren't the sympathetic type."

"You can't—"

"If you don't comply, a confidential report will be mailed anonymously to the revolutionary council, and within a few hours your father will be put out of his misery. In plain words, he won't be a lifeless vegetable anymore, he'll be a cold corpse. Though he will suffer some first."

Arman's eyes narrowed and his legs tensed.

"Don't bother to try," Zia said. "The report is in safe hands. It'll get mailed if I don't return within the hour."

Zia looked serious. Arman's father's distorted image appeared in front of him.

"Go on, Zia." He leaned back. "I'm listening."

★ ★ ★

Half an hour later, Arman was glaring at Zia. "And you think this will work?"

Zia stood at the bar, pouring himself a drink. "Why not?"

"For one thing, the landing spot they picked is dangerous. Yes Posht-e Badam is in the middle of nowhere, but it's subject to extreme weather conditions. During one of my desert trips I encountered one of the most ghastly storms I've ever seen. They're called *haboobs*."

"American choppers are powerful, Arman. Nothing will destroy them."

"You've never seen a *haboob*."

"I've never heard of a *haboob*. What is it, anyway?"

Arman sat with one leg swinging over the side of his seat, a drink in his right hand. The storm had intensified outside and rain beat against the large living room window. "In dictionary terms, *haboobs* are lens-shaped dust walls generated from the surface outflow portion of a mature thunderstorm cell. In real life, they last about three hours with an average velocity of about fifty kilometers per hour and dust rising up to a thousand meters. They're mostly found in the southern regions of North America and in Sudan, but I've seen them in Dasht-e Kavir. It's like a thick wall of dust coming at you. If you're caught in one, you won't make it."

Zia shrugged. "It has to be there."

"Why?"

"Did you ever hear of the Hoshmandi construction company in downtown Tehran?"

"I believe so. David Hoshmandi? An engineer? He was shot during the revolution in an accident of some sort."

"Not an accident, no. David was a CIA agent. The construction company was a front for a very sophisticated operation. The Shah and a few top generals were the only ones aware of it. David built a hidden runway in Dasht-e Kavir outside of Posht-e Badam. Another agent—apparently a double agent—learned about David and that's how David suffered his accident."

"And that's how the CIA knows about the runway."

"Correct." Zia sat down and sipped from a very large scotch. "It took David five years to construct that runway without being noticed by the authorities. He must've been unaware of these sandstorms, what did you call them, *haboobs*?"

"Why would the Shah want this runway anyway?"

"In case of an emergency."

Arman turned to face Zia and crossed his feet at the ankles. "What about the radar system the Shah purchased a few years back?"

"I don't think it's a big deal. I mean how advanced was it, anyway?"

"Advanced enough," Arman said. "The American government wanted to keep an eye on the Persian Gulf and the Gulf of Oman. The Shah extended it to the Strait of Hormuz and the Chahbahar port. I've been told that these radars are capable of recognizing a fishing boat pulling out of Dubai. The system also picks up radar communications in all wavelengths. Nothing can pass through this invisible electronic wall without waking up the entire country. So tell me, Zia, how do you get across the southern border without waking the entire Revolutionary Guard Corps?"

Zia finished his drink. "That's what I need you to find out, Arman." He stood and put his pistol in his pocket. "Don't bother seeing me out. This is a number where you can reach me." He handed Arman a note. "Call me every day by eight o'clock in the evening and don't even think of taking your old man out of the country. He's under close surveillance at the hospital. One wrong move and he's dead." He opened the door. "Anything else?"

"Yes."

"What?"

"Next time, knock."

Zia shrugged. "Talk to you tomorrow, Arman."

A moment later, he was gone.

★ ★ ★

In the bathroom, a handful of candles threw a dim romantic light on the bubbles in the tub. Julia closed her eyes, and tried to lose herself in the soft Spanish guitar music from the tape player on the sink. Arman walked in and pulled up a chair to the tub.

"Hello." She threw him her sexiest smile, then her eyes caught the two wine glasses in his hands. "What a lovely idea." He handed one to her. "Thank you, darling."

"Feeling better?" he asked.

"I'm still worried about Dad. I hope he's all right. Any news?"

"Nothing yet. Khomeini keeps playing his silly game."

"I wish there was something we could do."

Arman had not told her about the talk he'd had yesterday with the strange man who'd broken into the living room. He said she'd be safer if she didn't know anything and she trusted him. After all, it was his culture. Besides, all Americans were under suspicion, and if she were discovered she wouldn't be released until the end of the negotiations with the U.S. whenever that might be.

"What do they want from us, anyway?" she said. "I don't get it."

"It's a game. They say they want the States to return the Shah to Iran for trial, but I think they also want a formal apology from the U.S. for what they consider to be past exploitations."

"Carter should just send the army in and bring the Shah back."

"No, they're wise to negotiate. You saw the news, Julia. Any sort of rescue mission or military attack, and the students have threatened to kill the hostages. The U.S. needs to be careful."

"They're such peasants!" Julia slapped a hand to her mouth. "I'm sorry, Arman, I know they aren't typical Iranians. You have wonderful people, but these people are . . . terrorists."

"Don't you have a saying; one man's terrorist is another man's freedom fighter?"

"I guess that's true. But it doesn't justify what they did."

"No, nothing justifies it."

They were silent for a moment.

"How's your father? Any news?"

Arman shrugged. "He's still stable. His blood pressure is up a little. The doctors are what I think they call 'cautiously optimistic.'"

"I'm glad." She smiled. "I don't know why I always apologize to you when I get upset. Your mother was American." She laughed and brought the red wine to her lips, eyeing Arman flirtatiously over her glass. Then she sighed. "I wish we could go back. I wish we'd never come here."

"I know, Julia, I'm sorry. I wish there were something I could do. Maybe . . ."

"Maybe what?"

Arman put his wine glass on the table next to the bathtub. "Have you packed?"

"Not yet. No."

"You should. It's a two-hour drive from here to Karaj. Mrs. Karimi plans on you being there around nine."

"Who is this Mrs. Karimi anyway, some old lover of yours?"

"More like an old nursemaid, in the British sense. She'll take good care of you. Now, let's get going."

She stood and he wrapped her in a soft white towel and helped her onto the cream-colored stone floor. She looked in the large bathroom mirror and touched the tears gathering in her eyes. "I really miss Dad. It's all so terrible and I love you, and . . . do I really have to go?"

He turned her around to face him. "It's only for a short while."

"What's going on, Arman?" Tears rolled freely down her face now. "Ever since that guy visited yesterday you haven't been yourself. What's bothering you? Please, tell me."

He touched her on her shoulders, his fingers tense and rugged against her soft white skin. "You've got to listen to me. When I realized that he broke into the house with you here, you don't know how much it scared me."

She crossed her arms. "Why aren't you telling me everything? Who is he anyway?"

"He's a former SAVAK agent—"

"My God, not the one you told me about when we were back home? Who used to come by once a week and harass you?"

"That would be him."

"But I thought that was over." Her eyes opened wide. "You said that the Islamic regime would put an end to him. What does he want now?"

Since early that morning, he'd been trying to convince her to go to a safer place, even though she felt she should stay with him. Now maybe she could find out what was going on.

He sighed. "He's blackmailing me," Arman said softly.

She put a hand to her mouth. "Why? How?"

"He says that if I don't pay him he'll give information to the authorities that will put both my father's life and my life in danger. The last thing I need is for him to figure out that you're here. He'll use it as a weapon against me."

"Oh my God, Arman. I knew this would happen. That's what I was afraid of when you told me you were coming here, but you said it would be safe."

"I'm sorry, Julia." He couldn't look at her.

"No, no." Her voice became immediately soft. "I chose to come with you. I insisted, in fact. It's not your fault."

"I wish you'd stayed there."

"Well, I'm here now," she said. "We have to deal with it. Now what are we going to do?"

"I don't know. Until I figure something out I need to make sure you're safe."

"I'll do whatever you say, but please keep in touch. And promise me, you'll come and get me as soon as possible?"

He kissed her, holding her for a few long minutes. "I promise, Julia."

TWO

IT WAS A PLEASANT day after the intense storm of the past week. Spring had begun and the New Year promised to be prosperous for the revolutionaries. Hamid Rahimi breathed in the fresh air. He had risen rapidly through the Revolutionary Guard Corps hierarchy because of his intense involvement with the Islamic movement before and during the revolution. Lately he had been promoted to work as Lieutenant for Commander Shirazi of the Revolutionary Guard Corps, safeguarding the internal security of the country. It was a heady rise for a laborer's son from the Pakran estate.

He didn't think about the Pakran family much anymore. What was the point anyway? He had left on such bad terms that he was sure the general would never want to see him again. Last he'd heard the old man had suffered a heart attack. It was probably better that way. The older generation had to be replaced with new blood. Iran must learn to embrace its new identity, and that was hard to do when the old folks still hung on to the ancient monarchy. No, he had no interest in meeting the Pakrans again.

Besides he was very busy with his job.

He stepped out of the Revolutionary Guard Corps station and walked to the interrogation office conveniently located next to the notorious Qasr Prison. Since February 11 of the previous year, the executions had intensified, clearing away the remnant of the past regime—journalists, military officers and commanders, ordinary businessmen, writers, sport figures, and even moderate clergymen. It might seem cruel to some, but it was a necessary purge to make room for Iran's true future.

And now that what was left of the past regime had been dealt with, the government could concentrate on destroying the Mujahedin-e Khalgh, a Marxist Islamic movement formed in the 60s. Mujahedin-e Khalgh was one of the strongest and most violent movements against the regime. And since it contained a large number of revolutionary youth who had become disillusioned with the Ayatollah in the early days of the revolution, it was also one of the fastest growing. Therefore, the Revolutionary Guard Corps were given the mission of exterminating them immediately.

It had not proven to be easy.

The Mujahedin hid within the Caspian jungles, had stations in remote locations across Iran, and had already begun to find refuge in Iraq, receiving support from Saddam Hussein's government and funding, indirectly, from the United States. They were everywhere and yet difficult to spot.

Hamid ascended the steps leading to the interrogation office aware of the many agitated people waiting in front of the prison hoping to hear about their loved ones. Hamid also realized many were terrified of the interrogation office in this building and that was unfortunate. But it was an unavoidable by-product of the means they needed to use to get information out of their enemies.

Still, Hamid felt a chill pass through his body as he walked in.

There was no receptionist in the interrogation office—none of the hired receptionists had lasted more than two weeks here. He walked down a hallway crammed with boxes, papers, and books and peered into a small cramped corner office. A young slim man, dressed in black from head to toe, sat with a finger to his lips, staring at a pile of paper on his desk.

"Hi Jamshid," Hamid said.

Jamshid looked around, his dreamy eyes lit up, and he reached Hamid with two large steps. He grabbed his right hand in both of his as if they hadn't seen each other in years, though Hamid had been there only last week. Jamshid's hands were cold and then Hamid realized that the office, too, was extremely cold.

"My friend, Hamid." Jamshid shook his hand eagerly, his back slightly hunched. "It's so good to see you."

"Same here, Jamshid." Hamid pulled his hand loose.

"I have some tea brewing in the break room. Want some?"

"No, thanks," Hamid said. "Any news on the investigation?"

"Which one?"

"I spoke with Ali about it last week. We've been on the trail of a Mujahedin cell by the Turkish border."

Jamshid nodded and walked back to his desk. "He mentioned it. That's the base where they help refugees escape to Turkey, right? I hear that instead of asking for money they make the refugees join their movement."

"Quite an efficient way of gathering new members." Hamid chuckled. "We haven't had much luck finding their location. Ali thought Kia Vaziri might know."

Jamshid started to say something, then stopped, rocking back and forth slightly in a show of nonchalance.

Hamid frowned. "Everything all right?"

Jamshid didn't seem to hear him. Instead he looked up with a cheerful smile.

"Jamshid, if you know . . ."

"I don't know, Hamid. But between you and me, I don't think Kia Vaziri has anything to do with the Mujahedin. He's a businessman and he's paid his dues."

"Then why is Ali interrogating him?"

"Don't know." He shrugged and then sighed. "Well, maybe I do. You know his wife's story, right?"

Hamid knew some of the story. Ali had married Maryam who was from a "high class" family against her parent's wishes. Ali was considered a "low class"—that patronizing, dismissive term for a man who didn't come from the right side of town, never mind that Ali's father, a poor plumber, had died years ago, and his mother had raised him on her own. Caught up in the revolutionary movement, Maryam had eloped with Ali and was now pregnant with his child. As far as Hamid knew they had a good relationship and they were a good example of what the new Iran was all about.

"What has his wife got to do with this?"

"Maryam's last name is Vaziri."

It took a second for Hamid to see the connection, the news was so unexpected. "Kia Vaziri is her father?"

"He owned the Meli shoe store. He's rich and Ali hates him."

"I see."

"I've been talking to Ali, Hamid." He shook his head and for the first time Hamid saw the extreme anguish in his face. "Maybe you can mention it too. He's arrested her uncle also, Senator Zandi."

The name sparked a memory. Arman Pakran had been in love with a Melody Zandi. Hamid pushed the thought aside. "How's the senator doing?"

"Frankly . . . I wish they'd put him out of his misery. First they thought he was behind some sort of a coup. Now, Ali's just keeping him around. Last I heard, his crime was 'battle against Allah.'"

Hamid shifted uncomfortably from one foot to another. Even he knew "battle against Allah" wasn't an unusual crime to be leveled against officials of the past regime, whether they had worked for SAVAK, danced publicly on a stage, or ordered alcohol for a formal reception.

"I'll talk to Ali," he said.

He walked out and into a larger office at the other end of the hallway, which faced the front courtyard where crowds of people waited to receive news about their loved ones.

Ali Alizadeh sat with his back to the window. Unlike Jamshid, he had fierce aggressive eyes and he was tall for an Iranian and unusually handsome. Hamid had heard that Ali's great grandfather had been a Cossack. As Hamid walked into the office, Ali looked up with a pleasant smile, causing a chill to pass through Hamid's body. If there was one man known for his extreme measures against political prisoners, it was Ali Alizadeh.

"Good to see you, Hamid. Come on in. Take a seat." He gestured widely at the seat across from him, like a king welcoming one of his generals. "What's new?"

Hamid sat down on the leather chair, crossing his legs. "Have you learned anything about the Mujahedin station by the border?"

"Yes, in fact, Kia Vaziri finally cracked late yesterday and gave me a name, a General Jalili."

"General Jalili?" Hamid frowned. "The name sounds familiar."

"It would." Ali opened one of the drawers of his desk and took out a folder. "He's the one who gave us information on the last military coup. Take a look at his files. He must've been working with the Mujahedin, playing both sides for fools."

Hamid took the folder. "How did Vaziri know about this?"

"He said he heard something at a dinner party of a friend, probably the old senator. Doesn't want to admit it though, afraid to get his cousin in trouble. But I think he knows more."

"How can you be so sure Vaziri knows anything?" Hamid asked, browsing through the folder. "As far as we can tell he's just a businessman."

"He's not, I assure you." Ali locked his fingers together, leaning forward. "I know why you're concerned. Jamshid, right?" He lowered his voice. "I personally think Jamshid's getting soft. I've known him since we were kids. He's a great guy, wants to make sure we do everything right, by the book. You and I know it's not that easy."

"And your wife?" Hamid took a deep breath. "What does she think about all this?"

"She's all for it. She used to have a tough time at home. Vaziri did things to her . . . I don't even want to go there." He crossed his arms and leaned back. "She's known for a long time that he's been in the Mujahedin and communist circles."

Hamid stood up. "As long as you're sure he really is guilty."

"Trust me."

"All right then, I'll leave you to it. If you hear more, let me know."

"Sure will."

Feeling a little assured, Hamid peered inside Jamshid's office, but he wasn't there. Maybe the dark atmosphere of this office had finally gotten to Jamshid and, as Ali said, he was becoming soft in his duties before Allah. Maybe he would have a talk with him later. Ali could be a vicious bastard but he was first-rate at his trade.

★ ★ ★

Jamshid was in the break room pouring his tea, his back toward the door, when a voice said, "How's it going, Jamshid? Haven't seen you all morning."

Jamshid turned around as if bitten by a scorpion. It was Ali, looking open and friendly.

"Fine, thanks," he said.

"What's that small bruise on your forehead?"

He nervously smoothed out his hair. "Soccer. We got a little enthusiastic."

Ali, hands in his pockets, paced the floor. "You don't know how much I miss hanging out with you guys. It's a real hassle having a wife."

A real hassle? Maryam? What more could you ask for in a woman? She had class, beauty, intelligence. Jamshid shook his head. What had happened to Ali? They'd been friends since they were ten years old, played on the same soccer team. When they'd graduated from high school, Ali had entered law school and Jamshid joined the military under the command of Colonel Moradi. After the revolution they'd both become involved in the Revolutionary Guard Corps and then joined the interrogation team where Ali had become an interrogator and Jamshid his assistant. But sometimes, now looking at Ali, Jamshid wondered if he'd ever really known him.

"You can bring Maryam along, if you like," Jamshid said.

"Maryam doesn't like going out."

Jamshid knew that was a lie. Maryam had always been an outgoing girl. Not knowing what else to say, he said, "Tea?"

"No, thanks. I just came here to tell you I'm not mistreating Vaziri. It's just that Maryam has told me some things that make me pretty sure he's involved in the Mujahedin movement. We need to protect the regime, Jamshid." He shrugged. "That's all."

"I hope you're right, Ali." He took a sip of the tea. It tasted bitter and strong though he had added two cubes of sugar to it. "I . . . I just have a bad feeling about it. He looks terrible and the interrogation isn't going anywhere."

"Do you think I enjoy this? For God's sake I care about Maryam and this is her father we're talking about. But I'll do anything to make sure what we fought for is secure. Is he here now?"

"You said you wanted him, so they went and got him from his cell. He's waiting for you in the red room." The name of that room made him nauseous so he grabbed the bowl of sugar cubes and turned his back on Ali and walked out.

Ali called after him, "Why don't you come by for tea tomorrow, Jamshid? Maryam would love to see you again."

Jamshid did not respond but from the corner of his eyes saw Ali turn, shrug, and walk away. He shook his head and walked into his office.

★ ★ ★

Kia Vaziri shifted slightly and moaned. He suspected a few of his ribs were broken and one eye was almost blind. He hadn't eaten for forty-eight hours. At times, a glass of water was shoved through a hatch at the base of his prison cell door. His head throbbed as he looked at the red walls. He realized then that his interrogators would soon show up to beat another confession out of him. He tried to gather all his strength, but he had very little left. It had been eight months since he was taken from his home in the middle of the night on charges of "battle against Allah!" Since then he had waited for death but had only received torture, beatings, and humiliation.

He rubbed his fingers together. They were numb. Many parts of his body were without sensation, half of his face blue from severe beating. Worst of all had been the cries in the middle of the night, the cell next to him belonging to an old parliamentarian, an eighty-two-year-old with pneumonia. They had thrown cold water on him every night and he had screamed until he died.

Vaziri's eyes rested on the ceiling. With his one good eye he thought he saw a cockroach crawling in a corner. He concentrated on the movement of the insect to forget his current situation.

He'd been a successful businessman. He had come up with the idea of creating an Iranian factory for practical shoes that were affordable for the average citizen. His company had grown and branches had opened up in all parts of the country, even in little rural backwaters. His shoe factory had competed with foreign companies on price and quality. It had all been great, until he was arrested. Except for having a cousin in the Senate, Vaziri had nothing to do with politics. He had tried to explain that he didn't have any idea what they were talking about, but what was the use? None of this was about politics.

The door opened and Ali stepped in. He looked at his son-in-law. How could a man with a face like an angel be this lethal? Ali put his left foot on the table and leaned over his knee. "So, are we going to talk today, father?"

"I'm no father of yours, and I have nothing to tell you," Vaziri replied in a hoarse voice. "How's my daughter?"

"She's glad to hear of your punishment. Meanwhile she enjoys me lying on top of her and doing things to her you couldn't imagine."

Vaziri sprang forward. "You low-class scum!"

Ali planted his fist in Vaziri's face. Vaziri fell to the ground, his nose bleeding.

Ali stood over him. "Listen to me, you old piece of shit. You keep on calling me low class and by the time I'm done with you, you'll be wishing you were dead!"

★ ★ ★

Hamid found Commander Shirazi looking out of his office window. Commander Shirazi was a short middle-aged man, bald, with a full-grown beard—Hamid was of the opinion that Commander Shirazi hadn't shaved his beard for years. He had worked with the revolutionaries both inside and outside of Iran to help overthrow the Shah's government. Upon the formation of the Islamic regime, he was given a commanding position in the Revolutionary Guard Corps and his superiors were pleased that he worked with the same zealousness to safeguard the regime as he had to overthrow the Shah.

"Hamid," he asked without turning around. "Any news?"

Hamid told him what Ali had learned from Vaziri.

"Good. At least that's something. I'm glad that Ali's in charge of this. He's been good at getting information out of our political prisoners. Like last year he knew about the Mujahedin attack to Ayatollah Khomeini's residence a week before it happened and we took care of it."

"Yes, sir, he does well. But there seems to be a little concern about the way he treats his prisoners. He seems very brutal."

"He gets the information we require. The rest is between him and Allah. Now, tell me, what do you know about this General Jalili?"

"I did a little investigation before coming here." Hamid placed a brown folder on Commander Shirazi's desk. "General Jalili is from Rasht, near the Caspian. He became a general under the Shah in 1968. Two years later the Fadayan-e Islam recruited him, but since the revolution he's held a low profile. He's still somewhere in the city, but it seems he's deliberately pulling himself away from the regime. It's happened before. Sometimes they do it because they don't want family and friends to know that they've been traitors for years. Other times it's because they've changed their minds and joined another political group, which seems to be the possible scenario here."

"It may be then that the information is correct and General Jalili has turned mujahid. I guess we won't know unless we visit him."

"He's out of town currently, sir, in Germany. He's due back day after tomorrow."

"Put it on the schedule, Hamid. I'm coming in on this one with you."

"Yes, sir."

★ ★ ★

Arman poured two glasses of Remy Martin. "So what do you think, Kami?" he asked. He had returned late from a run in the park to find his friend at the door, waiting for him. They had now finished discussing the hostage rescue mission.

Officer Kami Brujerdi wore blue jeans and a black sweater. He was a pleasant looking young man with lively brown eyes and a large smile hidden behind a well-groomed mustache. "It's a bit crazy, but it's not impossible. The question is: how much can we trust Zia? Do you think he's telling the truth?"

Arman handed him a snifter and sat across from him. "I wouldn't bet my life on it. What bothers me most is that he said the CIA came looking for Nasiri and then, realizing he's dead, contacted Zia instead."

"Why would that bother you?" Kami asked.

"Because he said the CIA knew how close he and Nasiri were. They weren't. Nasiri couldn't stand Zia. In fact I even know that Nasiri tried to fire Zia once but couldn't."

"Do you think Nasiri himself worked for the CIA?"

Arman shrugged. "SAVAK was a creation of the CIA and Mossad. They had trained agents in the SAVAK." He sipped his drink and frowned. "I'd bet that Zia's the real agent, not Nasiri."

"Good old vicious Zia, a noble CIA agent?" Kami chuckled, leaning over to pick a few pistachios from the wooden bowl on the glass table. "For a country that pushes democratic human rights values, they have curious friends."

Arman licked his lips, deep in thought. Finally, he looked up. "Does it matter who the agent was originally? Zia says the CIA and U.S. government will assist with a coup, and I believe it. I mean the U.S. isn't happy about the screw up in Iran."

"And it *was* a screw up. Did you hear about Sullivan's interview?"

"No?"

"He said he was surprised when he was appointed as American Ambassador to Iran because his specialty was the Far East. He seemed to have very little understanding of Iran, which is why he was backing the revolutionaries." He chuckled. "He actually thought Khomeini was a Gandhi-like figure."

Arman laughed and shook his head, but he wanted to get back to the subject. "So what's your take on this?"

"Well, I don't trust Zia. For one thing, I don't even like the guy. I'd make contact with the CIA myself, but my contact is currently held hostage in the American embassy. Colonel Moradi may have some contacts. We can check with him. Otherwise all our communication with the West is severed and with all these killings going on, trusting Zia . . . " He shook his head. "Just the sound of the words sends chills up my spine."

Arman nodded and threw a few pistachio shells into the fireplace, listening to their crackling, enjoying the scent that immediately filled his nostrils, reminding him of the nights he and Hamid had camped in the desert. He shook aside the memory and leaned forward to place his glass on the table. "Do you remember the construction company called Hoshmandi?"

"Yes, why?"

"Zia mentioned that the owner used to be a CIA agent. I believe David Hoshmandi was shot around the time of the revolution."

"I knew David. Pleasant guy. Shocks me to hear he was with the CIA, though . . . come to think of it, he was raised in Florida for a good portion of his life. His father was half American and worked for the U.S. government."

"I'm just thinking, if David was shot by one of the officers we know, we should be careful. There are a lot of things going on here I'm not sure about. If there is a traitor among us, we'd better know about it in advance."

"I'll ask around and let you know if I find out anything."

"I appreciate it. So, do you think, even if you want to do this, you could recruit three hundred officers?"

"More like five actually."

Arman's eyes opened wide. "Five *hundred?*"

"Maybe more. Once I make contact with the military leads, they'll gather their teams. They've been waiting for this for some time now. I know one of the teams made contact with the White House, but they hadn't received any sort of confirmation . . . until now."

"Then that's what Zia was talking about. He said the White House had been contacted by officers here and, because of their frustration with the hostage negotiations, have now agreed to this rescue mission."

"Well, as long as they bring the weapons and equipment, we can take care of the rest. I wonder though how much we can trust the American government?"

"Why do you say that?"

Kami finished his drink. "Well, they didn't exactly come through when the country hit a crisis situation early last year. They kept pushing human rights and forced the Shah to leave Iran, and that was fine. But when they realized they couldn't even hold a decent conversation with the Ayatollah, they started to panic. Now they may have come to their senses, but I sure don't want another Bay of Pigs happening here. I don't intend to get my men massacred because the American politicians decide, at the last minute, that this isn't what they want after all."

Arman sipped his cognac. Kami had a point. The American government had a bad reputation, not only among fanatical revolutionaries, but also among their friends whom they had forsaken. Both domestic and foreign media had exaggerated the Shah's flaws and had turned the Ayatollah into a symbol of holiness. Even most Americans had begun to fall for the Ayatollah's charisma, which they called democracy at the beginning. Then they'd hit his wall of insanity during and after the November 4 hostage crisis.

"What's your decision then?"

Kami sighed, uncrossed his legs, and put his glass on the table. "I'm not sure about this. It has promise, but there are too many things I'm concerned about. It's not just my life at stake here." He pushed up his sweater's sleeves. "There are other ways of doing this if the American administration really wants to help. For one thing they can pass on weapons to us at the border, so we can pull off the coup and then release their hostages. The officers who requested the CIA's help mentioned this. I guess Carter decided differently. This rescue mission . . . doesn't sound right."

Arman leaned back. "Do you want the Shah back, Kami?"

"Of course. Don't you?"

"Honestly, no, and that's part of my problem with this, and one reason I didn't want to work with Zia. To me, Zia is one of the symbols of the corruption within the Shah's regime. He's everything I detested in that government and the very reason our people rose to overthrow the monarchy. In some ways I'm on the people's side."

"But?"

"The people overthrew the Shah and replaced him with a bunch of criminals. I think there are those in the government who are trying to make things better, but they're slowly giving up hope and that's the tragedy." Arman sighed. "Maybe someday it'll change from within. In my dream, someday we'll have free elections, hard working competent people rising through ranks, working to make it better for everyone. But now, every day, we hear of intelligent competent people resigning. That's what's wrong."

"I'm not with you."

"What I'm trying to say is, I don't want the Shah back and I don't want this regime, which makes my choices rather limited."

"I never thought of you as an idealist."

"Of course I am. So are you. I've always wanted Iran to be something it probably can't be for quite some time. Like all Iranians I want us to succeed, because we have it in us, but somehow . . ." His face flushed. "I hate watching innocent people executed, and I hate to see how a country as rich as ours falls into recession because of mismanagement. I hate what Iran has become and I feel I need to do something about it."

Kami stared at him for some time. "Though I know your old man is in pain and can't be moved and the bastard is blackmailing you, I think you're actually hoping that this coup will work."

To his own surprise, Arman laughed. "I guess you know me well. Yes, I want the coup to work, but I don't want the Shah back. I want a government where people can vote for their representatives. Do you think we can do this?"

"Maybe. We have a strong plan and if I agree to go along with this rescue mission and it's successful, I want that plan to be put into place."

"What's the plan?"

"We'll take over the government and the top three generals will temporarily rule until a new government is formed. There have been debates between officers about the Shah returning, but frankly he's sick and the thoughts are that he won't last long even if he does come back. This time, we'll have people vote for their leaders."

"In that case I'd be all for it."

"So what you're telling me, Arman, is that you're just like your father."

"What do you mean?"

"You love Iran too much." Kami stood and walked to the door.

"And you don't?"

Kami picked up his jacket. "No, I hate her."

"What in the world for?"

"Because lately she hasn't once loved me back."

Arman didn't say anything as he watched Kami button up his jacket.

"Let me think about it."

"There isn't much time, Kami."

"I'll get back to you soon, Arman. Goodbye."

★ ★ ★

Kami walked into Zafar Street. He breathed in the fresh air of the chilled starry night, a northern breeze from the Alborz Mountains descending on the town. A small flashlight in his hand guided him down the street, and he passed two pedestrians coming from the opposite direction. They nodded in greeting, but their eyes observed him cautiously. Everyone was suspicious. It was the mood of the city.

He then looked down one of the dead-end alleys and saw something that made him hesitate. A small crowd gathered in the distance, oil lamps and flashlights in hand. He heard a woman sobbing.

Kami automatically turned down the alley, walking toward her, to see how he could help. As he got closer and could see clearer, he paused. At the door of an apartment building, a knot of young people gathered, divided into two groups. One group wore red headbands, long beards, dark clothes, and slippers, and were holding flashlights—local revolutionaries, or Hezbollahies, as the citizens had begun to call them. The other was a bunch of young men in their midtwenties standing by an older couple, one of whom was the woman Kami had heard crying. In the light, Kami recognized a few of the young men and his heart skipped a beat. The young men had once been soldiers under his command and he knew them quite well.

"We won't let you take them, Mashallah," the old man said. "You know they're innocent. You're only doing this because you've been jealous of us—"

"Get out of the way." Mashallah, the middle-aged fat man with a beard, spoke from the crowd of neighborhood Hezbollahies. "They made a living serving the *moftkhor* Shah—"

"We left the military two months before the revolution," one of the soldiers cried. "It's not true that we served until the end. Even if we did, it was our choice."

Kami stood in the shadows of the maple trees, watching. Under the light, he recognized the soldier who had spoken. He had been under his command for a year and had been very good indeed.

"You shouldn't have been working for him in the first place. You're all evil!"

"You're a liar, Mashallah," the woman said. "This is just an excuse to do what you've wanted to do to my sons for a long time. Leave them alone."

"The pasdars are coming, Khanum. They'll take your sons by force, if they have to. No more useless trash, showing off to us in the—"

"You're the only trash around here. We all know that."

More people came out of their homes and took sides. A few rushed back and locked the doors. Two young girls watched quietly from a rooftop.

"What have you told the pasdars, Mashallah?" the woman wailed, her white veil falling back, showing gray hair. "What lies have you weaved—"

"Shut up, Khanum. It's Allah's will to get rid of all heretics."

"But what's their crime, Mashallah?"

"Battle against Allah!"

"You're a bad man, Mashallah. You've never made good on anything. Countless times you came here to borrow money and countless times my husband helped you. And now, this is how you repay us. This has nothing to do with Allah. May He not forgive you!"

One of the young soldiers bent toward his father who leaned against the wall, breathing heavily, a hand to his heart. "Let it be over with, Baba joon. It's been weeks now. I can't take it anymore and this isn't right for you or Maman."

"No." His friend put a hand on his shoulder. "First it's you and then the rest of us. These jerks won't give up until they kill us all one by one."

Another pulled out a knife from his pocket. "Let's see what you're made of."

Mashallah took a step back but one of his younger Hezbollahi buddies stepped forward. "Let's do it," he said.

The street fight began. The old man pulled his wife to him while he held up the oil lamp to watch the violent combat. The two brothers, their three friends, and a neighbor who ran to join them, fought the larger crowd, knowing that their chances were slim.

A Hezbollahi grabbed one of the soldiers from behind and pushed him to the ground. He sat on his back, took the soldier's neck, and pulled out his pocketknife.

Kami stepped out of the shadow and snatched the Hezbollahi's hand, pulling it back. The Hezbollahi struggled.

Kami gave a sudden tug and a twist and heard the bone crack. The Hezbollahi screamed.

Suddenly, Kami heard the alarm of jeeps belonging to the revolutionary guards. Two jeeps stopped and eight pasdars climbed out. Kami pulled the unconscious soldier into the shadows and waited. He knew that unless the soldiers were armed, they couldn't fight the pasdars, who not only outnumbered them but were also well equipped with AK-47s.

One of the young soldiers turned around and in his frenzy ran into the shadows and bumped into Kami. Kami recognized him. "Sergeant Abbasi?"

Abbasi glanced quickly over him. "It's a beautiful night to walk, isn't it Lieutenant?"

Kami looked at him in confusion. Over his shoulder, he saw a pasdar pull the youngest son by his shirt to the car. The young man struggled but the pasdar pushed him with the butt of his rifle into the backseat of the jeep. Another pasdar jumped into the front, turned around, and pointed his rifle at his face.

Another soldier was seized, a gun pointed to his head, while he kneeled on the asphalt, his arms wide open, his shirt torn in the back.

"See what you and your bosses did to us, Lieutenant?" Abbasi said.

"I—"

"We'd sworn to serve this country. We'd been trained by the best to defend our nation to the death. Then you all abandoned us. Why didn't you kill these crooks when you had the chance?"

Abbasi didn't wait for an answer. He turned and rushed back into the crowd.

Laughing loudly, Mashallah threw the pleading woman to the side. He had taken his sick revenge with the help of a government that now sponsored his vices. A pasdar was beating one of the young men in the face with his rifle.

Abbasi grabbed the pasdar's rifle from behind and hit him hard in the center of his spine. The pasdar moaned, and dropped to the ground. Another pasdar by the jeep pulled up his rifle and aimed.

The first bullet hit Abbasi in the heart. The next one, square between the eyes.

Kami brought up his pistol and aimed, but before he could fire, the pasdar jumped in his jeep and slammed the door shut. Kami knelt by Abbasi.

The world seemed to vanish before his eyes as voices of regret and fury filled his mind. Around him bodies fell, while the jeeps took off with the two soldiers. The local Hezbollahies disappeared into the darkness.

Kami hardly noticed. He shivered as his body became covered with the young soldier's blood.

★ ★ ★

Arman sat in the library, on a Louis Quinze settee on an Isfahan rug, staring out the French windows overlooking the backyard. He had showered and changed into jeans and a white tee shirt. On the Biedermeier table next to his chair sat the glass of schnapps he'd emptied three times over. The half-full bottle sat next to his pistol. Alcohol seemed to be the only thing that eased his mind. He had just spoken with Julia—well, at least tried to speak. She had been hysterical, crying, and wanting to see him soon.

He threw another handful of shells into the fireplace, drowning in the tide of memories—the exotic scent of burning pistachios brought her back. *Melody.* The only woman that—and he could barely admit this to himself after three glasses of hard liquor—he had ever truly loved. She had been the one person allowed to join them on their desert trips and she hadn't changed their routine, but become a part of it. Wrapped in a warm blanket, in the healing vast dry wilderness, the light of the fire illuminating her fine profile, she had transitioned naturally from artlessness to unpretentious sophistication when reciting words of poetry to them in French. Looking back, it would've been impossible not to fall in love with her.

He cringed with guilt and turned a page of the book he was trying unsuccessfully to read when the phone rang.

"Pakran residence," he said.

"And how are you today, my friend?"

"We already talked, Zia. What do you want?"

He heard a chuckle on the line. "I wanted to see how your little chat went with your buddy."

"None of your business."

"Oh, but it is, and you know that."

"I'll call you tomorrow." He did not want to explain it on his home line.

"Just tell me the outcome."

"I don't know yet. He's thinking about it."

"There isn't much time to think. Let me know when you know."

"Fine. Anything else?"

"I left a gift for you outside the door. I hope you like it. Goodnight."

The line went dead. Arman walked to the door and opened it. There was a small envelope stuffed under the doormat. He picked it up, walked back in, and closed the door. While he was opening the envelope the phone rang again. He walked into the library and picked it up.

"Hello, Arman."

"Kami?"

"Yes."

Arman frowned. "Your voice is shaking. Are you all right?"

"I just saw something on my way home that made up my mind for me."

"What did you see?"

"It's too long to explain. I'll tell you tomorrow. Meanwhile, I called to tell you I'm in. Your plan might not be perfect. There would've been other ways to make this work, but they won't agree. They don't see it the way we do. Anyway, I'm afraid, real afraid. It might all go wrong but I want to try and make this right."

"You sure?"

"It's time to get rid of these crooks, Arman. It's past time."

"Yes. Yes, it is."

"I'll call you tomorrow."

"Take care, Kami."

He hung up. What had made such a drastic impact on Kami? He opened the envelope and found a picture of the front gate of the American embassy. A note on the back said, "Where? How many?"

Arman threw the picture on the table. Zia was trying to tell him that the CIA was asking for the exact location of the hostages and the information on the guards protecting the area. Damn him! Couldn't he do anything himself?

THREE

THE HOUSE WAS DARK. A cold wind through a broken window blew the torn gray curtains aside, allowing the full moon to shine on the remnants of tragedy. The furniture of the once grand living room had disappeared except for a stained couch and a green marble table carelessly pushed against the hall wall. Bricks, rocks, and gravel were piled in the stone-carved fireplace. The beam of her flashlight wandered over the cream-colored walls, now covered with spiteful slogans against the household. Someone had printed his name in huge letters on the middle of the living room wall and dated it—February 11, 1979.

Hezbollah has been here.

Melody tripped over the three steps connecting the long hallway to the large cold living room but caught herself.

"Hello!"

Her voice echoed through the vacant house.

She spun around, pointing her flashlight at the entrance door at the end of the dark hallway. "Is anybody here?"

Silence.

She stood numb, her flashlight to her side, a knife in her other hand, her ears straining. Were they still here? Hiding? Waiting to ambush her? For five minutes she stood there, frozen.

Let them come. At least it would be over.

For months she had lived in agony with her mother in an old cottage close to Saveh. In that desert climate, they had waited patiently for news about her father. Senator Zandi had been yanked from his home the day before they were to fly to the States. That had been eight months ago, and they had not had news from him until a few days ago. Her mother had insisted they move to their old farmland in case the pasdars came after them as well—their passports were confiscated and they were not allowed to leave the country. They had finally received news about her father on April 8. He had stood in front of the firing squad on April 6, almost blind and certainly mad. But that had not been enough. Upon hearing the news, her devoted mother had suffered a heart attack and died on the spot.

She shivered as she looked around.

Silence—bleak solitary silence that had been her only companion for the last few days.

She turned around, her flashlight pointing aimlessly at the floor. Her eyes were adjusting to the darkness. She walked to the shattered window to look outside. In the glow of the dim streetlight she could see the garden pool with its once blue water, now green, empty coke bottles and newspapers bobbing on its surface. The pool chairs were stolen, except one, which was cut to ribbons. The teak lawn furniture had been used for a patio fire, two table legs still lying near the pile of ashes.

Melody turned around and walked up the stairs, which circled the remains of a Baccarat crystal chandelier, hanging loose and broken from the ceiling. She nudged open the master bedroom door with her foot. Her flashlight beam fell on the torn curtains, swaying in the wind. The beds were slept in, the sheets rumpled. The smell of rotten fruit filled her nostrils. A bunch of grapefruit, apples, some rice, and meat were thrown casually into a corner on the marble floors and now were covered with cockroaches and ants. She stepped into the bathroom. A strong scent of human urine hit her stomach. She pulled out a handkerchief from her pocket and flushed the toilet. On the mirror someone had written with her mother's red lipstick, "I hate you!"

She walked out and stood in the corridor, looking down. Her flashlight scanned the walls catching glimpses of pictures, slogans, and colors. Her tongue moved over her dry lower lip. It had been days since she'd taken a shower or had a decent meal.

She came to herself with a start. For ten minutes she had been staring blankly at a picture in the beam of her flashlight, a portrait of Ayatollah Khomeini taped to the wall. From a distance, the song of the *azan* calling the Moslem brethren to prayer, echoed through the house. She listened. That song she had once loved and cherished, that had meant the orange descent of the sun upon the sand dunes, now seemed to only spread terror from the dark tall tower of the mosque.

Her eyes went back to Ayatollah Khomeini. An old man, with a turban wrapped around his head, a white beard covering half his face. Watchful angry eyes. He was coming closer, pulling her to him, a pitiless smirk on his lips. He was insane, the phantom of Lucifer, a bloodthirsty creature here to destroy her like he had destroyed them. Around his face, the revolutionary colors glowed—green for Islam, red for blood, black for death.

Melody sank to the stairs, took her head in the palm of her hands, and wept.

★ ★ ★

Sunlight shining through the large open windows found her on the couch. She blinked. The house seemed more familiar now, less haunted. She could see the kitchen door and the cabinets, and from there she could see the apple tree her father had once loved. It had blossomed and a few apples hung into the kitchen through its window. But that familiarity made it all seem even more empty. A few objects she barely recognized stood in odd corners of the room. It was as if there were a major auction, and the only things left were the dregs that no one wanted.

The phone began to ring. She jumped to her feet and circled, trying to hear where the sound was coming from. Then she ran to the kitchen and found the old hand dial phone on the cabinet.

"Hello?" she said breathlessly.

"Melody?"

"Gilda." It was her older sister who had left for France a few months before the revolution. She hadn't wanted to leave the country but her husband had decided to escape until Iran calmed down. It had been a smart decision, one that their father, Senator Zandi, had not made.

"Oh my God! Melody! Melody!" Gilda burst into tears.

Melody stood, a hand to her head, leaning against the kitchen bar, listening to the distant weeping of relief. It was so good to hear Gilda's voice, a familiar voice in this unfamiliar world gone crazy.

"Where have you been? I've called and called for two weeks. Where in the world is Maman? Any news from Baba? All of us here have been worried sick. Melody? Talk to me. Where are you?"

"I'm here," she said, finding her voice odd, hearing it for the first time after so many days.

"Melody, are you all right? Is everything all right? You sound strange."

"Yes, Gilda. Everything is perfectly fine."

She looked around. Everything was fine except Baba had been tortured so badly he had been unrecognizable by the time they had finally shot him; Maman had had a heart attack and now rested somewhere beneath the old farmland; Uncle Kia was dead; cousin Maryam had disappeared, and their entire inheritance had been confiscated by the Islamic regime in the name of Allah! But at that moment, she just couldn't add the burden of a grieving sister. Any more, and she would break.

"Everything," she said deliberately, "is fine."

"Oh, God, I'm so glad. I've been worried sick. Pass the phone to Maman. I want to speak to her."

"She's not here."

"Where is she?"

"Gilda I . . ."

"What? Melody?"

"I don't know how to . . ." She stopped again, one hand to her head.

"How to what? What's wrong, Melody?"

"I don't know how to tell you this. I don't know how to—"

"Don't lie to me. Anything but that! Just don't lie to me!"

"I'll call you back."

"Don't you dare! I've the right to know. Get Maman on the phone."

Melody couldn't speak.

"Melody, please."

It was the pleading voice she'd heard so often when they were children. "Gilda, they're . . . they're . . ."

"Please, Melody. Please."

Melody looked at the still-white ceiling. Gilda needed to know. She was far from home and this would hurt more than anything in the world, but not knowing sometimes hurt even more.

"Baba was shot, Gilda love, and Maman passed away when she heard the news."

She could not say any more for Gilda was screaming and would not stop. Melody would have cried with her but she had no tears left. She stared blankly at the wall, merely listening to the tears of mourning, amplified by the cold, ruthless distance. After all, there was nothing left to say.

★ ★ ★

Colonel Moradi tasted the soup and grimaced. Since the maids had left last year, his wife was forced into cooking. Colonel Moradi dearly loved his wife, but it had only taken a few days of marriage to realize she could not cook. He saw his wife sneak a glance at him. She knew how he felt about her cooking, she even agreed. But he knew she knew how important this meeting was and had tried her best. From the corner of his eyes, Colonel Moradi saw the stiff expression on Officer Larijani's face and the amusement of Mr. Azadi, a once famous writer. They had the same opinion about the food, but would be polite enough to keep the thought to themselves. He looked back at his wife and smiled kindly. Mrs. Moradi smiled back.

The dinner gathering, which had started at seven thirty, had gone well until now, but since the soup had arrived a strong silence had descended over the table. Even Mrs. Larijani who never stopped talking, did not say a word. The only person who seemed undisturbed by the taste of the foul soup was General Jalili. In fact, the general looked as if he might be enjoying the soup. Too many years on army rations, perhaps.

Finally the phone rang.

Colonel Moradi sighed in relief and excused himself. He walked through the small hallway between the living room and the bathroom and kitchen, into the library, and picked up the phone.

★ ★ ★

General Jalili was confused about the silence at the dinner table. It may have been due to the foul soup but he was not one to show his distaste openly.

He sighed. Since the revolution the gatherings had become unbearably gloomy. He wished people would just cheer up. It seemed they walked, talked, and slept politics. General Jalili wouldn't normally have much problem with this. After all, he made good money off the tips he got from listening to internal information. That was how he had been able to tell his Islamic friends about last year's planned coup. And he was running short on cash; last week he'd lost his last penny to a game of poker he had played with his few good old friends who were still alive.

But he had had enough of the depression and pessimism at this table. It was time to go to the bathroom. He excused himself and walked into the hallway. Before turning into the bathroom, he paused. He could hear Colonel Moradi's voice coming from the library.

"When do you want to meet?" Colonel Moradi said. "All right. I'll keep that open. Just stop by . . . My wife will make you something . . . No, it's no trouble. You know how much she likes to cook . . . You want to bring Officer Pakran too? . . . Oh no, not a problem at all, how is old Pakran doing? . . . Oh, poor man. He used to be so strong . . . It's real important? . . . You're not trying to pull another Mossadegh off, are you? . . . I'm kidding. I'll see you tomorrow. Sleep well, Lieutenant."

Colonel Moradi hung up and walked back into the hallway and then the living room, humming "Strangers in the Night" under his breath. Behind him, General Jalili eased the bathroom door closed.

★ ★ ★

Commander Shirazi parked, while Hamid scanned the area. The affluent Framanieh neighborhood had been quiet since the early days of the revolution, since many of the wealthy had fled and the remaining few lived silently, in fear of the revolutionary guards that patrolled the area nightly.

General Jalili, one of the few, pulled up to the curb in front of one of the smaller houses, stepped out of his Renault, walked up the few steps, and closed the door behind him.

Hamid threw his cigarette out of the car window. "Just got home. Must have been out to dinner or something."

"With his Mujahedin friends, probably," Commander Shirazi said.

"Should we go in?"

"In a minute. Let him get settled first."

Hamid looked at his commander sideways and smiled. Commander Shirazi had a natural flair for this work. Their backup car pulled up behind them and turned off its headlights.

★ ★ ★

Commander Shirazi rang the bell while Hamid flattened himself against the wall.

"Who is it?" General Jalili shouted from behind the door.

"Revolutionary guards. Open this door at once."

There was a moment of hesitation and then they heard the lock turn. The door opened a crack. Commander Shirazi hit the door with his heel and pushed it open, Hamid right behind him. General Jalili, already in a velvet robe and silk slippers, lost his balance, but at the last minute grabbed the side of the table and stayed upright. A cat mewed and disappeared behind the sofa.

General Jalili held up trembling hands. "What's going on?"

"We're here to get some information, General. Maybe you can oblige."

General Jalili looked over their shoulders at the backup jeep parked across the road. Hamid watched the general's pale face turn paler, smelling the intense alcohol scent from his body.

"What do you want?"

"First let's take a seat." Commander Shirazi shoved against his chest. General Jalili fell on the sofa.

"What's going on?"

"Close the door, Hamid." Commander Shirazi leaned against the armoire. "We've heard you're doing some deals behind our backs."

Hamid left the door ajar, in case they needed their backup quickly.

"Deals? I've got friends in the Revolutionary Guard Corps and in the revolutionary council. I've been a lot of help to you people. I can give you names. You can check with them—"

"I've checked with them and they've confirmed my opinion of you, General—that you're a cunning son of a bitch. They've given me an open hand to deal with you."

"Oh God, no!"

Hamid threw a quick glance at Commander Shirazi, knowing perfectly well that he was lying. They hadn't had time to check on much before coming to the general's house. But he was smart enough to play along.

"So, you have to tell me the truth, General. What have you been up to lately?"

"Nothing, I swear. I just went to a friend's house for dinner. That's all."

"What friend?"

"Colonel Moradi."

"Is Colonel Moradi in this with you? Are you both working for the Mujahedin-e Khalgh?"

As if finally the whole conversation made sense, General Jalili breathed in. "You're crazy. I've never dealt with the Mujahedin. What the hell are you talking about?"

"Someone tipped us off. They said they've seen you make deals with them."

"It's a lie! I swear!"

"Come on, Hamid. Let's take him to the interrogation office. They'll get the information out of him."

"No. Please, oh God, no!"

"Shut up, you son of a whore!" Commander Shirazi slapped him across the face. General Jalili's eyes began to water. "Get up. We're going to the interrogation office."

"All right, all right! I'll tell you anything you want to know."

"Now, we're talking. Go on."

General Jalili's underarms were soaked. "It's not what you want to hear. I mean it's not about the Mujahedin—"

"Take him, Hamid."

"No, wait. Please. Wait. Hear me out. I've always been a good friend of the Hezbollahies. I was one of the few who gave information to your group before the revolution. It was my tips and insider information that helped your bosses get where they are now. Sure, they paid me a little here and there, but I did it because I believed in the cause. Really."

"Get to the damn point, General."

"I've got information that may be useful to you. But if I give it to you, you've got to believe that I have nothing to do with the Mujahedin."

"I don't make deals." Commander Shirazi grabbed him by the collar and threw him down. His face hit the table.

"Tell me what you know, General, or Allah knows I'll throw you in a prison cell and have those bullies deal with you. Do you know what they do to you in there? They beat you, until you can't feel your bones anymore, then they throw you into a cold damp cell and throw freezing water over your numb body. Then they come in and beat you some more, until they've had enough of you and then, only then, they start pulling out your nails, one by one—"

"I heard something while I was on my way to the bathroom. Colonel Moradi was on the phone. He didn't see me. He was talking to someone—"

"Who?"

"I don't know, but he mentioned some things that sounded like he and his friends were planning—"

"What?"

"A military coup."

Commander Shirazi paused for a moment, as the meaning of the words slowly sank in. This was much, much more than either of them expected from this little fishing trip. When he spoke, his voice shook. "What else did you hear?"

General Jalili swallowed. "That's it."

"And what makes you sure you were right?"

"Because of the way he said it. He was planning a meeting with someone on the phone. The person calling must've been some sort of military person, because Colonel Moradi addressed him as officer. He said it like he was joking, but he wasn't. He was serious, I could tell."

"What did he exactly say?"

"He said something like, 'you're not planning on pulling off another Mossadegh, are you?'"

Hamid was even more deeply shocked. When he turned to look at Commander Shirazi, he saw that his face had gone completely red. Hamid knew that look. It was the zealous outrage caused by the thought that any man could think of betraying the Islamic regime.

Commander Shirazi took another step forward. "What else did you hear?"

"Nothing. That was it."

"When is this meeting?"

"He said tomorrow afternoon."

Commander Shirazi took the general by his collar and pulled him up. The general was taller than Commander Shirazi but he didn't resist, especially with Hamid's pistol pointed at his throat. "When did you hear this?"

"This evening." Sweat rolled down the general's cheeks. "Otherwise . . . I would have informed you earlier."

"Where have you been since?"

"Nowhere. I just got home."

"Whom did you speak to since?"

"No one. I was planning on calling my contact at the revolutionary council tomorrow. We have a deal going. He pays me for . . ." His eyes locked with Commander Shirazi's and his voice faded.

Suddenly Commander Shirazi let go of his collar and the general fell to the ground. "I'll let you go this time, General, but next time you won't be so lucky. You hear something about this again, you call me immediately." He nodded to Hamid who put his card on the side table. "Let's go Hamid. We've got more important matters to get to. You'll be hearing from us soon, General."

Hamid opened the door and leaned close to Commander Shirazi. "Don't you want to investigate him further, Commander? He may be lying about his affiliation with the Mujahedin."

Commander Shirazi closed the door behind them. "No, Hamid, but I want the backups watching him. Anywhere he goes, they follow. They should report anything suspicious to us. This way he'll think he's safe."

"And what next?"

"I'd hate to say it but I think we need to dig deeper into this coup business. We're already busy, so we have to pass the Mujahedin case to Commander Habibi's team."

"So you think he's telling the truth?"

"I don't know, but one thing's for certain. If he is, I want no one else but me on this case. Last time they planned a coup, most of them got away. We can't let that happen again."

"I'll contact Commander Habibi today and pass the Mujahedin investigation on to him."

"Good. Meanwhile, let's make sure the delicate two-faced general is telling us the truth."

★ ★ ★

Ali threw the newspaper to the side. On the third page Kia Vaziri's picture stared back at him. The last time he had beaten Vaziri in the red room his threat had finally turned into reality. Kia Vaziri, after eight months of nonstop thrashing, had died. Ali did not care much—Vaziri had told him everything he knew, which was pretty much nothing—but he was irritated because he somehow had to give the news to his wife. Maryam was an emotional girl at the best of times, and lately it had gotten worse. She was either upset at him for correcting her, especially physically, or she was unhappy at being away from her baba's large mansion, or missed her cousin and best friend Melody, or complained that he had changed since marriage. He didn't think he could stand one more day of her whining. And now he had beaten her baba to death and would never hear the end of it.

His door flung open and he looked up in astonishment as Jamshid marched in and threw a letter-sized paper on his desk.

Ali frowned. "What now?"

"This!" Jamshid pointed at the letter. "I'll have no part in this!"

Ali glanced at Jamshid, then unfolded the paper and began reading. He looked up. "So?"

"It's the letter of arrest for Colonel Moradi."

"And?"

"He was my commander."

"Ah yes, of course. I thought I'd heard his name. It's amazing we've missed him till now. The other day I saw a pilot's name we'd missed. What was his name now, let me think—"

"Colonel Moradi was one of the most decent, kind, and brave commanders I've ever had."

"As you weren't in the military very long, my friend, you can't possibly have had much experience with commanders. Besides, even if he was as good as you say, we've got to check him out. We can't have him poking around, causing trouble. Why don't you take this down to Commander Shirazi to take care of?"

"This copy was sent to us to inform us that they're bringing him here for interrogation."

"This must be about the Mujahedin station by Turkey. General Jalili must have spilled the beans."

"Does it matter? We can't go around killing everybody just because we want to protect the regime."

"What better reason than that?"

Ali looked at Jamshid for a second. Jamshid's hair had grayed at the temples, odd for a man his own age. "What's wrong with you Jamshid? Are you all right?"

"I believe the colonel to be a good man," Jamshid said. "When I'd just begun my service, an older officer was abusing me. The colonel dismissed the officer and personally paid attention to my well being until I was back in shape to serve. I'll always be grateful for that."

"I see. So what you're telling me is that you're buddies with a monarchy lover who may be plotting against the regime with the Mujahedin?"

"What? You want to shoot me now too? Go ahead."

Ali burst out laughing. "Just do as you're told Jamshid and you'll be fine. If the order is to arrest him then it's their job to arrest him. And it's our job to get any information we can out of him."

"Ali, I want you to stop this!"

"How can I?"

"All right, you can't stop Commander Shirazi from arresting him, but I don't want any harsh interrogation and I want him to have a fair trial. He's not a mujahid, I promise you."

"What? You stake your reputation on this?"

Jamshid took a deep breath. "Yes."

"You're funny, Jamshid. I hope you do realize that all the evidence is against him."

"I simply want him to have a fair trial. I don't want him to end up like Vaziri."

"All right! All right!" Ali shook an angry impatient hand. Vaziri's name still touched a nerve. "We can promise him he'll have a fair trial and that he'll be set free if we can't find anything against him."

"Do you promise me, Ali?"

Ali's face broke into a wide grin. "Yes. You have my promise. Now go."

Jamshid opened the door. "I'm relying on your word, Ali."

"Everyone does. Now go, go! You know how much I have to do."

★ ★ ★

Colonel Moradi lived in the suburbs of Damavand. He had a small house, decorated in French style. Since the revolution, he had begun working for a friend's business. He was currently sitting in his office near a large globe-shaped lamp, catching up on his paperwork. His wife was in the kitchen, washing dishes. Arman and Kami would be here soon for afternoon tea.

The doorbell rang. Colonel Moradi heard his wife's shoes tap down the hallway. The door opened.

His wife screamed.

Colonel Moradi rushed into the living room.

Commander Shirazi and Hamid stood at the door. Hamid had a hand to his pistol. Commander Shirazi spoke, "We have a letter of arrest for Colonel Moradi. Is that you, sir?"

"Yes. That's me."

Mrs. Moradi began to cry and sank into a chair in the hallway. Colonel Moradi rested a hand on her shoulder. "On what charge?"

"We have information that you're involved in illegal activities."

"What activities?"

"We are not at a liberty to say."

"I have a right to know, sir."

"You don't have a right to know anything, Colonel. Let's go."

"I refuse."

"All right then." Commander Shirazi pulled out his pistol and aimed it between Colonel Moradi's eyes. "Let me convince you, Colonel."

★ ★ ★

Half an hour later Arman walked out of the shower and picked up the phone.

"Hello?"

"This is Kami. I just got some bad news."

"What?"

"Mrs. Moradi called to cancel our meeting. They've arrested Colonel Moradi."

Arman stared at the phone a moment. "What? When?"

"At one thirty today."

"How . . . on what charge?"

"They didn't say. They said they had information that he is involved in illegal activities."

Arman held his breath.

"I know!" Kami said. "We've got a leak."

"Who?"

"God knows! I've got three hundred and forty confirmations. Can be anyone really. I've asked my friends in the south to get us the information we need. They should be getting back to me shortly."

Arman knew he meant information on the radar system in the south. "Come by when you've got the info. I'll pass it on. Meanwhile, watch your back. We don't want any more casualties."

"No kidding." Kami hung up.

FOUR

IT WAS A HOT Tuesday afternoon. The spring sun flooded the Qasr Prison courtyard, burning off the damp. Flowers blossomed outside the prison grounds. Jamshid tried to concentrate on these things as he walked down the stairs into the courtyard.

Ali had just given him a letter to pass on to the executioner. This was not Jamshid's normal duty, but as the usual functionary was home sick, Jamshid had to cover for him. The smell of blood nauseated him. He handed the letter to the firing squad commander, pulling himself slightly back from his smelly body.

His eyes wandered to the bloodstains on the infamous execution wall, which had not rested since February 11. How many had died, like cattle in a butcher shop? Inside these hellish walls, no one had cared.

The gates to the prison cells opened and a middle-aged woman was shoved forward. Behind her, was a boy of thirteen. The woman's clothes were torn and Jamshid could see her bare and bruised hips and shoulders. A long scar deformed the right side of her neck. The boy was weeping and had already wet his pants.

"Who's that?" Jamshid found his voice slightly above a terrified whisper.

"Mrs. Sara Farman," the executioner said this like he was introducing her to an old friend. "Ran that show on television, what was it called now? *Woman's Voice* or something?"

Jamshid remembered the attractive face, the nice hairdo, and the pleasant smile of the journalist who had informed Iranian women of their legislative rights and compared those rights to Western law. She had been known for her intelligence, guts, and cleverness. The discussions on her shows used to get heated as she introduced new ideas and sometimes even ridiculed the machos in her society, but she was always polite and respectful to those who disagreed with her. Now, her long curly hair fell about her face and seemed to cover the only healthy part of her neck.

"What happened to her neck?" Jamshid asked.

"Oh. One of the Islamic militant women knifed her."

"What for?"

"Not sure. Probably jealousy. She was good looking and smart. My own sister used to get furious just watching her talk. Between you and me, these Islamic militant girls are just like any other chick. If a couple of guys hadn't stopped them, she would've been dead by now. Although . . . " He suddenly burst into loud laughter, a bit of spittle landing on Jamshid's cheek. "Wouldn't make a difference now, if you know what I mean."

Jamshid wiped the spit off his cheek. He would have taken a swing at the officer if the man wasn't armed. "Why the boy?"

"He's the son of Admiral Habiballahi who got shot the very first day of the revolution. I don't know if you heard, but the admiral was in his office when our boys walked in and shot him. His son was with him, so we took him. We've been trying to get information out of him, but I always knew the boy didn't know anything. They're finally finishing him off." He turned to his men. "In position!"

The firing squad fell into line and stood with their guns at the ready.

The commander unfolded the letter. "'Blood must be spilled. The more Iran bleeds, the more will the revolution be victorious.'" The executioner chuckled and folded the letter. "Came from Ayatollah Khomeini himself, you said?"

"What did?"

"What I just read. The letter. They've quoted him saying we need to double the executions. We don't have enough room in the prisons anymore."

Suddenly Jamshid wasn't sure which way was up. He could have fainted and not realized it. "What did you say?"

"What's wrong with you? You look pale, brother. That's what the letter says. Now if you don't mind, I've got a job to do. Ready!" He turned to his squad. "Aim!"

But he stopped. The woman had begun to laugh. It was a sinister laughter directed at Jamshid and when he looked at her, he could see she was completely insane.

"What by Allah's name . . ." the executioner said.

The woman stared at Jamshid and screamed, "You look like you hope God will forgive you. Don't presume any absolution, you killer. You'll be damned to hell, just like the rest of them."

"Fire!"

Blizzards of bullets hit the woman and she crashed to the ground.

"Bitch gave me the creeps!" The executioner spat to the ground. "Get the body out of here. Push the boy forward. Hurry up! We haven't got all day."

Jamshid turned and walked away.

"Help! Help! Maman, please help!" the boy cried.

Jamshid began to run. The faster he ran, the slower he felt he was moving. He heard the shots end the wretched screams. By the front gate he fell to his knees and puked. Then he trudged up the stairs.

He walked into his office and shut the door, leaned against it, and remained deadly still.

Merciful God, what had he become?

★ ★ ★

"Damn it!" Melody ran a hand through her hair.

She had tried calling her fiancé, Nader, whom she had not seen since they had moved to the farm but no one picked up the phone. She dialed again. Of course if he was there, he would immediately come to her and she would have to shower, do her hair, and put on her best dress. He would expect no less. But she didn't want to. She wanted to forget his class and prestige and remain as she was: real. Convention and the social niceties had lost their importance. But at least she was not alone. There was Nader, and he loved her. The phone kept ringing. Was he arrested too? Was he dead?

She called for the third time. Still no answer. She banged the receiver, picked it up, and banged it again, then threw it at the wall.

If only Arman were here.

She felt a pang that confused her. It had been so long since she had fallen in love with him. Where was he now? Baba had been against their marriage but she had never forgotten Arman and she knew he was the main reason she could never love Nader enough.

By God, had it been five years since she and Arman had lain by each other in a sleeping bag in the desert? He was a quiet guy normally, but he had talked that night. Then they had kissed and he had asked her to marry him. It felt so right until her father introduced Nader to her. Nader was a sweet man, but it had not been the same.

It was about then that Maryam tried to convince her father about Ali Alizadeh, a boy of lower class with whom she was madly in love. Her father was against Ali the moment he had laid eyes on him. They had argued, not only about Maryam's new love affair but also about the revolution, which Maryam believed promised equality and freedom.

"Do you really like Nader?" she had asked Melody.

"He's a kind man."

"And that's all? You love Arman and you know it. Nader isn't you. You two don't belong to each other."

"Baba likes him."

"And that's enough?"

"It must be, I suppose."

"It's not. You've given in. Our parents have no right to make these decisions for us."

"This is Iran. They'll always have a right, Maryam."

"Well, it's not fair. You've given in, but I won't."

"Won't what?"

"Give up. I won't give up on Ali. No matter what Baba says I *will* have Ali."

That had been a week before Maryam left to live with Ali. Melody had not heard from her since.

She picked up the phone. After all she had done to him, maybe Arman would not want to talk her. If he was still in Iran. If he was still alive. She put down the phone. Instead she climbed the stairs.

It was time to start over.

★ ★ ★

Jamshid banged on the door a second time. The house seemed quiet. The shutters closed. Only a moment ago he had received news that Colonel Moradi would be executed. It had taken the interrogators no more than a day to realize he didn't know anything. But instead of releasing him, they had attached some crime to him—"abuse of military authority to massacre innocent supporters of the great Islamic revolution"—and stamped an execution date on it. That had finally thrown Jamshid over the edge.

The door opened. The woman who appeared did not look at his face but kept her green eyes on his shoes.

"May I come in, Maryam?"

"I . . . I don't know."

"You don't know?"

"No, I don't." She stared at the ground beneath his feet, her eyes blinking uncontrollably. "Ali isn't here and he doesn't like me alone in the house with anyone. He gets mad."

"Let me in, Maryam. Don't you think we've known each other long enough?"

"I don't think. Not anymore."

"Please, Maryam."

She turned and walked in but left the door ajar. He stepped in and looked around. Dim light found its way through the glass above the door. A half-empty box of Kleenex lay near a rocking chair covered by a black shawl next to the old heater. A photo album stuck out from under the sofa, its pages open and a few pictures thrown on it in disarray. Jamshid had seen that album before and knew it belonged to Maryam. Ali had tried to take it away many times, perhaps to erase her memories. He turned to look at Maryam. When she finally looked up, he saw the dark bruise around her left eye.

"When's the baby due?" He tried to keep his voice cheerful.

"The doctor says any moment really." She waved him toward a brown chair. "You can sit here. Ali doesn't normally sit on this seat. Tea?"

"No thank you, Maryam. I'm all right."

"I'll get you tea. He gets mad if his guests don't get tea."

"Maryam!" He took her by the shoulders and spun her around, forcing her to face him. "Are you listening to yourself? Where is the Maryam I knew? What has he done to you?"

She began to cry. It came slowly and then intensified into loud sobs. He pulled her into his arms, caressing her black hair under the scarf. Apparently, Ali would not even allow her to go around the house without a scarf anymore. It slipped down and her hand moved to pull it back over her head. He took her hand and gently pulled the scarf off her head, letting her hair fall around her pathetic face.

He breathed in. The windows had steel bars on them. He had not noticed that before. The house was dark and stuffy. There were no pictures on the walls except of Imam Ali. The book of Koran lay next to a vase of dead flowers. Some clothes hung to dry on lines strung in the hallway and patio; Ali did not believe in using washing machines or dryers, or any other western technical equipment if he could help it. "You came from such a place to end up here, Maryam. You had so much. Why do you allow him to do this to you?"

"He . . . he . . . " She choked over the words.

Jamshid's eyes caught a picture of her on the side table. Next to her was her cousin . . . Melody, he recalled. She was pretty, but more than that she had her head together. She had been a thinker, not like Maryam who lived for love and passion. Melody saw what she saw, not what she wanted to see. Behind them stood a man, his eyes the same color as Maryam's. Jamshid recognized the face—Kia Vaziri. It seemed so different from the swollen broken figure he had seen coming out of the red room. Jamshid was sure Maryam did not know her father had been imprisoned, tortured, and was now dead.

"Maryam, listen to me." He pulled her back to look at her face. "Have you contacted your family since you left them?"

"I . . . I can't. There's no phone here and he leaves me no money and he . . . he would know."

"Not even coins?"

"Nothing. Just food. He fills up the fridge like . . . like I'm a dog. And I'm afraid to go back. I was so angry and I told Baba Kia off and I just can't go back. I'm so ashamed."

"Sometimes Maryam, we make mistakes because we think we understand something we don't. I've done the same, believe me. You have to return to your family."

Maryam looked blank. "But how?"

"I'll tell you what." He pulled a small role of notes—twenty-five tomans—from his pocket. "Here is some money. Put it aside and get a taxi when he's gone. Go to your cousin Melody or any other relative you may have."

Maryam took the money. "Thank you. I can go to Baba Kia."

"Maryam, I don't know how to tell you this, but I must because—"

The sound of the entrance door closing brought them to themselves. She pulled herself away from him. "He's here!" She rushed into the kitchen as if the devil himself had arrived.

And perhaps he had. Ali walked in. Tall, handsome, secure, self-assured, he had a smile so warm and innocent you'd think he just stepped out of his cradle.

"Jamshid? By Allah! What a pleasure to see you out of the office. You hardly visit us anymore. Sorry you were out sick this morning." He threw his wallet and keys on the sofa.

Jamshid's eyes followed the wallet and then crisply returned to Ali.

"Tea?" Ali asked, and before Jamshid could respond, he shouted, "Khanum! Bring some tea."

"No, thank you, Maryam," Jamshid shouted in turn. "I don't want any tea."

"Sorbet, then?"

"Nothing. Thank you."

"I shall have something then. It's getting hot out there, isn't it? Hey, Khanum, bring some sorbet and some of those sweets I bought this morning. I'm thirsty. Have you tried the sweets from Haj Mammad's store? They're homemade." He bent toward Jamshid and whispered, "His eighteen-year-old daughter makes them."

There was a message of some kind in that, but Jamshid could only guess what it was. He gave it his best shot. "You seem to like Haj Mammad's grocery store. You were there yesterday at noon for a couple of hours."

Ali put a finger to his lips, then shouted, "Bring some tea, Khanum!" He bent forward. "I want to keep her in the kitchen. She doesn't know yet."

"Know what?"

"I proposed to Haj Mammad's daughter."

"The eighteen-year-old?"

Ali nodded. "Her name is Fati and she looks as beautiful as Saint Fati herself."

"You must be kidding me. You're married."

"So?" Ali put his hand in a bowl of sunflower seeds and picked up a handful.

"You have a wife."

"So?" He spat the shells into the dish in front of him.

"So what are you doing with another woman?"

For once Ali caught the sarcasm in Jamshid's voice and looked up. "It's completely respectable and Islamic, Jamshid. Prophet Mohammad had plenty of wives. I'm just following his path. That's why we've finally made it legal in the Islamic regime. You can have as many wives as you can afford and if not you have the option of a temporary marriage and an immediate divorce. Everything is Islamic."

Jamshid shook his head. "And is she happy with this Islamic arrangement?"

"Maryam?" Ali frowned. "Why? Has she told you any different?"

"No, she hasn't. But you can't really miss it if you look at her."

"Well I can't divorce her to marry Fati. I mean what would she do? She can't go back to her father. He's dead. Her uncle is gone too. All her relatives have fled or died. So it's just me left and I've got too much heart to kick her out."

"When are you going to tell her about her father?"

"Soon. She doesn't get the newspaper, so she doesn't need to know immediately."

Maryam walked into the room. Her hands shook as she placed the tray on the table.

"Where's the pastry, Khanum?"

"I'll get it." Maryam turned and accidentally hit her shoulder against the doorway.

"Now, see," Ali said, "that's the difference. I mean Fati serves you like it's second nature. There's no confusion in our roles. So I think it'll be good for Maryam to see how a proper housewife should be. She's so clumsy."

"She wasn't raised to be a housewife."

"All women should be raised to be housewives, to stay in the kitchen and shut up. Don't need their silly gibberish around town. Besides Fati is pure."

"Pure?"

"Never been touched. I prefer women that way."

"Maryam was a virgin, too, till you slept with her."

"Yes, but that was before we got married."

"But . . . she married you."

"It's not the same is it, marrying somebody who's not a virgin? It's so vulgar, somehow whorish."

"Let's clear this up. You're the only one she ever slept with and she married you."

"If she wasn't a whore, she would've waited till we got married."

"You're sick."

Ali laughed and spit the rest of the sunflower seeds onto his plate.

Jamshid decided to change the subject before he said something he'd really regret. "What happened to Colonel Moradi? I heard he's on the list to be shot."

"Oh yes. We interrogated him, but he didn't know anything. It was pretty obvious. So we're getting rid of him."

"On what grounds?"

"He was the Shah's colonel and can be dangerous to the regime."

"Who made the decision?"

"Commander Shirazi. He thought it best to get rid of him, just in case. I agreed, so I pushed for it. It's cleaner this way."

"Being in the army before the revolution is not a crime."

"It is as far as the regime is concerned. Why are you so bothered?"

"I want you to release him."

"Impossible."

"If you talk to the judge in charge of the case, you can do it. You've got enough pull. I know he's innocent. I'm asking you to set him free."

Ali shook his head. "Impossible."

"I served in the military too. When do you plan to kill me?"

"Don't be ridiculous." Ali chuckled, wiping his mouth with the sleeve of his uniform. "Where's the tea, Khanum?"

"Ali, he's an ordinary man, a good citizen. There's no reason to kill him. He has a family."

"He's evil. What's wrong with you anyway?"

"You don't have to take your bloody revenge on everyone. You know perfectly well that most of these people haven't done anything wrong. Is this what we fought for?"

"I see that my guess was right." Ali leaned back. "You have become soft. To protect the regime we need to get rid of these people—"

"You're getting rid of all the educated trained professionals. We're losing them in the navy, the air force, and ground troops.

We're losing our best physicians, our scientists, our journalists, and businessmen. We're losing them in the judiciary and the government. How do you think you'll replace them?"

"Eventually we will."

"But when? We need these resources. It's insane to kill for the purpose of killing. For years, these people have worked and gathered experience. You won't be able to replace them overnight. In the long run this will destroy the regime, not protect it."

Ali shrugged. "I do it all for Islam, Jamshid. Allah expects us to get rid of the heretics. It is so written in the Koran. Everything I do is for Allah."

"You're destroying Iran's past."

"Isn't that the point?"

Jamshid squeezed his eyes shut. "A few nights ago I had a nightmare."

"What about?"

"I dreamt of a bunch of men walking around, their heads cut off. They were confused, asking directions from each other, but none could find the way. They were all lost."

Ali burst out laughing. "Well, they would be if they couldn't see anything."

"Exactly."

"I don't get it."

"You never have."

Ali looked puzzled and then shook his head. "What do you want from me?"

"I told you. Let Colonel Moradi go."

"I can't, it's already been decided."

"There's ways around it. We both know that."

Ali sighed. "I've known you for a long time Jamshid and I know you're a kind person. You're shocked by what you see in the office, and I agree. It's not pleasant but it has to be done. It's for Allah and Islam. More so it's for the Islamic regime. You should know that, you're the most religious of us all. You haven't missed a single prayer since you've been a child. So I don't understand why you're the one questioning these rules. In Koran, Allah says that all enemies and heretics shall die by the sword of the followers of Allah. We're just doing what we're told to do—"

"Words!" Jamshid said. "You go on talking rubbish and wrap it in words like Allah, Heaven, and Koran—"

"I do what Islam says. Everything I do is for Islam."

Jamshid looked around him, breathing heavily. Suddenly he pushed the coffee table over. The sunflower seeds went flying. The red sorbet splashed across the floor like blood.

"Now see what you've done," Ali said. "My carpet!"

"Red goes with your life, Ali. Don't tell me you don't like it."

"You act like this is my hobby, as if I enjoy . . ."

He stopped as his eyes met Jamshid's. Jamshid stood facing him, only a step away.

"I'm sick and tired of you and your words Ali. I'm tired of superficiality and lies. I want decency, dignity, truth. Those are the backbone of Islam. Those were the things the revolution promised us. Where did those promises go?"

"I'm tired. We'll talk about this some other time."

"No, Ali. Remember the banners we held when we ran in the streets? They said 'equality, liberty, justice.' Has this regime provided us with any of that? No. There is no more equality today than there was in the past. Instead of the useless nobility, now we have guys like you, ten times more dangerous and bloody, with the same arrogance toward the poor. Do we have liberty? From the West maybe but not from our own selves. Justice? You told me today you're killing an innocent man because it's convenient. If it wasn't so sad, I think I could laugh."

Jamshid could see the momentary discomfort in Ali's eyes. Ali stepped back. "I don't know what you want. We're doing everything we can. Besides what's your problem? Your salary has doubled since you got this job—"

"You're a disgusting sick man and that's why you do so well in this insane government. There was always something inherently wrong with you that we ignored and now it all comes out. This regime has given you the power to do whatever you want, and look what you're doing."

"Get out, Jamshid."

"Repent, Ali, before it's too late. Tell Maryam what you've done to her father and uncle. Tell her how you buried them alive in a cell and humiliated them until they broke. Tell her how they begged for death by the time you were done with them. Tell her, Ali. Tell her how you never loved her but hated her for all she was and the life she had that you longed for and didn't have and will *never* have, Ali, no matter what you do. Because, brother, you don't deserve it—"

A loud noise brought Jamshid to himself. He turned to see Maryam standing in the kitchen doorway, a hand to her mouth, her green eyes wide. The tray in her hands had crashed to the ground.

"Ali? Tell me this isn't true. Please tell me."

"You're fired!" Ali shouted at his friend. "Get the hell out of my house."

Jamshid hesitated for a second, disturbed by the anguish he saw in Maryam's face, but he could not stay any longer. He turned on his heels and walked out.

★ ★ ★

It had just turned dark when Arman heard the knock on the door. He was in his workout clothes. He pulled off the towel around his shoulders and draped it over his pistol. He hesitated for a moment in the hallway, looking at the door. "Who is it?"

A voice from behind the door said, "Jamshid Mahmoudi. I'm a friend of Colonel Moradi's. I need to speak to you, Lieutenant."

Arman could not recall the name and neither did he like a visitor this late at night, especially a man who claimed to be a friend of a friend who was recently taken to jail. Arman thumbed the hammer on his pistol.

"What do you want?"

"Please, Lieutenant, I have to speak with you."

Carefully Arman pulled the door open and looked out. The face of the young man standing in his long ill-fitting green jacket seemed familiar although he couldn't place it.

"I was told you might be able to help me," Jamshid said.

"With what?"

"That's what I'm here to talk about. Can I come in please, Lieutenant?"

Arman hesitated but finally stood aside. As Jamshid walked by, Arman put his pistol against his spine.

Jamshid chuckled. "You're fast."

"Not as fast as I'll be if you make a wrong move, Pasdar Mahmoudi."

Jamshid raised his arms. "I'm clean."

"I'll decide that."

Arman searched him but Jamshid had no weapon. He returned his wallet. "Who gave you my name?"

"Mrs. Moradi."

"Mrs. Moradi?" Arman became less guarded as he locked the door. "Take a seat." He signaled with his pistol and Jamshid sat down. "Now tell me what this is all about."

Jamshid's eyes moved away from the pistol and toward the pictures of the family yacht on the walls. "You're a sailor?"

"Yes."

"How far have you gone?"

"Indian Ocean. Reunion Island."

"I prefer motor boats."

"Why's that?"

"They're fast and powerful."

"It depends on how you define power. But you're not here to discuss sailing, are you?"

"No."

"All right then." Arman sat across from him, his pistol still in his hand. "Get on with it, Pasdar Mahmoudi. You are a pasdar aren't you, or are you wearing that charming outfit for show?"

"No, I'm afraid I'm a pasdar."

"Okay, honesty is a good start. What can I do for a powerful militant of the Islamic regime?"

"I'd like to start from the beginning, Lieutenant."

"Start wherever you want, but hurry."

"If I don't start at the beginning you won't believe me and won't agree to cooperate."

"Depends on what you want me to cooperate with."

"Saving Colonel Moradi's life."

Arman narrowed his eyes at him. "Why?"

"I'm afraid it's a call of my conscience."

Arman eyed him quietly for a few more minutes.

"Please Lieutenant," Jamshid finally said. "Give me a chance to explain."

Arman crossed his arms. "All right. Start from the beginning."

And Jamshid did.

★ ★ ★

Half an hour later, Arman put down his glass of water. "I don't see how I can help you."

"You were a navy officer, you were a friend of the colonel, and he trusts you. On top of that Mrs. Moradi thought you'd be able to help."

"But it's not so easy. We have to somehow get into the Qasr Prison, put him into a car, drive him—hoping no one will see us—to the airport, and then somehow get him on a flight without being recognized. How do you intend to do all this?"

"You forget I'm a pasdar. I may have been fired last night but the prison guards won't know that. I can drive him probably even close to the airport, but after that I'm stumped. How in the world do I get him on an airplane and out of the country? That's where I need some creativity, some help. So, I went to Colonel Moradi's house to warn his wife. She was devastated. She told me he had mentioned your name. She seemed to think you had some sort of connection."

Arman frowned. "What else did she say?"

"That was all. She said the Colonel was not a man to talk much and I don't think she was quite comfortable with me . . . "

Arman glanced over Jamshid's military boots and green jacket and chuckled. It wasn't a surprise Mrs. Moradi wouldn't trust a defecting pasdar.

"So you see, Lieutenant, this is an act of desperation. I came to you because of a simple hint and because I have no one else to go to. Can you help me?"

Arman was still not sure he could trust Jamshid. Jamshid seemed to realize his suspicion and sighed. "You still don't believe me, do you?"

Arman did not respond.

"I left because I hate this business. This regime has nothing to do with Islam. They use it as a symbol to do as they please. I've seen too much to ever go back."

He could be lying and Arman knew that. But the fact that he was unarmed, wore his Islamic uniform when he came, and seemed genuinely honest made Arman hesitate.

"What can I do so you trust me?"

"Why the colonel? A lot of innocent people have died or are in jail now."

"I can only do so much. I didn't know the rest. I don't know their crimes, but I do know the colonel and I know he's innocent."

"I see. So we just rescue our friends and to hell with the rest. If it was up to me, I'd free most of them, but then again, you're right. We can only help so many. And as you're the one getting him out of prison, I won't be too demanding."

"So you'll help?" Jamshid looked up with childish eagerness.

"What's your plan?"

"Day after tomorrow is his execution day. If we want to do anything we need to do it tomorrow. I've checked the flights. There is a flight to London leaving at ten o'clock tomorrow night. If we can get him on that, he'll make it."

"What about Mrs. Moradi?"

"I asked her to leave the country but she refuses. She says she wants to wait for her husband. But you know if we manage to get Colonel Moradi out, the authorities will immediately arrest her to get him back. I was hoping that since you're an old friend, you could speak with her."

"There can be no harm in that."

"Will you help me, Lieutenant?"

Arman took another glance at him and finally made up his mind. "If you were trying to find an excuse to put me into prison, I'm sure you could have managed that without going through all this trouble. Nowadays a charge of 'battle against Allah,' seems to be sufficient. On top of that only a fool would come here wearing a pasdar uniform asking for assistance from one of the Shah's naval officers."

Jamshid turned pale from the insult but did not respond.

"So on another note, you told me you were involved in the November 4 American hostage taking, is that correct?"

"Yes."

"All right then. If I help you with this, I'm putting my life at risk—"

"Yes, but you're doing it for a friend."

"Jamshid, two of my uncles and five of my closest friends were executed, and the only thing the rest of us could do was hope they wouldn't come after us. Maybe if you'd been here then, it would've been different, but I have my responsibilities and I'll be putting my life in danger."

Jamshid did not respond.

"So in return for my help, I want something from you."

"What?" Jamshid asked.

"I need the exact location of the American hostages and guards."

"Why? They're very well guarded. You can't possibly get them out."

"Who said anything about getting them out?"

"Then why do you need the information?"

"I'm writing a novel."

Jamshid eyed him for a second and then shrugged. "I don't care what you want it for, Lieutenant. I'll get it to you. It's the least I can do."

"Good." Arman stood up. "It's a plan then."

"Do you mind telling me how you're planning on getting the colonel on the plane?"

"You do your part, I'll do mine. Come back tomorrow morning at eight o'clock and I'll have more information. And Jamshid, wear something less noticeable, will you?"

Jamshid looked at his green uniform and military boots. "Anything else?"

Arman unlocked the entrance door. "Bring me a pasdar uniform just like the one you're wearing. Size large."

"And weapons?"

"I can find my own."

Arman opened the door.

"Thank you, Lieutenant," Jamshid said, walking out, "for trusting me."

Arman refrained from saying that was stretching it a bit far. He closed the door behind Jamshid. Then he walked into the library to make a phone call.

FIVE

ON APRIL 7, GENERAL Kramer, the commander of the Joint Task Force called a meeting to review the American hostage rescue plan. Colonel Jerry Wilson, the deputy commander, caught a flight to Fort Bragg to attend the meeting. Now, the colonel walked into the conference room and looked around in surprise. He had never seen this many people here. Most field and staff units associated with the mission were present.

He took a seat in the back of the room. Everyone looked exhausted. Since early November when Iranians had taken American diplomats hostage, most hadn't had a good night's sleep. The meeting started off with an intelligence report. It was not a happy situation. Intelligence information was difficult to get from inside Iran. The hostages were well guarded in the embassy compound. Tehran was crammed with four million people but it was isolated and surrounded by about seven hundred miles of rough terrain in every direction. There was no easy way to do this.

Parachuting in an elite army special forces team was suicidal. The only workable solution was a complex, two-night operation. An army rescue team would fly into Iran with a combination of RH-53Ds and C-130s. C-130 Hercules could operate from rough dirt strips and could airdrop troops and equipment into hostile regions. The plan was to have the Hercs fly the men into a staging area from Oman. They would load the rescue team on the helicopters, refuel the choppers, and then the choppers would hide about fifty miles outside of Tehran. On day two, the Iranian agents would escort the army team to the embassy in trucks.

It was an ambitious plan. For one thing, the men had to fly using night-vision goggles, which was almost unheard of until today. There was no way to refuel the helicopters at remote landing zones. Nothing of this nature had ever been done. They were making it up as they went.

As if the hostage catastrophe in Iran was not enough, one month later, several hundred aircraft flew about five thousand troops from the Soviet Union into Kabul. These troops had helped support the Afghani communist party to overthrow the government. Any military movement by the United States in the proximity of Afghanistan would attract the attention of the Soviets—already, a huge Soviet fleet was off the coasts of Pakistan, India, Iran, and the Persian Gulf watching the Americans.

Only this morning, Colonel Wilson had received news from the *USS Nimitz* that a Soviet Bear Bomber flew a scant five hundred feet overhead monitoring their activities, which made it difficult to test the rescue mission choppers in daylight.

"Before you know it," Colonel Pade, the helicopter mission commander, had said with a frown, "they'll be landing right next to us, asking questions. Last night we heard the Soviet AGI picked up our radio transmission again. Makes you think they'd even pick up our God-forsaken trash to see what's in it."

Colonel Wilson shook the thought aside. He had too many responsibilities to be worried about the Soviets. Keeping track of their activities was the intelligence service's job. The colonel was here to ensure that the mission went smoothly.

He turned to look back at General Kramer who was going over the plan. The more Colonel Wilson thought about this, the more he was convinced that this plan required not only teamwork and experience, but more important, luck.

★ ★ ★

"We'll take two cars, a Peykan and a Mercedes—government officials love Mercedes. We need to rent them from two different shops, so they'll be harder to track. I'll pick them up. I'll drop the Peykan off in Tajrish, east of the bazaar." Arman put his finger on the Tehran map. "Right here. You can pick it up. The key will be under the seat."

Jamshid nodded. They were in Arman's kitchen and the blinds were closed. A bag rested on one of the barstools at the cooking island.

Mrs. Moradi had left early that morning for London. At first she had resisted but finally realized the sense of the move. Tonight at nine o'clock they would implement Moradi's escape. Jamshid appeared worried. Arman took a quick glance at him. "You're still in this with me, Jamshid?"

"Of course."

"Did you bring what I asked of you?"

Jamshid picked up the bag on the stool and pulled out some clothes. "A pasdar uniform, size large. I've also got a clergy uniform with a turban, and a tiny book of Koran and a prayer chain for Colonel Moradi."

"Good."

Jamshid frowned. "How are we getting him out of the country?"

"With this." Arman threw a red passport on the table.

Jamshid looked at him in surprise and picked it up. "Ayatollah Rahbari." He studied it closely, feeling the quality of the paper. "It seems absolutely authentic. How in the world did you manage this?"

"I've got friends in low places." Arman fought a grin. It had been Zia who had agreed to do this in return for the internal information Jamshid was to provide about the embassy.

"I'm really impressed, Lieutenant."

"Cut the Lieutenant, Jamshid. My name will do just fine."

"All right, Arman. So you said we'll be changing cars?"

"Yes, right here." Arman put his finger on the map. "A few blocks east of Qasr Prison there's a street that has been renamed Shahidi. It's a dead end. I went there last night around midnight and took a look. It's dark and quiet, and it's right across the road you'll be coming out of. You turn your headlights on and off twice. I'll do the same. You pull in here, right next to me. There is a large vacant building on the left side of the road with an extended front wall. You can park behind the wall. It'll take them awhile to find the car and will give us time to get him out."

"They'll know it's me anyway. My boss, Ali, will come after me immediately."

"It's better not to leave evidence at the table."

Jamshid shrugged. He looked exhausted. He had told Arman that he had barely slept the entire night and every time he had dozed off, he had woken up from a nightmare.

"When you join me in the Mercedes, you'll have to help Colonel Moradi change into his clergy uniform. We'll drive straight to the airport. At the gate, my friend, we'll find company. A dozen or so of your old buddies will be standing with AK-47s, guarding the entrance door to all airlines. It's up to you to pull it through there, Jamshid. You talk their talk, Colonel Moradi and I don't. We'll be relying on you there."

"I'll do my best. Will you leave then too, Arman?"

"Not yet. I've got some unfinished business to attend to."

"That would have nothing to do with this insider embassy information I just gave you, would it?"

"You do your thing, Jamshid, I'll do mine. I don't like my part of the deal any better than you, but sometimes you've just got to do what you can. If that makes any sense."

"I think it does. I wish you the best in whatever it may be, Arman."

"Thanks. I'll see you tonight as planned. Remember to pick up the car in two hours in Tajrish. Meanwhile I think you should be the one trying to get out. Once Colonel Moradi's free, you can be sure they'll come after you. I can arrange something for you, if you'd like."

"For now, I only have the colonel on my mind. After that, I'll think about myself."

"Don't you think that's a bit shortsighted?"

Jamshid did not respond.

"I hope you won't end up regretting this later on."

"Regret?" Jamshid broke into hollow laughter. "How can I regret the only right thing I've done so far?"

★ ★ ★

Even in the best of times, Tehran's hospitals were overcrowded and understaffed. It grew worse when most specialists left the country after the revolution.

Arman walked into the second floor waiting room. Crowds of patients and their families sat, while exhausted physicians and nurses ran from room to room. He approached a pretty secretary sitting behind the counter. She looked up and smiled at him.

He leaned on the desk and smiled back. "Is Nurse Fathi back?"

The girl giggled. "She's still on leave of absence. Instead Nurse Leila will be taking over from tomorrow on. She's really nice. Your father has met her. I'm sure you'll like her."

"And where will you move to when she takes your spot at this desk, Shiva?"

The girl blushed. "Just down the hall, Arman. If you'd ever like to stop by . . . "

"Maybe I will." He grinned. "Can I go in?"

"The door's unlocked. The doctor just visited your father."

"How's he doing?"

"Not bad. The doctor said his condition is improving, but if you'd like more detailed information, you should speak to the doctor. He's in surgery now. You can call him later."

"Sounds good. You're perfect, Shiva."

Shiva giggled again. Arman winked at her before entering his father's room. He pulled the curtain aside and immediately dropped the amused look. His father lay on the hospital bed attached to a nest of tubes and wires. Some entered under his collarbone, with a few in his groin that threaded into his heart. They were all attached to monitors that measured his heart rate. Needles connected IV tubes to his right arm, with which he had held rifles and fought the communists and the fundamentalists. But that was ages ago.

Arman pulled up a chair and sat by him. The old man opened his eyes and looked at him. That was all he could do. He could not talk, he could not move. His once agile and athletic body was nothing more than a prison. Arman tucked his blanket around him.

"*Salam*, Baba."

The old general's eyes opened and closed in response. But they were questioning him. The old man's brain was as sharp as it had ever been.

"I meant to come by this morning, but I was busy." He sighed. "I'm doing a dangerous thing tonight, Baba. Not too far off from the adventures you had not that long ago. It's for Iran, Baba. Kami came by the other day and told me that I'm just like you."

Arman saw the puzzled look in his father's eyes.

"It's ironic. Especially that we argued about it so much before this happened to you. He said I'm like you because I love Iran too much—too much for my sanity."

Arman paused. His father was still alert, waiting.

"I hope I'll be able to come back tomorrow. But if I don't, you must understand that I've always loved you. No matter what I've said or how I've behaved. I was in a turmoil deciding whether I should forget it all and try to take you out of this place, but I'm afraid it won't work and you wouldn't want it anyway. You would want me to do what I'm doing. I know you'd join me if you could."

He could feel the muscles of his father's arm become tense, as tears gathered in his eyes.

"If everything goes fine, I'll be back early tomorrow morning. If not, please think of me fondly and forgive me."

Tears rolled down the old general's cheeks as Arman put his face in his father's chest and remained there.

★ ★ ★

Commander Shirazi and Hamid pulled their green jeep up in front of Colonel Moradi's residence. The area seemed very quiet, but Hamid had noticed that neighborhoods got quiet when a pasdar jeep drove through. Though there was always a young man or a child who would sit by the *joob,* the channel of running water, watching the pasdars curiously. Today as well, a young man dressed in an old gray tee shirt and faded dark blue pants and slippers, sat across from the colonel's house, watching.

Hamid knocked on the door.

"Try ringing the bell," Commander Shirazi said.

Annoyed that the interrogators had been unable to get the necessary information out of Colonel Moradi, Commander

Shirazi had decided that perhaps Mrs. Moradi would be able to pass on some information.

Hamid rang the bell again.

"Where the hell is she?" Commander Shirazi frowned. "Probably gone shopping." He sighed irritably. "Get Abdullah here. Tell him it's urgent. I'd rather not make noise and break this door down."

"Yes, sir."

Hamid turned on his walkie-talkie and gave the orders for Abdullah, an employee of the Revolutionary Guard Corps, who could open any lock in Tehran, to immediately drive to Colonel Moradi's residence. He gave the address to the pasdar and then signed off.

"Let's wait in the car." Commander Shirazi walked down the steps to the jeep parked across the street. "Maybe Mrs. Moradi will show up."

★ ★ ★

"Hello?"

Melody's heart beat madly from hearing another human being's voice, especially this one. She had finally found the courage to call. Her voice trembled as she whispered his name, "Arman?"

There was a momentary pause on the other end of the line. "Who is this?"

The memory of their last argument made her hesitate. Then she took in a deep breath and dove in. "Melody. This is Melody, Arman. How are you?"

"My God, Melody." She caught a slight shiver in his voice. It had been over two years since they had spoken. "Where are you?"

"Here in the house."

"Are you alone?"

"Yes."

"I heard about your father. You don't know how sorry I am."

"You mean it?"

"Of course. Where's your mother?"

"Passed away. She had a heart attack."

"Oh, Melody." He was silent for a long while. "And Nader? Is he there with you?"

"I can't find him. He's disappeared." She knew something was bothering Arman. His sentences were short, carefully self-censored for those listening on the tapped lines.

"I'd come over this second, if I could, Melody."

"I understand."

"No, you don't. Not right now, anyway. But I'll explain later. I'll be there tomorrow morning. One more day of loneliness my brave lady, and you'll be fine. That's a promise."

She hung up, relieved to have spoken to somebody. She felt a warm feeling pass through her body. All the memories of him she had buried so deep in her mind now flooded back. In the light of the oil lamps, she could see the green and red colors painted by the Hezbollahies on her living room walls. Furiously she said out loud, "I'll paint these damn walls one more time, after I get myself some food. And then I swear I'll survive, because I'm sure that's exactly what you don't want me to do."

Then she wondered why Arman's voice had not seemed very sure when he had said he would be there tomorrow.

★ ★ ★

Arman hung up. Oh God, he would have liked to rush to Melody. Her voice had been crisp and somber but Arman had lived too long not to be able to read her. The tragedy that had befallen her had been too great and she must be in an awful state. For a fraction of a second, he wished he could drop it all, tell all the political crazies to go to hell, and get in the car and drive to her place. Together, maybe they could forget the madness surrounding them. He hesitated for a second, looking about him. Then his eyes rested on the plastic bag Jamshid had brought with him that morning. The thought of his old friend Colonel Moradi in jail woke him up. It was time to act. Melody could wait one more day. That is, if he survived tonight.

He picked up the bag and walked out.

He drove the Mercedes toward downtown. At the intersection of Gheytarieh, he saw large groups of pasdars, searching cars driving through the crossroad. He took a back street and found his way past the side streets and large shops to the Tajrish area. From there he headed toward Qasr Prison.

★ ★ ★

Colonel Moradi looked up as his cell door opened. The guard stepped in. Although Colonel Moradi had been beaten during interrogation, his face had been untouched. Just a bruise near his right eye gave any indication of the pain and fear he felt down deep in his bones.

"Someone from the interrogation office is here to see you," the guard said hoarsely. "Get up and get ready. They've got some more questions to ask you."

Colonel Moradi almost laughed. Get ready? How did you get ready for a beating? Especially if you didn't know how much more you could take? He had thought they were done with him when they had set his execution day. Maybe there were new developments. He hadn't given out Arman or Kami's names, since like most of his military officers he believed in honor first. Besides when they had arrested him, he came to the conclusion that even if he died, it would be worth it to see Arman and Kami pull off the coup. Although he still didn't know what the reason for the meeting had been, he had a feeling that it was about overthrowing the new regime.

Outside, stood a young man who had once been a promising sergeant under his command, but then had joined the revolutionaries. Jamshid Mahmoudi, that was his name. Colonel Moradi did not look at him. The sight of any pasdar disgusted him.

"Take off his handcuffs," Jamshid told the guard. "I'll take it from here."

The prison supervisor held out a sign-in sheet. "Signature, Pasdar Mahmoudi?"

"Don't you people know me by now?"

"Yes, sir. Sorry sir. But it is procedure."

"I understand." Jamshid signed and then nodded to the guard. "Take him up. I haven't got all day. Pasdar Alizadeh wants him there immediately. There have been new developments."

"Really?" The guard looked interested as he pushed Colonel Moradi forward. "Do they think they figured out about the Mujahedin?"

"This is a different investigation, brother."

As they walked up the stairs, the supervisor asked, "When will you bring him back?"

"When we're done with him. Hopefully no later than midnight."

★ ★ ★

"Here he is, finally!"

Commander Shirazi walked out of the car and slammed the door shut. The van stopped and a short thin man jumped out. Abdullah had been a government employee for the last twenty years. He also knew he was irreplaceable and could afford to be lazy. He had not yet made it to any meeting or appointment on time.

"Where the hell have you been?"

"I'm sorry, sir. My van broke down and then I was stuck in traffic—"

"Excuses as usual! Hurry up, Abdullah. Open this damn door."

Abdullah bent in front of the door and within seconds flung it open. Commander Shirazi stormed in, Hamid in his wake. They both stopped just inside the door.

The furniture was covered with a white cloth. The curtains were pulled, and only a light in the kitchen was on. Hamid walked to the bedroom. The closets were half empty. There were gaps on the bureau and night table where photos and jewelry cases had stood.

He walked back out. "She's gone."

Commander Shirazi stood by a desk, looking through documents pulled out from the drawers. "What?"

"Her clothes are gone. So's her jewelry."

"But where in the world would she go?"

"She flew out of the country?"

"Call headquarters. Ask them to check the departure flights. See if her name is on there. Otherwise, she may still be here. Meanwhile, check out the colonel's room. Let's see if he's left any notes around."

★ ★ ★

Arman turned off the engine and headlights and pulled back his seat. Jamshid would show up any minute. If not, Arman would have to run for it. He heard the sound of laughter and breathed in, focusing his eyes on a group of students walking casually past. One of them looked up the alleyway. They had their school bags on their backs. Suddenly, he leaned forward. A white Peykan—Iranian-made shoebox sedan—drove in from across the street. Its headlights turned on and off twice. Arman repeated the signal. The Peykan parked behind the construction building and two men sprang out, running toward his Mercedes. They both jumped in the back.

"Arman?" Colonel Moradi's voice shook.

"Greetings, Colonel."

Arman drove toward the airport. "Everything went fine?" he asked Jamshid.

"Yes," Jamshid said. "I told them he's going to the interrogation office. They didn't doubt me."

"How much time have we got?"

"I'd give them till tomorrow morning to put two and two together."

"Good. Listen to me, Colonel."

"Yes, Arman." Colonel Moradi leaned forward.

"Jamshid will help you put on the clothes in that bag. You've got to be fast. We haven't got much time."

"These clergy clothes?"

"Yes and Jamshid is here to help you wrap that turban around your head." Arman chuckled. "You're holy now. Congratulations."

Arman drove while Jamshid helped Colonel Moradi put on the clothes and glue on the fake beard. "Your name is Ayatollah Rahbari and you're from Qom. You're going for a short visit to the Islamic Cultural Center in London to give a talk. This is yours." He handed back the red passport. "You're fifty-two years old. You were born on October 11. You have a wife and five children, three boys. Don't say one word, unless absolutely necessary. Jamshid's doing the talking. Any comments?"

"Where is my wife?" Colonel Moradi asked, while he put on the robe.

"In London. Anything else?"

"Yes."

Arman waited.

"Thank you," Colonel Moradi said, his voice quivering.

"You're welcome. It's a pleasure to be working with you again, sir."

"The feeling is mutual, Lieutenant."

"Thank you, sir."

★ ★ ★

"I was just told, Commander Shirazi, that a lady with the name of Parvaneh Moradi boarded a London flight at three thirty-five this morning. She flew via British Airways."

Commander Shirazi browsed through the papers on Colonel Moradi's desk in his study. It was dark and there was a power outage again. They both had their flashlights on.

"I wonder why she escaped like that?" Hamid said.

"Probably got scared. You know how women are."

"Yes, but don't you think it's a bit strange?" Hamid frowned. "I mean, she could've at least waited until he died. There is no reason to escape unless—"

"Unless what?"

"She knew something we don't."

"Like what? Frankly, I think this is all a fairy tale made up by General Jalili to get himself off the hook. Though . . . if there were nothing to hide, she wouldn't get out so fast. Maybe you're right, Hamid—"

Commander Shirazi's walkie-talkie came on line. He answered. "Hello?"

"Commander Shirazi, this is Sergeant Taheri calling from the base. I have Mr. Taji on the phone. He would like to speak to you."

Hamid's eyes met Commander Shirazi's. He knew he was thinking the same thing. What did one of the most powerful members of the revolutionary council want from him?

"At this time of night?"

"He's here, Commander. Please hold."

"Commander Shirazi?" The deep voice of the representative of the revolutionary council came on line.

"Yes?"

"This is Mohsen Taji."

"Yes, sir."

"I think you should come to the station at once, Commander. We need to talk."

"May I ask what about, sir?"

"When you get here, Commander."

"I'll be there at once, sir." He turned off his walkie-talkie. Hamid stared back at him. Commander Shirazi stood and walked out of the house, with Hamid following close by.

★ ★ ★

Groups of pasdars stopped the cars on the freeway to the airport. Arman slowed down. One of the pasdars separated from the crowd and walked forward, shining his flashlight on them. Arman stopped the car and pulled down his window.

"What's happening, brother?" Jamshid appeared angry.

The pasdar's eyes rested momentarily on Jamshid's uniform and the beam of his flashlight fell on the backseat where Colonel Moradi sat in his clerical uniform.

"We're checking every car tonight, Haj Agha. It's the order."

"Whose order?"

"Ayatollah Khomeini's, sir." The young man's eyes rested on Jamshid once more, this time recognizing the badge of rank attached to his uniform.

"All right then." Jamshid waved an agitated hand. "Hurry up."

"May I ask where you're going, sir?"

"To the airport."

"Where are you flying to, sir?"

"London."

"Who is flying out?"

"The Ayatollah Mohammad Rahbari traveling to the Islamic Cultural Center in London to exhort the faithful to hold to the glories of Islam in the midst of western corruption. Do you have a problem with that, brother?"

"No, sir. Passport please."

Jamshid handed over Colonel Moradi's passport. The guard looked through it quickly.

"These are questions I need to ask, sir. I apologize in advance. But how long will you be in London, sir?"

"Are these questions necessary, young man? It is obvious who we are. If you must know, the Ayatollah will remain in London long enough to do the work of Allah. We're running late. Now, are you done?"

"Yes sir! Thank you, sir! Good night, sir!"

Jamshid rolled up his window. Arman drove off.

"You were terrific, Jamshid."

Jamshid grinned. "It's a gift, God help me."

"Now the airport."

Arman parked the car in a visitor parking spot in front of the entrance gate. It seemed more crowded than before as guards fortified the building. At the entrance door to the airport, a pasdar looked up sharply but then smiled as he saw the clerical figure. "*As-salam-o alaykum*, Haj Agha."

Colonel Moradi smiled and mumbled something humbly under his breath to sound like a man of God.

"Passports, please."

Jamshid handed him the passport. His eyes met Arman's. This pasdar was older and more competent. He would not be as easily manipulated as the young man on the road.

"Where to, Haj Agha?"

The pasdar looked at Colonel Moradi. Jamshid couldn't jump in without seeming suspiciously arrogant.

"Under Ayatollah Khomeini's supervision and holy shadow," Colonel Moradi said, "with the righteous work of his guardians, such as yourself, my son, I am going to London to speak at an Islamic gathering about our country and our view of the Islamic world."

The pasdar's expression became softer. "Allah bless you, father. This is a true Islamic government. This is the government of Allah. What else could a society ask for?"

"That is why I'm going, my child, to show the world what they are missing."

"A few days back in the mosque, father, I heard a terrible report about how in the Western world, they do horrible crimes against humanity. This girl was raped in America, in New York, Allah forbid, and nobody stopped in the street to help her. It disturbed me and I thought then of how much better the world would be with our religion. Maybe then the world would see the light."

"I'm proud of you, my son, to have such understanding of our religion. Islam is a fantastic religion and that's what I'm taking with me to share with the world in London."

"Oh, how I wish I were there, but nevertheless I wish you a great trip, father." He kissed Colonel Moradi's hand and gave him back his passport.

"May Allah be with you, my son."

"You too, father. Pray for my family."

"Of course, son. I pray for all humankind."

They walked on and as Arman heard Colonel Moradi take a deep breath of relief, he chuckled.

At the ticket registration desk, Jamshid's pasdar uniform worked against him. The airport police had no fondness for the revolutionary guards. The airline worker, a clean-shaven man with a neatly ironed white shirt said, "I need to see the Ayatollah personally, to check him in."

"What's your name again, Mr.—"

"Farshi."

"Well, Mr. Farshi, I don't know where you've been hiding, but Iran is a place where we now rule. I'm telling you, as a government official, to check in his Excellency, and you'll do it." He smiled cheerfully. "Even if I have to make you do it."

The man's eyes rested on Jamshid's pistol and he checked in the Ayatollah without further questioning. But then the sound of shouting and gunfire froze them in their tracks. All people turned to look at the door. Six pasdars rushed in and pushed aside two passengers who fell to the ground; one an older woman who screamed.

"Make way! Make way!" the head pasdar shouted. "Make way for the Ayatollah's son."

The airport police officer who came forward to object was knocked aside with a rough kick to the stomach. Guarded by these vicious pasdars was an obese clergyman, walking grandly past the queues.

Jamshid wiped the sweat off his forehead with his handkerchief. "Just what we need. Sheikh Mohammad Ringo."

"Who?"

"The son of one of the great supporters of Ayatollah Khomeini. A crook. Lives off of drugs and gambling. His organization operates like the mafia."

"Nice," Colonel Moradi said.

"I have an idea," Arman said. "Follow me."

The two men followed Arman who walked with one hand to his pistol. Mohammad Ringo's bodyguards shoved the airport police aside, making so much noise that the entire airport was in chaos. Arman fell in behind the last pasdar in the Sheikh's team. As they walked through the lines and groups of pasdars standing in corners, and the airport police, everyone thought that the three of them were part of the Ringo team and didn't bother to stop them. The gate to the airline had just opened. The passengers began to climb down the steps into the shuttle, which drove them to the airplane.

"Come with me, Arman," Colonel Moradi said, "before it's too late."

"I can't. I have things to do."

"Whatever it is, Arman, it's not worth it."

Arman did not respond so Colonel Moradi added, "My wife and I would love to have you if you ever plan on visiting London."

"Thank you."

"You don't know, both of you, how grateful I am. Words cannot express my gratitude."

"Give my love to your family," Arman said. "Go on and live, Colonel."

"I'll try, Arman." Then he turned to Jamshid. "Thank you Jamshid. You were a good soldier under my command and I'm glad to see you are still a good man."

"It took some time to find myself, sir."

"Go, Colonel. Get out." Arman pushed him to the gate. Colonel Moradi soon vanished between the passengers and entered the shuttle. In the airplane, he was out of Iranian territory. He was a free man.

"You should have gone with him, Jamshid," Arman finally said.

"And leave Iran? Iran is my life."

"You may end up dying for it."

"Better die for something you believe in than live for nothing, don't you think? Lieutenant?"

"Doing nothing is sometimes better than doing the wrong thing."

"You aristocrats!" Jamshid shook his head. "You're so damned arrogant! You think you're the only ones who've got nationalism toward this country, who've got thoughts and ideas, who've got opinions to share. Well let me tell you something, Lieutenant Pakran, you're damn wrong. It's people like you who've got us into this mess now. What you don't get is that you've got the big voice, the big cars, the big money, but it's always been the ordinary Iranian who makes the difference in the end. You're the first ones to get out and then you shout your opinions at us over the radio or from another country, sitting on your luxurious sofas. We stay. We fight. Maybe because we just don't have the means to run."

"Is this for Iran, Jamshid, or for Islam?"

The airplane began to move on the runway. Soon it would fly toward the horizon, promising liberty and bliss.

"They're one and the same to me. It's love, you see, the kind of love you're ready to forfeit your life for. And I tell you why, because it's the ultimate love; it's past the threshold when you recognize all the flaws of your beloved and yet go on loving and you dream that someday you'll be given that chance to finally get it right. Because that's our problem, Lieutenant, isn't it? Somehow we never manage to get it right."

★ ★ ★

Commander Shirazi walked into the conference room where Mohsen Taji of the revolutionary council waited. Taji stood with his back to the door, looking out the window and at the busy downtown street. Commander Shirazi closed the door and Taji briskly turned around.

"Take a seat, Commander."

"Thank you, sir."

Commander Shirazi sat on one of the chairs of the conference table and eyed Taji, a well-known intellectual and religious scholar. "Sorry to intrude on you at such a late hour, Commander, but this is urgent."

"No problem, sir."

"I received a call from General Jalili a few days back."

Commander Shirazi clenched his fists.

"I understand that he has been under suspicion by your station, Commander?"

"Yes, sir. During a prisoner's interrogation his name was mentioned as a Mujahedin collaborator."

"That's ridiculous. I want these charges dropped."

"I'm afraid I cannot—"

"Listen to me, Commander." Taji stepped forward, tiny eyes glaring at him from a round fat face. "He was invaluable during the days of the revolution. He was our man planted amid the monarchists. He gave us any dirty little information we needed. It's because of men like him we were successful. I can personally vouch that he's not with the Mujahedin. My men keep track of him—"

"Your men, sir?"

"My guards. I can assure you he's clean, so I want you to drop the investigation."

Commander Shirazi hesitated for a second and then looked at Taji's determined face. Why did Taji think this was important enough to come here personally? "Consider it finished, sir."

"Good. Now we can get to the real reason I'm here."

"Yes, sir?"

"He called me. We have this deal going. He gets me info. I pay him. It's clean. It gets the job done."

"What information, sir?"

"He said that during your interrogation he did not state one fact."

"What was that?"

"He had overheard more than he admitted."

"I knew it!"

"Well, yes, Commander. Maybe if you had given him a chance to speak, he would've told you."

Commander Shirazi did not react to this statement. Instead he asked, "Do you care to tell me what he said, sir?"

"That's why I'm here, Commander. I want this thing stopped. If this is a planned coup, we've got to get to it before anything happens."

"What did he say, sir?"

"He'd heard Colonel Moradi mention the name Pakran on the phone. Seems he may have had a part in this somehow. I remember General Abdullah Pakran, one hell of a fighter, a man who didn't give up easily. I would define him as a dangerous man. He's an old man now but he has a son and the son is in town, and by God, if he has anything in common with his father, we're in real trouble."

"What has the father done?"

"He was one of the men who brought the Shah back in 1953 with the help of the CIA. I've seen him in combat, when he had to make tough decisions. His comrades and military staff loved him. There was a time when one command from him would have united the entire military under one cause. That's why the Shah hated him."

"I'll have the interrogation office try to get more information from Colonel Moradi. I'll also go personally after Pakran—"

"Yes, you will. Meanwhile I don't want you going around harassing General Jalili. Any communication with him goes through me. Is that understood?"

"Yes, sir."

"And I want you to get Pakran, Commander, dead or alive. He's a hazard and needs to be stopped."

"I'll do my best, sir."

"Your best may not be good enough, Commander. Get him! That's an order and if you can get the names of others working with him you'll be highly rewarded. I'll personally make sure of that."

"Yes, sir."

Commander Shirazi stood, saluted, and walked out of the room.

SIX

EARLY NEXT MORNING, MARYAM rubbed her hand across her stomach and winced. The child hadn't moved—not in the forty-eight hours since Ali had thrown her in this room and locked her inside.

She fell from her bed and crawled to a tray of food placed for her on the floor in the center of the room, grabbed the bread hungrily and shoved it down her throat. Then she drank the cold tea. Her hands were scabbed from knocking on the door and her throat dry from screaming. Until the moment Jamshid had spoken she had not realized the wrong that had been done to her. Ali had not changed. She had been used from the beginning. But what she was not still clear about was her father's situation.

The shadow of the window bars fell upon the machine woven carpet. Ali did not see the necessity of buying handmade Persian carpets. She wiped her mouth with the back of her sleeve. Then she gasped. The doorknob turned and the door opened. She clung to the bed.

Ali peeked through the opening of the door and smiled warmly, the same smile she had fallen in love with. It was the smile of the man who had carried her books for her at the University. "And how are we today, Khanum?"

She did not respond.

"Still angry?" He looked at her as if looking at a lost kitten. She pulled herself back in fear. "It's not my fault, you know, that your family fell into this mess. It's their own doing. I mean so what if your father is . . . hurt. You shouldn't really care after what he's done to you."

Not care?

"Come! Let me help you up." He pulled her by the arm. "Here you go. Let's go to the living room and get my little wife some sweets."

He put her on the sofa. She watched him pour hot tea for her. His gentleness was somehow more terrifying than his madness.

"What's going on?" she asked.

He sat by her. "What do you mean?"

"You're too nice. Why aren't you beating me up?"

"Nonsense. Just because every once in a while you displease me doesn't mean I don't care for you."

"Don't touch me!"

He pulled his hand back.

She looked at him with ice-cold eyes. "I want a divorce."

Ali blinked. "Impossible!"

"You don't love me, Ali, and I don't—"

"What has love got to do with it? You're my wife."

"I don't love you."

Ali shrugged. "In Islam when you marry, you marry for good. I promised to take care of you and I will. That's that."

"I have a right—"

"No, you don't. You have no rights anymore, woman. The revolution took them all away. Now you're my wife. You don't have the right to ask for a divorce."

"What?"

"You've been in the house way too long, Khanum." He chuckled. "A woman can't ask for a divorce. A man has to give it. Your word has half the value of mine in court. And guess what? When our son is born, even if I permit you a divorce, you'll have to leave the child with me. It'll belong to me."

"I'll get out." She put a hand to her face, her voice shivering. "I'll leave Iran."

"You can't, Khanum, not without my signature. You'll need your husband's signature to leave the country or renew your passport."

"This is not what I fought for, this is not what I wanted when I ran in the streets with you—"

"This is Islam. This is the way it should've always been."

"But Ali you don't love me and I'm so miserable. Please—"

"Love has nothing to do with it. You're my wife. You belong to me—"

"I don't belong to you. I'm not a cow or a horse you own and treat as you like. I'm a human being. I have rights, Ali. *Rights!* Where is my father, Ali? What have you done to him?"

He put a handful of sunflower seeds in his mouth. She hated that. She abhorred watching him crack those seeds between his yellow teeth, his saliva running out. She smelled his odor and felt nauseous one more time. He barely showered and at night when he slept next to her, forcing her to sleep with a scarf on, his body smell was so intense she would turn from him to hide her face in her pillow. He also ordered her not to wash her clothes too often to save water and energy.

"You did so much," she said.

"What?"

"You went so much out of your way to impress me. You spoiled me, you brought me flowers, and you made me dinner. You did so much, Ali, just to seduce me, to get me to marry you. Why? Because of my father's money? Because you had a complex? Because you hated me and Baba?"

He did not respond.

"Is Baba Kia still in jail?"

"No." He did not look at her.

"You let him go?"

"Yes, we did." He stood and walked toward the television.

"What happened?"

"We just let him go, that's all." He picked up the remote and turned on the television, clicking through the channels.

"He's free?"

"Yes."

She did not love him anymore but that caused her to jump to her feet and rush to him. "Thank you! Thank you so much! I knew you couldn't have harmed him. I knew I couldn't have been that wrong—"

"I said we freed him, I didn't say how."

"What do you mean?"

"What do you think I mean?" He put the remote back on the television, which showed a mullah giving a speech in a mosque.

"Come on Ali. Don't do this to me. Did he escape?"

"Not alone."

"With whom then?"

"Your Uncle."

"My uncle?" She had forgotten that Senator Zandi, Melody's father, had also been in prison. "Did they go to the States?"

"Further than that."

She was openly shivering. "Where are they, Ali?"

Slowly he began to laugh. "They are dead, woman."

She stepped back, her chest heaving up and down. She leaned against a chair for support. "What did you say?"

"They're gone. All of them. And they deserved it."

"But Baba Kia . . ."

Baba Kia . . . dead?

She turned away, a hand to her head, bending. Poor Baba Kia who had done so much for her—spoiled her, loved her, gave the world to her. Dead?

The room began to turn and the images of her father's loving face flashed in her memory. She clung to the air for protection as she ran from her husband. He tried to grab her, but she freed herself, and fell to the floor. And there, gratefully, she passed out.

★ ★ ★

A few hours later, Hamid drove toward the Pakran residence. Commander Shirazi had gone to visit Colonel Moradi at the Qasr Prison, so Hamid got the job of finding Arman. As Hamid drove in the green and white jeep with Pasdar Moshiri, he thought of Arman. The shock he had first felt when Arman's name was mentioned had been vast, but seeing the determination on his commander's face had made him keep his mouth shut. After all, there was no need for anyone to know about his childhood friendship with Arman. Besides, Hamid was not sure it even meant anything anymore. So many things had changed since the revolution. Made you wonder what friendship was all about, anyway.

He turned on Zafar Street when his walkie-talkie went off and then died. He parked by the curb and Pasdar Moshiri ran to a telephone booth to call headquarters to make sure nothing urgent had happened. He came back a few minutes later and Hamid started the engine. "What's going on?"

"You won't believe this."

"What?"

"The prison guard went in this morning to check on Colonel Moradi, bring him his breakfast and prepare him for execution and—"

"Will you get to the point?"

"He wasn't there."

Hamid stepped on the brakes. The car skidded to a halt. Behind him a driver swerved his car around him but didn't dare to blow his horn.

He looked up. "What do you mean he wasn't there?"

Pasdar Moshiri let go of the handle of the door. "You're going to kill us, the way you drive—"

"What do you mean he wasn't there?"

"He escaped."

"How in the world—"

"They said one of the guys at the interrogation office has also disappeared. They think he may have been involved in it. Can't believe it, thinking—"

"What's his name?"

"Who?"

"The guy from the interrogation office, obviously, who else?"

"They said Jamshid Mahmoudi, though I can't be sure. There was a lot of noise on the call and with the traffic on the road. They really should do something about Tehran's traffic—"

"Moshiri!" Hamid leaned forward, resisting the urge to slap Moshiri until he got focused. "Have they found Jamshid?"

"Nope. The guy on the call said we should be on the lookout for him, though they seem to think he's left the country too. He came and got Colonel Moradi last night around nine or so, claiming to be taking him to the interrogation office. Since then nobody's seen either one of them."

"Fantastic!"

Hamid made a sharp U-turn against the upcoming traffic to head back to the station. Cars pulled over to let him pass.

"Where are you going?" Moshiri asked, holding tight to the sides of his seat.

"To headquarters. I want to make sure we find Jamshid."

★ ★ ★

Arman walked past the pond where children threw pieces of bread at the ducks. The park was as crowded as usual. He walked up the steps leading to the highest area of the park where a big lake was constructed. Next to the pedal boat rentals, he spotted Zia on a bench, wearing sunglasses and a leather jacket, eating an ice cream. A girl with a balloon ran by Arman laughing and her mother called her back.

Arman sat on the bench next to Zia and looked straight ahead at the citizens who continued to enjoy themselves even while increasing numbers of their neighbors were disappearing.

"Do you have it?" Zia asked without looking at him.

Arman put the folder on the bench between them.

"The complete information. All hostages are kept in the Chancery building. There is more in here, including the number of guards and their schedules."

"Good job." Zia smiled. "I've got bad news."

"What?"

"Your cover was impeccable during Colonel Moradi's escape, but unfortunately they're on to you."

"How?"

"Somebody informed them. You've got to avoid your home. They're spying on your house, waiting for you. Continue calling me at the same hour from a different location."

"How do you know all this?"

"I have my ways."

Arman did not like the non-answer. Even now, he couldn't bring himself to completely trust Zia. "Anything else you need?"

"How many men have you recruited?"

"Four fifty."

Zia laughed. "Incredible. I knew you were good." He frowned. "Be careful. Somewhere in that crowd is someone we can't trust. I don't know whom yet. Do you have the list of names of the officers?"

"Not with me, no."

"Get them to me as soon as you can, so I can check them out."

"It's a long list. I'll get it to you when I can."

"Good. I passed the radar info to the boys. They were very appreciative. They'll be getting back to me tonight. And I've taken care of the rest. The trucks and jeeps are ready for the mission. Kami has been a lot of help. Thanks for connecting me with him." He picked up the folder. "I'll send the rest of this to them tonight."

"What's the plan?"

"You and six other officers be at location Desert One on the twenty-fourth." He looked at his watch. "That's in exactly fourteen days. From Desert One you'll be distributing the weapons to your men. You decide where they'll be positioned."

"That's already been decided."

"Perfect. You'll get the marines to the embassy to get the hostages out. They'll be flown out of there with choppers. Meanwhile you and your men have the weapons to finish the regime."

"That's all we want."

"Where are you going now?"

"To an old friend."

"A lady friend?"

Arman did not respond but smiled faintly.

Zia chuckled. "Keep in touch." He stood, patted the little girl's head who was holding the balloons and walked on. Arman stood up five minutes later and walked in the opposite direction.

★ ★ ★

The doorbell rang. Melody hesitated and then walked toward the door. She looked through the opening and then immediately flung the door open with a warm smile.

"You're a mess," Arman said and then smiled.

Melody laughed and was shocked by the sound of her own laughter. She was wearing dark blue jeans and a tee shirt. Her hair was in a ponytail. She would have said the same to him, except that it wouldn't be true. He was impeccably dressed in jeans and a black shirt. Only with careful attention could you see wrinkles of worry around his eyes.

"Come in, Arman."

He walked in and shut the door. He then looked at her face with amusement and wiped off a spatter of paint from her nose.

"Eggshell?"

"Yes."

He nodded with a faint approving smile.

"Had to. It still looks terrible here with all the colors and the slogans on the walls. It looks nothing like the house I left seven months ago."

"You left? Where did you go?"

"Remember Zarin Abad? My grandparents had a cottage there they'd abandoned. We moved there because Maman was scared about the pasdars coming after us. I think she was more worried for me than herself."

"She seems to have been right, considering what they've done here."

"A drink?" She led him into the kitchen. "As you're well aware, you can't buy any alcohol publicly, so juice or water?"

"Water is fine."

She poured him a glass of water in a heavy tumbler.

"All those wine glasses . . . "

"They were in tiny pieces when I got here. How have you been, Arman?"

"I've been better."

"I heard you lived in California. How was it?"

"Great. I worked at Digital Equipment but then I came back for Baba—"

"How is he?"

Arman shook his head. "Not well."

"I'm sorry."

He nodded. "It was a good job but I believe they've replaced me since we haven't been able to go back." He stood with his hands in his trouser pockets, still looking around.

"We?"

"Oh, right. You haven't met Julia. She's my girlfriend."

"Another one of your flings?" She regretted the words as soon as they came out.

Arman frowned. "I thought we're over that."

"How can we be over that? You went out on me!"

"I went out with another girl after you told me that you're going to accept Nader's proposal." He shrugged. "As far as I was concerned, we were over. I did *not* go out on you, Melody."

She knew he was right but it still infuriated her and she wasn't sure why. "I hadn't accepted Nader's proposal yet. I was considering it. You helped make up my mind for me. You could've waited a day or two before . . . " She couldn't finish the sentence. She turned her back on him.

She heard him sigh. "Melody, can we just let it go? Does it really matter anymore?"

No, it didn't. Besides the truth was she wasn't being fair. He wasn't the only one who had hurt her. She had hurt him first. She looked over her shoulder and couldn't help but smile faintly. "So back to Julia. Is she here now?"

"She came here to visit me before November 4. Her father worked at the embassy. So . . . " He gestured the rest.

"I see. And now you can't go back, because she can't go back?"

"Exactly."

"Sounds almost as bad as my situation." She put a bowl of pistachios in front of him and he smiled like he was remembering something. "How are you feeling, Arman?"

"How much time have you got?"

She grinned. "All day."

He said in a soft voice, "I've missed you, Melody."

She looked at him for a moment, eyeing those broad shoulders, strong masculine arms, and deep dark eyes that seemed to look right through her soul. She felt a chill pass through her body. She wanted to respond, but instead poured him more water.

"Married yet?" he asked.

"Engaged. We had planned it for March last year but with the revolution—"

"I see."

She looked away. "Well, yes, it all seems insignificant now."

"Your father was an excellent man."

"It's nice of you to say that considering he never treated you very well."

"It hurt, but he only wanted the best for you. I understood that."

"I miss him. I miss them."

"I know."

He walked over and took her in his arms. "It was bound to happen, Melody. The Shah and his advisors made too many mistakes. They had fooled themselves by making it all sound too good to be true."

"I know, but I don't understand this, this *hate*! Were the people so poor and so needy that . . . that . . . "

"It's a transition Iran is going through, Melody. We have to learn to live with it. At least that's how I've come to terms with it."

"I don't know if I ever will."

"Can't you go to Gilda?"

"I'd like to but, no. The man who arrested Baba said that I was also on their targeted list and if I showed my face at the airport, they'd immediately arrest me. Maman checked afterward through a gentleman we knew and he said it was true. So, I can't leave. I'm stuck here until things get better."

She was not sure she wanted to leave. She looked through the kitchen window where a red-breasted flycatcher perched in the apple tree her father had planted. Her mother had at times picked apples from the kitchen.

"But you can't live here anymore, Melody."

"This is my home. I won't leave it, unless they kick me out."

"You haven't changed."

"And that disturbs you?"

"On the contrary it delights me."

She laughed with him and then pulled herself reluctantly away.

"All right then," he said. "Would you mind taking care of Julia, Melody?"

She felt as though he'd stabbed her in the heart but she wasn't about to show it. "Why?"

"I took her to a friend of mine out of town for a few days, but I have to go get her soon. I promised her. I think you'll like each other and she'll be a good companion for you."

Melody sighed. "If she doesn't mind this mess. I mean this house isn't exactly comfortable at the moment."

"She'll do just fine. She's a tough girl, although it's not an easy time for her. We need to do all we can to help her, Melody. It's awful that our people have done this to her father. It's unforgivable."

"I know what you mean."

She stood next to him, while he sat on the barstool. His face seemed older, and there was an air about him, like a man who had lost much, but gained even more in the struggle. It was the sense of aptitude and determination, together with an unbeaten will to survive. She realized he was smiling at her.

"What are you thinking?" he asked.

"Tell me, Arman, what's bothering you?"

"It's a long story."

"That bad?"

He nodded.

She sighed. She was glad that he was here. Nothing else seemed to matter that much anymore. "All right. I'll be happy to have her here. Are you picking her up tonight?"

"Honestly, no. Today I'd rather stay off the streets."

"But you don't want to stay at your place either, do you?" It was more a statement than a question. "You can stay with me here and help me paint."

He laughed at her as she put the bucket of paint on the bar.

★ ★ ★

They worked quietly and peacefully. The bond of friendship they had known since childhood had not been damaged even by the way they had hurt each other. Dinnertime he took the brush from her, threw it on the ground, and pulled her to him and held her close. Then they washed and he made dinner for them.

She looked at him in amusement as he walked out of the kitchen with a pan of pasta, an apron he had found in one of the drawers wrapped around his waist. She was once more barefoot with her jeans rolled up. He put the pan on the table and opened the last bottle of red wine they had found in the basement. He poured it in two tumblers. "Not quite the ideal wine for the meal, but it has to do I'm afraid."

She grinned. "It looks delicious."

They began to eat.

Fresh air blew through the open living room window. Her eyes rested on the remains of the chandelier. She could still remember the effort her mother had put into convincing her father to buy it. Now it was hacked to bits, twisted, and—

"You have to learn to forgive eventually," Arman said, stroking her hair.

She came to herself. "Forgive?"

"Whomever you're hating now."

"Never," she said. "I don't think I can ever forget, and there is no forgiving without forgetting."

★ ★ ★

Fire glowed in the darkness; a man was running; a woman screamed. Melody woke up and gasped in the heat of the night, panting. Sweat covered her entire body. She looked around her in terror. The oil lamp next to her bed had gone out. The wind blew through the open window of her bedroom. She was home and in her bed, but it all looked so unfamiliar.

Resting her bare feet on the marble floor she walked quietly out of the room. At her parent's room she stopped. The door was open and Arman was lying in bed, asleep. He had no shirt on and in the heat only a thin cream-colored sheet covered his tanned body glistening under the moonlight shining through the open window.

Long ago she had learned to live only for the past as if she did not exist in the present. Now the present seemed . . . possible, a place she could finally go.

He opened his eyes. "Melody?" he murmured.

Why had they all died?

"Come here, Melody," he said. "Come to me."

She walked to him, barely seeing him. He pulled up his sheet and made room for her. Her skin was fresh and soft, she smelled like soap, and her hair was still damp from the shower she had taken a few hours ago. Her hands rested on his chest without seeing him. He did not say anything. She would not have been able to respond anyway. She had not come here to make love. At some level, she was not even aware that she was here, in his arms. Under the moonlight, her eyes closed, she felt like a lost little girl.

"Where are you, my love?" he whispered and pulled her to him, warming her body. Gently he rested his lips on her forehead. "Do you know what you've done to me? How much you've hurt me, Melody? Do you know the intensity with which I love you?"

But she had already fallen asleep.

★ ★ ★

When he awoke, his left hand automatically felt for her, but she was gone.

Had she fled? Had she been taken, made to disappear in the night like so many? He threw his sheets to the side, and rushed to the corridor. But he stopped. Classical music played in the kitchen and he could smell fried eggs. He chuckled and returned to his room to shower.

In the kitchen he found her in shorts and a khaki pullover, looking refreshed. He sat on the only barstool left, his hair messy from the quick shower. She turned to him and her white teeth sparkled against her bronze skin. "Breakfast?"

"Sounds great."

"You look tired. Didn't you sleep well?"

He smiled but did not respond. He'd slept much better after she arrived, but it seemed ungentlemanly to say so.

She put two eggs on his plate and handed it to him. Then she poured some tea. Any other Iranian woman would have been nearly crippled by shame about what may have happened last night. After all, the society still required women to remain virgins until the day they married. But she just sat across from him, on the kitchen counter, her legs dangling in front of her like a child. She had cut an orange and was peeling the inside of it with her teeth.

"How are *you* feeling this morning?" he asked.

"All right, thank you." She smiled back. "Care to tell me what happened last night?"

He looked at her, trying to appear confused about the question. She laughed and he grinned. "You came by around midnight and slept next to me."

"That's all?"

"If you're asking me whether we made mad, passionate love, we did not."

He would have waited for a look of relief on any other woman's face. He was sure she was a virgin. She had to be, otherwise Nader would not marry her. But the relief never came. "You don't seem to care?"

"Should I?" she asked. "Besides with you I don't have to act. I can be who I am."

"And why is that?"

Her eyes laughed at him. "Because you've always seen me as I truly am, Arman love."

"And what is that?"

"A woman with too few inhibitions, too outspoken for her own good, too much of a tomboy to even peel an orange the right way." She tossed the skin of the orange into the sink. "There is no fakery in our relationship. It wasn't my family name, my father's money, or his title that grabbed your attention, so that you had to pretend it was me you were interested in. You've never been one to be impressed with such things anyway. That's what I've always liked about you and that is . . . " her voice faded, " . . . what has been hard to let go."

She was right. It was her honesty, easy attitude, and boyish mentality that had captured his attention the very first time. She didn't play the silly flirtatious games of most girls. That was the reason they were such good friends since childhood. She was part of the gang, not a little girl he had to protect.

"And Nader?"

"Nader." She sighed, looking at the ceiling, waving her left leg back and forth. "Nader . . . thinks I'm fragile, a girl who he needs to take care of. He thinks I'm better than I am, but I'm afraid he is in love with a dream. I'm not good enough for him. But enough of this. I assume you'll be heading out soon?"

"Yes." He didn't look at her as he wiped his mouth with a napkin. And then after breakfast he walked to the door.

"When will you be back?" she asked.

He knew that she must be afraid of being alone in the house, but she did not show it. "Tonight."

She smiled and looked relieved.

"I'll bring Julia with me when I come. Is that all right?"

"Fine. I'd be happy to have her here. May I ask something of you in return?"

"Of course."

"I've been trying to find him and I can't. I've called but he's never there. I even drove to his house and rang the bell but no one answered. I'm really worried about him. He talks big but I know he's a sensitive man and I don't know how he is handling all this. Change doesn't come easy to him—"

"Who?"

"Nader." She paused for breath. "Will you please try to find him, Arman? I'm really concerned and I know you can help. You know your way around. He's probably already totally lost."

He felt numb to his bones. "I'll do that only for you, Melody." He closed the door behind him, taking a last look at her petite figure alone in the emptiness of the house.

★ ★ ★

Commander Shirazi parked near a Toyota pickup truck. Hamid stepped out to look around. It was early Saturday morning and from here you could see the airport. They had hoped that Colonel Moradi was still in the country, but this morning they had received confirmation that a mysterious clergyman named Ayatollah Rahbari had boarded a flight on the night of Colonel Moradi's escape. According to their records, Ayatollah Rahbari had died at the age of ninety-two, ten years ago in Qom and didn't have a son. He clearly couldn't have flown to London recently.

The arrival of two men in green uniforms had its effect. A few women adjusted their scarves, a man turned and walked the opposite direction, a child stopped laughing. Hamid and Commander Shirazi stepped into the airport. The guard at the gate immediately saluted.

Commander Shirazi nodded in return. "We're here to investigate the flight of a refugee. He escaped from the Qasr Prison on Monday night some time after eight o'clock. We believe he caught a flight to London at 10:05. We'd like to check your official records."

"Impossible, sir. No one can go through this gate without my own personal interrogation. I can assure you, sir, that I did not see any suspicious characters in the last week."

"Our understanding is that he may have been posing as a clergyman, an Ayatollah Rahbari."

"An Ayatollah? Let me see . . . " The guard looked through his books and then his face went slightly pale. He cleared his throat. "I do recall him, sir. He said he would be giving an Islamic talk at a London Islamic association this coming week. As far as I could see, sir, he was . . . above suspicion, sir."

"Who was with him?"

"Two men." The guard's forehead covered now with sweat. "They showed me official papers. They were part of the Revolutionary Guard Corps, sir."

"What's your name?"

"Husseini."

"Well, let me tell you something, Pasdar Husseini. Passports and official papers can be falsified. That's why we've got people like you guarding this damn place, so if you see something suspicious you report to us."

He stood to attention. "Yes, sir."

"So we need you to use every diminutive cell in your tiny brain to analyze anything you see. Even if Allah Himself wants to walk through this door, it's your duty to thoroughly check Him."

"Yes, sir."

"Good. Now, did you see anyone with him?"

"Yes, sir. They were two men with him. His guards."

Hamid made a note.

"What did they do after the Ayatollah flew out?"

"They walked out, sir."

"So, you mean to tell me they didn't leave with him?"

"No, sir."

"No, sir, they left? Or no, sir, they didn't leave?"

"No, sir, they did not leave with him, sir!" Sweat was now openly rolling down Pasdar Husseini's face.

"All right. Now I need two things from you—"

"Yes, sir!"

Commander Shirazi looked annoyed and Hamid suppressed a smile. "First I need you to double-check all official airport books. Make sure those two men didn't in fact leave the country."

"Yes, sir."

"I also want you to talk to your boss and get someone to replace you—"

"But sir." Pasdar Husseini's voice trembled. "I'm sorry about the confusion—"

"Listen to me, Pasdar. I want you to tell your boss to replace you temporarily with a colleague. Then I want you to get your stuff and come with us to the station. We want to get details from you. Meanwhile, we'll talk to some other officials who may have seen something."

"Yes, sir."

The guard spun and practically ran away.

Commander Shirazi sighed and turned to Hamid, a twinkle in his eye. "Let's see if he's smart enough to at least recognize a few faces from our official pictures."

Hamid laughed.

★ ★ ★

Maryam remembered as soon as she woke up. He had told her he was to marry a second time. Ali was like that. He gave you the bad information in large doses, so that you could take it all in at once. That was only if he slightly cared for you.

Maryam did not care if he married again. She had lost her love for him and her own self-respect, so what did it matter? Instead, she asked him to leave her and go to his second wife, so that she could have some peace. He had done just that. For the last two days he had not visited her.

Maryam forced the kitchen window open, although the bars still blocked her view. Every so often, a crack or a noise in the empty house would rush a chill of terror through her veins for she was afraid he had returned. She did not want his filthy green uniform touching her fresh clean skin while he entered her through the open zipper of his trousers.

Suddenly pain hit her stomach. She dropped the plate she was washing into the sink and gasped—it hurt so much she couldn't even scream. She looked down.

Blood dripped down her thighs.

Tearing her clothes off, she ran to the bathroom. She stepped into the bathtub, opened her legs, and shrieked.

★ ★ ★

Arman had dropped off Julia at Melody's house. Now he was standing by a yellow phone booth when the phone rang. He walked in, shut the sliding door, and picked up the phone. The collar of his leather jacket partially shielded his face. He waited for the other end to start speaking first.

"Arman?"

"Kami?"

"What's going on? Where have you been?"

"They know about me," Arman said. "They're watching my place. I wanted to tell you so you wouldn't go there."

"Too late, but it's all right. I could see them from a block away. They're not trying to be discreet—two jeeps are parked right across from your entrance door. What happened?"

"Don't know. A leak somewhere. Again."

"This is bad. We have only thirteen days left till the mission and if there is a traitor . . . " He didn't finish his sentence. "Unless Moradi spoke."

"He said he didn't—I asked him before he left. He didn't even have a chance to speak, he said." *My God. Only thirteen days left till the mission? Time was flying by so fast it was hard to imagine they'd be ready for the U.S. Marines by the time they arrived.*

"How come?" Kami asked.

"Somebody overruled the interrogators. The order came from higher up. They wanted him dead."

There was a slight pause. "That's odd."

"Yes, it is. Have you got the rest of the radar information? We don't have much time."

"Yes. I'll drop it off at the place we talked about," Kami said.

They had planned to meet in the Jamshidieh Park at a secluded bench. It seemed safest and had worked before.

"Is that all, then?" Kami said.

"Until the date, yes. We should meet one more time to go over details."

"Let's do it tomorrow."

"Sounds good. See you—"

"One more thing, Arman."

Arman could hear the concern in Kami's voice. "Is everything all right?"

"Remember you asked me to get details on David Hoshmandi's construction company?"

A woman in a long black veil knocked on the phone booth. Arman signed that he would be done in a minute. "Yeah. Any news?"

"It was no accident. David was shot while buying fruit at a store. A motorcyclist gunned him down. It was hushed up because of the sensitivity of the issue."

"When was this?"

"February 1, 1979."

Ten days before the revolution.

"The person I talked to didn't have any info on it. He said SAVAK tried for those ten days to find the murderer but failed. It's not a surprise considering the turmoil the country was going through at the time. So, the case was dropped and forgotten."

"Convenient. Do you know who did it?"

"Not sure. Whoever it was must have had a real good reason for killing him. They say he was on some sort of a case when he got shot, investigating courtiers and military personnel."

"For what?"

"There was a bunch of top military commanders who wanted to capture the courtiers they believed were traitors to the Shah. He was helping with that, digging in the past. Maybe he dug too far and ended up knowing too much."

"Who knew about the case he worked on?"

"Four people as far as I could gather. One was the big guy." He meant the Shah. "All right."

"And it wouldn't be him. Why should he? He wouldn't double-cross himself."

"I agree."

"The second," Kami said, "was Admiral Habiballahi."

"He got shot right after the revolution. They gunned him down in his office. Come to think of it, I think I heard in the news that his thirteen-year-old son recently got executed."

"That would be him. My theory is that if he'd been working for the Islamic fundamentalists undercover, they wouldn't have killed him. Well, not so soon, anyway."

"Right. And the third?"

"Is the guy who I've been waiting to hear back from. He's traveling right now. He left with the big guy to his exile. He was with him throughout the whole thing. If he was a traitor he could've killed him there. I trust him. I talked to him last night. I've known him since we were kids."

"And the fourth?" Arman held his breath.

"I didn't even know he knew about David. He's currently a member of the revolutionary council—"

The black-veiled woman pounded on the door again and waved an angry fist at him. Behind her, in the line that had formed while Arman wasn't looking, a man shouted something he couldn't hear.

"What did you say?" Arman asked.

"I said the fourth one is currently a member of the revolutionary council."

"No, his name. I didn't catch his name."

"Taji. He's a known Islamic intellectual and a fundamentalist. He was also part of the committee the government put together the last days before the revolution to ease public frustration. He was told about David's investigation in the hope that he would convey that to the revolutionaries, to buy the monarchy time. Didn't work, of course."

"I see."

"What's that noise in the background?"

"Some people waiting in line to use the phone. So you think . . . "

"I don't know what to think. We have to investigate this fellow a little more. One thing that I do know is—"

The woman began pounding on the telephone booth again. "Hold on, Kami." Arman slid the door open. "Give me a moment, please."

"You've had all the time you need! I have to use the phone. I've been waiting twenty minutes. You don't own the telephone booth you know."

"One more minute. Just one more minute!"

"No!"

"My grandfather is dying, Khanum. Just a minute more please."

There was a moment's hesitation, which allowed Arman to get back in and slide the door closed. "Talk fast," he said to Kami.

"Okay, one more thing I learned."

"What?"

"David was investigating a person before his death. Some of the SAVAK agents believed that this was the man who finally killed him, because David dug too much into his past—"

"How do you know this?"

"It's the last thing David wrote in his dossier before he was murdered."

The woman knocked on the door again, slapping her own face.

"Would it be too much to hope he left a name?"

"He only referred to him as Nightshade. From the way he wrote about him, seemed he found Nightshade to be quite the double agent."

A pasdar jeep crossed the block and parked on the other side. The pasdars were looking at a map. Arman turned around, his back toward them. "I've got to go, Kami. I'm being watched. I'll call you later."

He hung up, walked out, smiled at the annoyed line of people waiting to use the phone. He turned his back toward the pasdar's jeep, traveling down the Gheytarieh intersection, disappearing into a crowd.

SEVEN

"**THANK YOU FOR HAVING** me here," Julia said again as she put the two plates she dried by the sink.

"Not a problem." Melody passed her a glass she had rinsed. "Have you known Arman long?"

"About a year. We met at an embassy party. He was there with his father. We hit it off right from the start, then I moved in with him. We've had a lovely time."

"That's good." The truth was, now that Julia was here, it didn't hurt as much. She seemed like a nice girl, much nicer than some of the other girls Arman had gone out with, and in some way Melody was happy for him.

"What about you?" Julia said, her eyes fixed on Melody's face.

"We go a long way back."

"How long?"

"Let's see . . . over twenty years."

Julia put the dishes in the cupboard. "How did you meet?"

"My mother was a friend of his mother. We used to go to their Yazd estate when I was a kid. And they'd come here and visit. When we went to college abroad we lost touch but then met again years later when we were back in Iran . . . "

"How did you meet again?"

"It was his parents' anniversary and we were invited." She chuckled. "It was funny because even after so many years of marriage, they were like high school lovers. I liked his father. He was a Bakhtiari."

"What's that?"

Melody rubbed the grease off a plate. "Oh, sorry, one of the tribes. The Shah's father annihilated most of them. They were warriors."

"I can see that in him."

Melody hid a smile. "Can you?"

"What happened then?"

"We didn't exactly hit it off. He was here for a summer visit from UC Berkeley and had strong opinions about almost everything. I guess we had both changed and I found him insufferable. We argued for days and I thought he hated me . . . "

"And then?"

Melody passed the plate over. "Then he surprisingly asked me to go on a desert trip with him."

"He told me he doesn't like taking anybody with him on those trips. He must have liked you after all."

"He tolerated company then, it wasn't only me. He used to go with a friend of his. Hamid Rahimi."

"He never mentioned him. Who was he?"

"The son of his mother's maid. They'd been friends since childhood. Those two had a bond—"

"Where is he now?"

"Hamid? I heard they had an argument. Hamid joined the revolutionaries and moved here, to Tehran. I don't think they've spoken since."

Julia dried the dish. "What was it like?"

"What?"

"The desert? Being with him . . . out there, I mean."

Melody paused a minute, thinking. "I think some people may find the silence in the desert disturbing, but Arman never did. He enjoyed it. Maybe it's because he doesn't like crowds. The desert was magnificent of course but . . . what was it like being out there?" She bit her lip. "It was peaceful. And you almost felt as though anything was possible."

"How so?"

"It was haunting sitting by the fire, in the quiet desert nights. The sky was full of stars. You forgot there was a real world out there. It all seemed like a beautiful dream." She shrugged. "Then one night, he asked me to read him a French poem. Baudelaire." She looked up and saw Julia was still drying the same plate absentmindedly.

"Were you in love?" Julia asked.

She'd gone too far. "Who knows?" She laughed it off. "We were young, that's all there was to it. A year later I became engaged, and now Arman loves you very much."

A blush swept across Julia's face as she tried to hide her smile. She put the plate in the cupboard. "Yes, we've had great times together. I wish we could go back. But you said you're engaged. Where is your fiancé?"

"I don't know. Arman said he'd try to find him. We got separated when my mother and I left Tehran. Now . . . " She folded her dish towel and turned around. "I'm tired. How about you?"

"Terribly. I guess we should take these oil lamps with us upstairs. How do hospitals function in these circumstances?"

"Not easily, I guess."

They walked up the stairs and went to their bedrooms, each holding an oil lamp.

Melody got under her sheet. She could smell the roses from the yard, hear the crickets, the singing of the birds. It was a warm night. She tried to read, but after a few seconds, she closed the book, turned sideways, and shut her eyes.

Ten minutes later her bedroom door was flung open. She turned in alarm and sat up. Julia stood barefoot and in a tee shirt, her long blond hair wild around her, her brown eyes stared at Melody in open horror. "Someone's at the door."

"What?"

"Someone's knocking on the door."

Melody pushed aside her sheets and stepped onto the cold floor. She pulled up her blue jeans, her ivory tank top falling over them. And now she could hear the knocking for herself.

"There it is again," Julia said, her voice quivering.

Melody held up the oil lamp and headed for the stairs. Before descending, she turned to Julia. "Stay here."

"I will. But what if it's the . . . "

Melody did not have an answer, so she started down the stairs.

The knocking echoed through the empty house. Her shadow holding on to the oil lamp reflected on the large living room window, opening to the yard. She stood a few steps away from the door.

"Who is it?" she asked.

She turned the handle of the door and stood in the doorway in the complete darkness of the night. She saw what frightened her most—absolutely nothing. A gentle breeze shook the branches of the maple trees.

"Who's there?" she cried peering into the darkness.

It seemed quiet enough. She turned back, already thinking of her bed and the safety of her home when a hand grabbed her right ankle.

She gasped and kicked. Staggered, she looked down. At her feet, a figure gradually took shape in the night. It hugged the corner of the wall and only a hand extended out toward her. It was wrapped in a long dark cloth, trying to warm its wretched body from the summer night's breeze. Not an attacker. Something . . . else.

"Who are you?" Melody said in a voice hardly above a whisper. She held up her oil lamp to look closer. She realized then that Julia was standing behind her. It gave her a secure feeling to know she was not alone.

"Oh my God! Don't get close, Melody."

They saw a pair of miserable green eyes staring at them through the wrapped cloth.

"Who is this?" Julia's voice trembled but it managed to pull Melody out of her trance.

The figure in front of her was a woman.

"Help us," the woman said in soft, sibilant Farsi. "In Allah's name, have mercy on us."

"What is she saying? Melody . . . "

"Maryam," Melody bent toward the pitiful woman. "Just please tell me it's not you. My beautiful cousin Maryam, what have they done to you?"

Maryam cringed, trying to pull herself from her cousin.

"Give me your hand, Maryam. Come in. You're home."

"Melody, who is she? Is she okay?"

"My cousin," Melody said in English.

Suddenly, from between the layers of Maryam's veil, Melody caught the sight of a tiny white and red object. She pulled back the veil.

Julia put a hand to her mouth.

"Get up, Maryam. This is Melody, your cousin. Come in."

The name seemed to awaken memories because Maryam's eyes showed amusement, the way they had as a child whenever they met. Maryam leaned forward and placed the bloody infant in Melody's extended arms. Melody did not look at the child. She turned and handed it to Julia.

Julia stepped back but then allowed Melody to place the infant in her arms. Melody pulled Maryam up. Maryam could barely stand and put her hand on Melody's shoulder for support. Melody shut the door with her left foot and turned to face Julia's terrified stare. "Oh come, Julia, it's just a child."

Julia held the infant at arm's length and her voice came hardly above a whisper. "It's not that."

"What is it, then?"

"It's dead."

"What?"

"It's dead." Julia turned her head away from the infant. "Poor thing must've died some time ago."

Maryam growled and sprang forward. Julia danced away. Melody pulled Maryam back. "Calm down, Maryam. Stop." She turned to Julia. "Give the child to her."

Julia took a couple of deep breaths, then stepped forward and placed the child in Maryam's arms. Maryam then became quiet and calm. They led her up the stairs and Melody helped her to her parents' bed while Julia watched from the doorway. Melody finally came out and shut the door behind her.

"I'm sorry about this, Julia. Thank you. Please go to bed and lock yourself in."

"No, I'm sorry I couldn't be of more help. I wish I understood the language. She looks sick. Is she all right?"

"I'm not sure. We'll see how she is tomorrow morning."

"I'm scared, Melody." Tears gathered in her eyes. "I'm just so scared."

"I know. I am too. Go and try to sleep now. It'll all be fine. She'll be okay tomorrow morning."

"What happened to her?"

"She ran away from home with a boy she loved. That was over a year ago. I haven't heard anything from her since. Her father was executed. She has nowhere to go. I'm not sure what's happened to her. I know you're scared but I guess we have to deal with it—"

"I think it's easier for you to deal with all of this." Julia frowned. "This is your home. Your country. I'm halfway around the world. I don't even speak the Goddamn language. My father is still a prisoner and he might be dead for all I know . . . "

Before Melody could respond Julia burst into tears, ran to her room and locked herself inside.

★ ★ ★

By the next morning, Commander Shirazi and Hamid had personally interrogated the airport guard. Finally, they had him describe the faces of the three men, including the man impersonating the deceased Ayatollah Rahbari. When the police sketcher had handed the drawings to them, they both recognized Jamshid immediately.

Hamid frowned. "We should have moved him from the interrogation office. That wasn't his type of job."

"I know you were a friend of his, Hamid," Commander Shirazi said, looking out his office window at the crowded streets, "but you need to forget that. We've got to find him. If you're not up to the job, I'll find someone who is."

"No, sir. He made his own bed, now he's got to sleep in it."

"Good. I'm glad to see your dedication to the Islamic cause. Your religious and governmental duties should be far more important than your personal relationships."

"Yes, sir."

"Now, we're sure of Jamshid, and once we took the turban and the beard off the clergyman, we can be sure of Colonel Moradi. So who was the third? The guard didn't seem to have a good recollection of him."

"Seems the guard did most of his talking with Jamshid and Colonel Moradi."

"Would make sense, I guess." Commander Shirazi put a hand to his waist and turned around. "Let's get Pasdar Husseini into the conference room and show him the slides. Let's see if he'll recognize any of them. Meanwhile, let his boss know that he needs to be better trained before he's put back into position."

Hamid was certain the guard would take this as a personal insult. But then, Commander Shirazi was not known for his compassion.

Five minutes later they gathered in the conference room. With Commander Shirazi and Hamid came Pasdar Husseini, the airport guard, and the technician in charge of the projector.

"Put up slide number two first, please." Hamid said.

The technician put in slide number two and turned on the projector.

"Recognize him?" Commander Shirazi standing in the back asked Pasdar Husseini.

"No, sir. Not at all."

It was the picture of a young man in a pilot uniform. Hamid was checking the accuracy of Husseini's statements. So far, so good. "Put slide number one on." The picture of a man carrying a grocery bag flashed up. "Recognize him?"

"Never seen him in my life."

"Pay close attention, Pasdar Husseini. He may have changed his appearance."

"I'm sure, sir. I'm sure it's not him."

"Put the third one up, please." The picture of a young man in navy uniform, standing on the deck of a ship, with a wide smile on his lips was flashed on the screen. It was the money shot—Lieutenant Arman Pakran. "You recognize him?"

Hussein paused. "Seem to . . . yes, sir. He was the third man. He had a mustache and this person doesn't and his hair looked different but it's the same eyes, sir, and he smiled at me. That's the smile, all right."

Commander Shirazi's eyes met Hamid's.

"Good job, Pasdar Husseini. You may go now," Hamid said.

Pasdar Husseini and the technician walked out. Commander Shirazi stood with his hands behind him. "Arman Pakran."

Hamid stared at the picture. He was now fighting against one of his closest friends. He tried to hide his shock. After all, Commander Shirazi knew about his friendship with Jamshid. If he heard that he even slightly knew Arman, he was sure to replace him with another revolutionary guard, and Hamid was too interested in this case to walk out of it so easily. He was a man who finished anything he started and he wanted to finish this.

"What information have you received from our guys?" Commander Shirazi said.

He meant the team watching over Arman's house. "He hasn't been home. We've been searching the area and haven't found him."

"Tell them to break in and report anything they find. And look into the files, Hamid. Dig into his past. I want to know his friends, where his relatives are, where old Pakran is. I want to know what his habits are—when does he sleep, what does he eat. Anything and everything!"

Hamid put his notes back into his cream-colored folder and tucked it under his arm. He walked to the door.

"You know, Hamid," Commander Shirazi said, "we're dealing with something much bigger than I anticipated. We must stop this coup before it's too late. Do you know that Taji called me this morning again to get an update on the case?"

Hamid stopped and frowned. It seemed strange that Taji worried so openly about this case. This wasn't the first planned rebellion they'd encountered and, so far, wasn't the most dangerous.

Commander Shirazi rubbed his beard with his right hand thoughtfully as Hamid turned and walked out the door to speak to the man in charge of the political files, many of which were inherited from the SAVAK.

★ ★ ★

A golden blanket had been spread across the country for years, covering the grime and filth so well buried into the heart of this land that it had fooled them all.

Slowly Melody placed the spoon in the cup of *ash-e reshte* soup and brought it to her cousin's lips. Only when Maryam would open her mouth to take in the spoon, would their eyes meet wearily.

The Shah had done it and the royal family and in fact government officials like her own father had made them think they lived in a progressive society, while underneath there had been nothing but mayhem and ignorance, whether they wanted to accept it or not.

"Eat," Melody said. The more Maryam ate, the livelier she became. "Why did you leave?" Melody was talking to herself more than to her cousin. "There was a time I thought you were dead. I used to tell Maman that you might be dead, that's why you hadn't called us. She told me once you were probably better off dead. I didn't agree then. I told her they kept reminding us that we're different. It's the symbols that are attached to us that manipulate our society. High class; low class; religious; farmer; *dahati;* peasant; *bazaari*. They make sure, we make sure, the lines stay in place. We want the lines there so we don't have to leave our comfort zone. That's the real tragedy. But you saw it way before I did. That's why you left, isn't it?"

Maryam's lifeless eyes stared straight into Melody's.

"Last spoon. Please. Good. I feel dead. I feel as if I've been buried alive. But what frightens me is that I think you actually have been buried alive. You are already dead. What did they do to you, Maryam?"

Maryam finally fell asleep.

Melody walked out and closed the door. She met Julia halfway up the staircase. "Is she feeling any better?"

"Seems to be, yes."

"Oh, thank God. Shouldn't we call a doctor?"

"She won't let a doctor near. We have to have her checked pretty soon, though, considering she gave birth on her own. But I'll give her till tomorrow morning. I don't want anybody to know of her whereabouts." Melody remembered Julia's outburst from last night and suddenly felt ashamed of her country and her people. Nothing justified the way the Islamic revolutionaries had mistreated the Americans. "I'm sorry, Julia. I was thinking once she gets better, we could try to move to my family villa in Karaj. It's two hours away. I'd thought till now that they've probably confiscated it, but I think it's worth a try. This place is unlivable."

"How can we be sure it's safe?"

"When you feel all right staying with Maryam alone, I'll drive there and take a look. Then we can move."

Julia looked as though she thought there was very little chance she would be comfortable alone in the house with Maryam. She finally sighed. "All right, I'll do what I can. This has turned into a living nightmare. I was looking at the news the other day and they said the negotiations are still going on. I don't even know if Dad is alive."

"From what I've heard they haven't physically abused the hostages." She walked into the kitchen and put Maryam's tray of food by the sink.

Julia followed her in. "I don't understand how this could all happen. Iran seemed so lovely. It still does. I mean when you go in the streets, people are so nice and hospitable. Tehran is green and beautiful. How did it all go wrong? You know, in the States, this would never happen. We have laws and a constitution. You can go to a court and demand your rights."

Melody rinsed Maryam's soup bowl.

"I wish Arman would visit."

"He will soon." Melody dried her hands while Julia leaned against the kitchen counter. Her head ached and she had a big lump in her throat. She found it harder to breathe the more Julia talked.

"Have you been to the States?" Julia asked.

"I lived there for several years. I got my MBA from the University of Washington. It was very different from my studies in Paris."

"Did you like it?"

"Paris or the States?"

"The States."

"Yes, it was very nice. I liked it."

"Why did you come back?"

"Because, believe it or not, this place is my home."

Julia played with her ponytail, her eyes distant and nostalgic. "I used to love coming to Iran for summer vacations. But now . . . I think Arman should move to the States. He's half American. He doesn't belong here. You don't either. What's the point of staying here anyway? These people are so primitive. I mean is it lack of education? Or is the culture—"

"Look!" Melody spun around in rage. Julia recoiled.

"What we have become," Melody said quietly, "your government helped us become. We're both at fault here—us more than you perhaps, but those people you call primitive so freely are what they are because they're torn between two cultures. And one of those cultures was forced upon us by your politicians and our own. Don't disassociate yourself so proudly from what is upstairs. It's as much a part of you as it's a part of me. The only difference is you've been ignorant of it."

"Melody! I had nothing to do with this!"

"No, but your government did and still does. Ignorance about other countries, meddling in their affairs for oil, is as bad a folly as us being confused about our own identities."

"I . . . I'm proud to be an American no matter what you say," Julia said.

"Yes and I love Iran despite everything," Melody said. "Why is this so hard for you to accept?"

★ ★ ★

That evening, General Jalili walked under the bridge past the traffic and turned up a narrow steep road. Then he took a right again and ended up by the International School. He pushed open the gate and walked into the playground. He had been here several times and knew his way quite well—the meeting was to take place next to the gym. When he got there, he stopped and looked around him, then checked his watch. 9:07. Sure, he was seven minutes late, but Nightshade should have been here already with the money.

General Jalili's hand shook as he threw his cigarette to the ground and crushed it under his Gucci shoe. He liked to gamble but the habit had put him in financial embarrassment before. And even though money was now flowing in, General Jalili was still scared. He knew what he was up against. Though once he too had been party to great things in the military—had been a commander in His Majesty's Imperial Guards for a short period—very little of that past courage had stayed in him.

Where was Nightshade?

General Jalili looked at his watch. Eight minutes past nine. He chuckled at his own cleverness. It had all been so obvious to him the moment he had encountered it, though no one else had figured it out. Of course, he hadn't known of the code name. He had come across that when going through the files a few days ago. Nightshade's identity had been in the highly confidential files he had managed to take from the royal court before the revolution. His hand moved to his inside jacket pocket and found the picture—a personal joke. He smiled.

He looked at his watch again.

With the cash he received last time from Nightshade, he paid off his debts to the city sharks, who of course were now employed by the government. A night later he had unfortunately fallen into more debt. So, he had called Nightshade once more. With the new facts he had on him, Nightshade had to comply.

But he was still scared. Where was Nightshade?

The shadow of a hand holding a knife fell across the gym wall. General Jalili was grabbed from behind. The knife cut straight through his neck and he fell to the ground, motionless.

Nightshade stood over him until he died. Then he turned and walked away.

★ ★ ★

At dawn, Jamshid sat on the damp ground by his University friend, Firooz. When Colonel Moradi had fled, Jamshid contacted his old friend Firooz and asked if he could hide with the Mujahedin-e Khalgh for a little while. Behind them green tents were set up in the Caspian jungle spreading across the entire Alborz chain of mountains, separating Tehran from the Caspian region. It was a wild area few civilians ever visited. A handful of young men and women with AK-47s on their backs stood in circles, talking. Firooz whittled a piece of wood with a knife, turning it into a small delicate goldfish. It was very humid and Jamshid's back was soaked.

"I wouldn't mind getting out of here." Jamshid chuckled. He hadn't joined the Mujahedin because he believed in their cause, but because he had nowhere else to go.

"You know it was my birthday last Friday?" Firooz said in a cold voice.

"Oh, God, I completely forgot. I'm sorry."

"The sad thing is I forgot too. I just remembered half an hour ago while I sat here carving this stupid fish."

"You're doing well with that wood."

"At least there's something I'm good at."

"Maybe that's what you should be doing."

"Instead of fighting, you mean?"

"Yes."

Firooz grinned. It was a bitter grin below innocent brown eyes. "It'll be good for *Noruz,* New Years, you know. I didn't celebrate last New Year. There didn't seem to be much point celebrating when our country was heading for destruction. I'm going to send this to my grandma. It'll make her happy to know her last living grandchild is thinking of her."

"She understands, Firooz."

"No, she doesn't. Everything has changed so much. I haven't visited her for a year now."

"Why don't you take leave—"

"You don't get it, do you Jamshid? This isn't summer camp. Once you get in, you don't get out."

"You wanted to talk to me?"

Firooz sighed. "They want me to talk to you."

Jamshid waved away a fly buzzing around his head. "Who does?"

"The leaders. Who else?"

Jamshid nodded. He had been waiting for this. He had tried to distance himself from the Mujahedin missions and Firooz, who had been an old friend, had tried to shelter him from the violence and the battles. But he had known it could not last this way forever.

"What do they want?"

"You know about the next attack, right?"

"I've heard of it, yes."

"That's the trouble."

"What is?"

"You hear too much here. The guys wonder why you're here if you don't want to fight your old comrades. They think you're a spy."

"Rubbish!"

"I know that, because I know you. I've been holding them back because I know how you feel and I sympathize with you, believe me, because I know where you're coming from. I've been there, remember? But they won't listen anymore."

"All this blood, all this hate, Firooz, for what? I'm so tired of it all. I'm simply tired . . ."

"I know."

"We just kill ourselves every time we fire a bullet. When we kill a man who could have been our neighbor, we just kill a part of us. And that's a part we'll never be able to revive again."

Suddenly Firooz was on his feet. "You think I don't know? You think I don't look back and realize I was stupid to ever get involved in the revolution? I mean I didn't agree with the Shah. He was a puppet of those Americans. They said jump and he'd throw himself off a bridge, and you can't have such a fool ruling a respectful country. But at least then I went to University and held a decent job. I had a reasonable life. Now, I'm stuck in this godforsaken graveyard of a jungle with bugs flying around my head, sweat running down my face like I'm standing under a shower, and the only hobby I've got is carving this stupid fish. I haven't showered for three weeks and I even forgot my own damn birthday. You think I like it?"

"Let's get out of here, Firooz. Let's find another place—"

"Wake up and smell the blood, Jamshid. There's nowhere to go, brother. You leave this hellhole and you've given up your last support. These guys may not be perfect but at least they try to attack the Hezbollah, which is more than the others do. At least we're trying to make things right again. We're doing something, not just talking."

"You're just as fanatical as the revolutionary guards, Firooz. I mean, Islamic Marxism? It makes absolutely no sense. You can't mix one of the strongest religions in the world with an ideology that doesn't believe in any God."

"Listen." Firooz bent forward, his face in Jamshid's, his normally innocent brown eyes harsh and angry. "They're ruthless, you fool. They'll kill you if they hear you talking like this. You've got nowhere to go. It's either the revolutionary guards or these guys who'll finally kill you."

"So you're asking me to take one side or another to stay alive?"

"No, I'm telling you."

Firooz put the carved fish in his pocket. "The message they want me to pass on to you is: with us or against us. Choose your way."

"There's no gray?"

"That's life I'm afraid, Jamshid."

"Our life anyway. Till when do I have to make this decision?"

"Midnight. Tonight."

Firooz walked away, his rifle on his back. His boots sank into the mud but his walk was the same as the lighthearted boy of a year and a half ago. But Jamshid knew there was now nothing light about his soul.

★ ★ ★

The doorbell rang once more. Julia waited in her room while Melody rushed down the stairs. The electricity was on tonight, so she turned on the porch light and looked outside.

It was Arman.

She flung the door wide open. Her warm smile froze when she saw him supporting Nader whose head dropped forward, his mouth open.

"Nader!" she said. "What in the world happened to you?"

"Do you mind if we skip the romantic reunion?" Arman asked. "I'd like to get out of sight."

Melody slung Nader's other arm over her shoulder and they carried him in. She shut the door with her foot. "What happened to him?"

Before Arman could respond, Julia rushed down the staircase and fell into his arms. "Arman, my God! I've been worried sick. How are you?"

Arman managed to keep his balance. "Fine, Julia, thank you. Let's take Nader upstairs first."

"What's wrong with him?" Julia asked.

"Drunk, that's all."

They took Nader upstairs and laid him on one of the guestroom beds. Melody opened the windows for fresh air and to let Nader's alcoholic odor escape.

"Where did you find him?" Julia asked.

"In his house."

"Really?" Melody looked surprised. "I went there several times and no one answered the doorbell."

"Well, you can see why. He was luckier this time."

"How so?"

"Because I promised to bring him here. Otherwise, frankly, I'd have no problem seeing the fool drink himself to death. He's the sort of idiot who would do just that."

"Arman!"

"He spoke to me before he passed out. He's been drunk for days now. It'll take a miracle to get all that alcohol out of his body."

"We all have our ways of dealing with stress, I guess," Julia said.

"Did you talk to him before he passed out?" Melody asked.

Arman nodded. "He said he's been too alone and scared. 'Scared like shit!' was the phrase he used. He'd gone to a friend of his whom they'd released from prison about a month ago. The guy must have looked a wreck. That's how it all started."

Melody looked at the saliva dripping from Nader's open mouth and his yellow shirt that had not been changed for days, if not weeks.

"You're right. I guess we all have our way of dealing with stress." Melody stood. "We should leave him to dry out. Nothing else we can do right now. Would you like tea or coffee, Arman?"

"I'd die for a cup of coffee."

"I'll get it for you." Julia rushed out.

Melody's eyes followed Julia, then turned to rest with amusement on Arman.

"What?" he asked, his eyes widening.

"She's been talking about nothing but you since she got here." She could hear the irritation in her voice and hated herself for it. "You should probably spend some time with her."

"I will. What's it to you, anyway? I thought you were engaged." He chuckled and then threw a glance at Nader. "Take a good look at your handsome prince, Melody. Is he all you dreamt of?"

"Oh shut up." She turned to walk out of the room.

He put his hand out, grabbed her by the arm, and pulled her harshly toward him. His body odor mixed with alcohol reached her nostrils. Apparently, he had had a few drinks himself.

"Let me go." She pushed against him. "You smell."

"Did you miss me, Melody?" He was leaning toward her now. She knew she should push him away. She was engaged and her fiancé was lying on the bed in this very room. But somehow, she couldn't find the strength to fight him. She closed her eyes, her body relaxing, yearning for his lips to touch hers.

But the sound of footsteps running up the stairs brought her back to reality. She looked at him in alarm and he released her.

Julia ran into the room. "Coffee's ready." She turned to Melody. "By the way, I heard some noises from . . . " She nodded toward Maryam's room.

Arman frowned. "What noise?"

"Maryam is here. Julia can tell you the rest." Melody walked out and into Maryam's bedroom.

The curtains were pulled and the room was dark. Maryam was on the bed, sobbing loudly, holding her child's cold corpse, rocking back and forth. A fresh breeze blew through the open window, cutting the foul smell. Melody shut the door behind her and walked toward Maryam in the darkness.

"You know, Maryam," she said gently, "there was a time you'd never shut up. I used to fall asleep at night before you'd stop telling me stories. So what can I do to make you talk now, girlfriend? I've tried. I've tried everything I can. When they died, they still loved you. Uncle Kia, you know, Baba Kia, spoke of you often. He never forgave your stepmom for treating you badly. He didn't love her like he loved your mother, Maryam."

Melody stopped. This was the first time she had talked about the dead ones. Now she realized it was the right move because Maryam's sobbing got louder until it turned into shrieks. Maryam rocked back and forth faster as if in physical pain.

"Maryam, love, don't do this to yourself. We didn't know. You didn't know. It's not your fault. Baba Kia knew that. We all understood, more than you thought we did. You have to learn to forgive yourself, Maryam. Please, Maryam, for God's sake, stop this."

Maryam dropped to the floor and crawled around like a wild creature. She seemed to be grubbing for a way to hide from the pain that Melody could feel was so severe it had become physical. Melody grabbed her cousin's back, but Maryam was so intent that she dragged Melody with her. It was a strange portrait of two women in the shadow of the room rocking back and forth.

Maryam mumbled something between her sobs, but Melody could not make it out.

"Talk to me, Maryam. Tell me. Don't be afraid. We had a treasure chest, remember? We hid it in the villa, underground, two meters deep. We promised we'd be the only ones who'd ever know. It had a twenty toman bill in it. We divided it in half because without one side, the other would not be complete. That's how we defined our friendship. We thought our friendship would never die. And it hasn't."

Maryam was trembling now and Melody held on to her tightly. She pulled her cousin's hair back from her face, her lips close to her right ear.

"Your father was proud of you. He enjoyed watching us play in your backyard. He said you were the prettiest girl on earth. Until the end, Maryam, he loved you and he wanted you to be happy. That's why, for him, you must learn to be happy again."

"Oh God! Oh God!" The cry eventually turned into words. "Oh God. Forgive me. Baba. I'm so sorry. So very sorry."

Melody held her. Slowly the cry turned from shrieks into silent moaning and then soft, healthy weeping.

★ ★ ★

Mrs. Sadeghi, the PE teacher at the International School, opened the gate and walked in. She liked to come in earlier than the other teachers to work out a bit before classes began. Before the revolution she used to go for a run in her neighborhood, but since the enforcement of the veil and restrictions on women's outdoor activities, she had gotten into the habit of coming to school early for her daily exercise. The principal of the school, a friend of hers, had finally agreed to give her special privileges and a key to the gym.

Her bag on her back, her running shoes tied to the handles, her ponytail stuck out from under her scarf, she rushed through the school playground. She stepped into the hallway to the girls' gym.

She shook her head. It was a pity that the students, girls or boys with potential, could no longer get quality professional training in competitive sports—especially the girls, thanks to the pressures from the Islamic regime. She put her bag down on one of the side benches and changed into her tennis shoes. Then she tied her scarf around her shoulders so it would be available in case one of the other teachers, some of whom had high Islamic beliefs, accidentally walked in.

She ran in the woods surrounding the school playground. Although a political nightmare, Iran was still a safe country for ordinary citizens. From the corner of her eye, she thought she spotted something. First, she ran past it, then turned back. Then she stopped running. It was a shoe and then . . . she saw the hand.

Mrs. Sadeghi was not a woman to lose her nerve easily. She walked closer. Perhaps it was the gardener who came by on Fridays to do extra work. She knew he had heart problems. She bent down and turned the body over.

The man's throat was cut with a knife . . .

She gasped, turned around, and ran faster than she ever had.

★ ★ ★

Melody swept the kitchen tiles—their vacuum cleaner had also been stolen and she had not yet bought another one. Arman had left early after they had buried Maryam's child in Behesht-e Zahra cemetery and watched her weep. He'd told her that, as she couldn't leave Maryam or Nader with Julia, he would check to see if her Karaj villa was available so they could move to it. They had all come to the conclusion that even with the fresh paint and supplies Melody had bought, this house was still terrible to live in. More than that, it was depressing.

She thought of her conversation with Arman last night. They had sat on the patio overlooking the unkempt but still beautiful garden while Julia had watched a movie Arman had brought for her, along with his own VCR and television. To the sound of *Gone with the Wind*'s symphony, he had told Melody everything, from his father, to Zia, to the rescue mission plan.

"It doesn't seem to shock you," he had said in the end.

"Not much shocks me with you, Arman."

"So what do you think of this whole thing?"

She had hesitated, then looked up at the starry skies, her left leg swinging back and forth as it normally did when she was thinking.

"I think it's risky," she finally said. "But I agree with Kami. It's not impossible. The issue is if, after all this, the Americans will go through with it and won't pull out at the last minute."

"That's what concerned Kami as well."

"What do you think?"

"They won't back out. They want the hostages freed. Carter's desperate. We have enough officers to pull it off once we get the weapons and the backup from the Americans."

She had turned to him for once in worry. She knew he had known what she was thinking. "Please be careful, Arman. I believe you can pull this off. I believe you can do whatever you set your mind on, but you're a good friend and I don't want to lose you. I'm sure Julia feels the same."

He grinned. "I don't want to lose me either, Melody."

"What will you do if it all goes wrong?"

"I've spoken with a friend. His name is Jamshid Mahmoudi. He helped get Colonel Moradi out of Iran."

"Yes, you told me about him."

"I talked to him before I came here tonight. He's joined the Mujahedin." Arman crossed his arms, his chin tucked into his sweater, like a little boy, staring into the night.

"Oh, no!"

"Apparently he had a friend there and that was the first hiding place that came to mind when the pasdars showed up at his house. Anyway, he was given an ultimatum today to join the Mujahedin or become their enemy."

"Pleasant choice. What did he decide?"

"He says he knows the pasdars will find him anywhere he goes, so he decided to stay with the Mujahedin only if he can work at their base by the Turkish border. He's heard during his work at the interrogation office that that's the most decent place to be a mujahid."

"They help get refugees out of the country?"

Arman nodded and Melody looked at the shining stars and breathed in the night's dry air. As a child she had slept in a mosquito net on this same patio, staring at the same stars. She had dreamt of beautiful things then, and could not even imagine today's ugliness. "So what do they want for getting you out?"

"Why? Are you thinking of getting out?"

"If I do," she said, "it won't be the Mujahedin I'll ask for help. I'm as frightened by them as I am by the Hezbollah. I'm just curious. I've come to believe that no one in this world does anything without getting something in return."

"They want people to join them for a short time."

"Pleasant." She laughed. "So why did he tell you all this?"

"He suggested that if I ever needed to get out fast, I should give him a call. He gave me a number to some cement factory, which is a front for their operation. He said they could get a hold of him immediately. If I say code name *pardees*, he'll arrange the rest."

"*Pardees*? Paradise?"

"I guess they must think their ideology takes them to paradise."

They had both laughed, but then Melody had turned serious. "I want you to know that despite everything, I'm glad you're back in my life again, Arman. You are back in my life, aren't you?"

"I seem to be. Yes."

Their eyes had met and a heavy silence had fallen between them, when the patio door abruptly opened and Julia looked out. "Arman, where are you? Don't you want to watch the movie with me?"

Arman had stood and an understanding glance passed between him and Melody. Julia was jealous, and Melody could not honestly blame her.

"I'm sorry, Julia," she said. "It's been a long time since we talked. I'm afraid it's been my fault. I've been chatting endlessly."

"I understand but I haven't seen him for a long time either. I'd appreciate if you'd give him back for a while."

And Arman had sat on the couch with Julia and watched the rest of *Gone with the Wind* while both he and Melody had felt like guilty children.

She heard a voice and looked up. Then she leaned her broom against the wall, tidying her hair and clothes. It was Nader's voice coming from the living room. He seemed to have finally woken up. She let him make his way to the kitchen.

"Good God!" Nader said walking in, a hand to his head. And then he looked around. "What in the world am I doing here?" He put a hand to the wall to balance himself. Then he rushed to the sink and threw up. When he looked up, she was standing there with a towel.

"Thanks, Melody. Tell me, are we in heaven?"

She grinned. "Far from it, I'm afraid."

"I feel dead, that's for sure."

"Anything to eat?"

"Tea. I need tea."

She began pouring him tea from the samovar.

"I was so sure I'd die." His voice shook.

She put the glass of tea in front of him. "Drink up, Nader. You are very much alive."

He became quiet suddenly, watching her. She knew that something about her puzzled him. And she wondered if like Arman, he could see the grief lines by her mouth and the slight flicker of hate in her eyes, which spoke of a struggle and a grief he knew nothing about. It wasn't only a few pages of her life that he had missed but an entire novel.

"I saw an American girl out there," he said. "She seems familiar. Who is she?"

"Daughter of Frank Hutchinson who worked at the American embassy. You may have met her at one of the embassy parties."

"Could be." Tears of despair gathered in his eyes. He sipped his tea. "How did I get here? Last I recall someone walked into my living room."

"That must have been Arman."

"Arman?"

"Arman Pakran. Navy officer. Remember him?"

"Oh yes." Nader frowned. "Your friend."

"Yes, my friend."

"The one who went out on you."

Melody nodded with a faint smile. "The one who went out on me."

"You know I would've never done that to you."

She turned to look at him. "I know, Nader."

He shook his head. "It's a bummer I should be saved by that asshole. I don't like him one bit."

She laughed.

"I still remember the first time I met him. You and I were engaged and you left me for the entire day."

"We were racing," she said. "I forgot the time. And you're exaggerating. It was only a couple of hours."

"The way you rode that horse, I'm amazed you didn't break your neck. Even your father was worried."

"He was worried because you were so petrified. He'd seen me on a horse since I was nine. I think he knew I could handle it."

He shook his head. "I still don't get why you hang out with Arman. After the way he treated you. Besides, he's not at all concerned about your safety. He forgets that you're a beautiful and sensitive girl. I get so worried about you—"

"You shouldn't—"

"Of course I should. You're my fiancé, my future wife, and it's my duty to protect you. I really don't want you to continue with some of the things you used to do. Especially when we have children, you have to put aside some of the dangerous activities—"

"Like horseback riding?"

"And river rafting. It terrifies me every time you go down Karaj River."

Melody laughed.

"What I'm trying to—"

He winced, putting a hand to his head.

"Here! Take some aspirin. This is a silly argument to have now."

Before he could answer, Julia rushed in. "Melody, she's coming downstairs!"

"Who?" Nader swallowed the aspirin with his tea and grimaced.

Melody walked out of the kitchen and saw Maryam walking down the stairs, holding on to the rails, her back bent. The doctor had left this morning with prescribed medication.

Maryam laughed at herself. "I feel like an old woman. I can barely walk."

"You look much better though. Did you take the medication the doctor gave you? I left a glass of water by your bed."

"I did. Thank you, Melody."

"Hungry?"

"Yes."

Melody held her by the arm and they walked toward the kitchen together.

"Your house looks so . . . "

"Terrible?"

"Yes. I'm sorry Melody. I know how much it must hurt you."

"It does."

Warmth covered her. It was good to have Maryam back, to hold her hand and smell her familiar body scent. It was nice to see the old liveliness in her green eyes.

"Tonight," she suddenly laughed, "we'll sleep in the same room and talk about everything like we did when we were kids. Well, almost everything. It'll make us both feel better, I'm sure."

"Agreed. It's good to see you again."

"I'm very glad to see you too, Maryam. Don't you ever run away like that again."

Maryam laughed as they walked into the kitchen.

"And what the hell is *she* doing here?"

They both looked up in surprise to face Nader's glare.

"Nader. This is Maryam. I'm sure you remember her—"

"Remember her? How could I forget? How could any of us ever forget? That's why I demand to know what the hell this whore is doing here?"

"Nader!" Melody had never heard Nader speak like this before.

"She ran away from home, had sex with a tramp who supported the revolution, and ended up joining their cause against her own family, her own poor father, and now that it hasn't turned out to be as great as she thought, she's back here begging for help?"

Melody felt Maryam tremble next to her. She was beginning to tremble herself, but not from fear.

"Nader, let me explain—"

"I don't want you to explain anything, Melody. Tell me, Maryam Khanum, isn't your lovely husband a pasdar? Are you here to trap us so he can come and kill us?"

"Nader," Melody yelled. "Shut up!"

He took a step back in complete shock. "But Melody," he said in a softer voice, "are you telling me you allow this whore in here after all she's done? She had sex before marriage, did so many disgraceful things, and then she killed her own father."

"Enough, Nader."

"People like this bitch and her fanatic husband did this to us. Don't you see, Melody?"

"Sit down, Maryam. I'll pour you some tea."

"No, you will get her the hell out of here! Now!"

Maryam turned and ran upstairs. Without thinking, Melody pulled back and slapped Nader in the face with everything she had.

His hand moved to his cheek and stayed there.

Melody turned, walked out of the room, and caught up with Maryam. "No, Maryam, wait. Ignore him—"

"It was stupid," Maryam said. "Insane to think that I'd ever be able to return and be accepted. I should've known."

"No, Maryam. Listen to me. Wait."

Maryam rushed into her bedroom and ran to the window, but a step before it she stopped. Melody followed and closed the door behind her. Maryam turned around.

"Am I a whore to you, Melody?"

"Of course not. He's an idiot. Don't—"

"Ali calls me a whore too. You know why?"

Melody shook her head.

"He calls me a whore because I slept with him—him, the bastard—before I married him. He says I should've waited my turn, when society allowed me to offer my body to him, so that I could be a woman worth his esteem. He calls me a whore and treats me accordingly."

"So leave him!"

"You think I don't want to? Have you seen the bruises on my body? Oh, but you have. This body doesn't belong to me, Melody. This regime I fought for, gave up my University life for, Baba for, tells me that my votes, my rights to travel, my divorce, and my own body belongs to my husband. He hits me when he's angry and he's angry often. And I can't go to court, Melody. There's nothing I can do."

"Stay with me."

"And Nader?"

"Forget Nader. I'll speak to Arman. I'm sure he'll have a good idea."

Maryam watched Melody for a few seconds. "You don't love Nader, do you? It's always been Arman, hasn't it? When are you going to wake up girlfriend? But then who am I to talk. I've made too many mistakes."

Melody could not look back into Maryam's eyes.

"There was a time, Melody, when I looked at the midnight blue of the sky above Tehran and thought of liberty, equality, the opportunities a revolution would bring. I dreamt of freedom, democracy, and classless societies. Now I realize that an idea that can start with a dream can end in a nightmare."

"You couldn't have known, Maryam."

"No, I couldn't, because I was an idealist. Now I know. And those are the same nights now that I wish I were dead. I remember how things used to be and I simply want to lie down and die when I realize what I've done. I miss Baba and I missed you and the way you used to laugh."

Melody opened her mouth to say something but could not find the right words.

"And then I decided not to kill myself, not because I wanted to live anymore, but because that's what Ali wanted. What he had done to my father hadn't been enough. He wanted to torture me until I gave in, and I won't give in. Do you know what Ali's greatest gift to me has been Melody?"

"No."

"Hatred. I never felt it, never understood it, until I met Ali. Ali's entire existence is based on hate. His father was an opium addict and used to beat him as a child. And when he died his mother took over and treated him the same way. This is his revenge. But I understand him more than I ever did before. I know what hate is, Melody. It eats you up inside and destroys every piece of dignity or humanity you have within you. You only live for one thing and that is revenge."

"He's not worth it—"

"Baba's life is worth it."

"Your father wouldn't have wanted this."

"Poor Baba. I'd always been a stubborn child. But one more time, Melody, I'm going to be stubborn. I want this."

Melody held her breath. "What are you planning to do?"

"Ever since I heard of Baba's death, I've been planning. Before, you see, I had the child, and it gave me some sort of hope and more of a desire to live in order to protect it. But now, I'm free."

"Hate brought us here, Maryam. Please, stay here and try to forget and we'll start all over again."

"And allow him to go on making a mockery of my life, after what he did to my father?"

"To destroy him, you have to become like him, and that's not in you. I know that."

"No, Melody, you don't understand." Maryam's voice was eerily calm, like she was explaining how to cook some simple dish. "I won't be able to go on until he suffers the way he's made Baba and me suffer."

"And then? What happens after he's gone?"

"Only then, Melody, can I try to start over again."

"By then it may be too late. But you're right, you won't listen. You never have. I don't want you to do this, but I can't stop you. If you ever need me don't hesitate to come back. You know I'd always be here for you."

Maryam smiled. "You always are. Thank you, Melody."

EIGHT

HAMID HEATED UP LEFTOVERS from last night. It had been a long day. He sipped his glass of water and stirred the chicken soup. The radio broadcast a speech by Ayatollah Khomeini. Papers were spread across the table, clothes to be washed stacked in a corner. An old couch from his college years and a television were the only furniture in his living room. Pinned to the white walls were a few unframed posters, and pictures of his parents lay on a side table next to the couch. The only part of the house that seemed to be lived in was his bed, next to which lay a pile of books, notebooks, official reports, pens, pencils, and an eraser.

The phone rang.

"Hello?" he said.

"Hello, sir. This is Pasdar Taheri from headquarters, sir."

"This late at night?"

"It's important news. We just received it from the police station. I thought you might want to know. Sorry for the inconvenience, sir."

Hamid turned off the radio. "What's up?"

"A teacher at the International School rang up the police station this morning around five."

"What is a teacher doing at school so early in the morning?"

"Getting exercise. She's a PE teacher."

"Five in the morning?" Hamid who was a late riser himself asked. "What's the problem?"

"She found a dead body. His throat was cut with a knife, sir."

Hamid began pouring the soup into a bowl. "All right, the police are taking care of it, I assume. What do you want from me?"

"They've been working all morning to figure out who the dead man is and they came up with a name. General Jalili, sir."

Some of the hot soup dripped on Hamid's hand. "Ouch! What did you say?"

"The dead man's name is General Jalili. I knew you and Commander Shirazi were doing some sort of an investigation that involved the general and I thought you might want to know."

"Has Commander Shirazi been notified?"

"No, sir. I thought I'd ring you up first."

"Thanks, Taheri. I'll give him a call myself. It's too late to do anything tonight. Why did it take them so long to notify us?"

"The officer in charge told me they were doing a proper investigation, sir." Which meant they were trying to figure it out for themselves before transferring it to the Revolutionary Guard Corps. The police resented the pasdars meddling in their important investigations.

"We'll have to deal with it in the morning. Where's the body at the moment?"

"At the police station. The doctor is examining him."

"Tell them to keep him there. If they don't want him there, transfer his body to headquarters but don't let them do anything else with him until we give official orders. Meanwhile, I'll get a hold of Commander Shirazi."

Hamid hung up. A second later he called Commander Shirazi and gave him the news.

★ ★ ★

Maryam arrived back at her home. At the door she stopped to take in a deep breath. The door was slightly ajar and she could see the gleam of an oil lamp in the living room. She pushed it open and stepped inside. Ali stood in the kitchen doorway with a dish towel in his hand.

She gasped. She assumed he might be there, but the domesticity of the scene caught her off guard.

"What?" He dried his hands on the towel. "You're even afraid of your own husband?"

"I'm not." She folded her veil. She was wearing an ivory shirt and blue jeans borrowed from Melody.

He looked at her for a few moments. "Where the hell have you been?"

"Somewhere."

"Somewhere, where?"

"Somewhere, you son of a bitch, where I could get help."

His eyes rested on her stomach where the infant had once been and finally got it. "Where is it?"

"It?"

"The child. My boy . . . "

She nodded. "It was a boy. Now it's your son? It wasn't your son when you threw me around and beat the crap out of me."

"I do as I please with you, Khanum. You belong to me and so does that child. Where is my son?"

She had gained back the confidence she'd lost on first spotting him and could see that he was bothered by the missing baby. She bent to pick up a match from the ground and carelessly threw in into an ashtray on the living room table. Then she turned and looked at him and her hands moved to her neck, opened the knot on her scarf, and pulled it off with one hand. Finally she loosened her ponytail and shook her hair, which fell around her casually. Her eyes turned to him confidently and saw the contempt in his eyes, feeling his hatred for the class he so detested.

"I don't belong to you," she said.

That awoke him. He walked toward her and reached for her arm.

She turned around, facing him squarely, and slapped him.

"It's dead, you bastard," she said. "You low-class scum who I sold my body to only to be called a whore. It was a boy and it's dead. It died before it was born. Remember the way you pushed me around, stepped on me, and threw me against walls? That's what did it. While you were out somewhere fucking a child, here I was giving birth to the son you killed."

"No!" he suddenly cried, real pain in his voice.

She stepped back. Once again in her naiveté, she had underestimated the value of a son to a man such as him. He turned himself around once in agony and then faced her. She smiled watching his pain, but then he took her by the hair and threw her against the wall. She grabbed on to the couch and fell onto it while he moved toward her. She knew he wanted her to beg for her freedom, but instead she remained on the couch, one hand holding her head sideways with a luscious careless smile on her lips.

"You witch," he said, his nostrils opening wide, breathing heavily. "You snobby shit. You're a whore now. You belong to me."

"You wish." She laughed at him and he snatched her shirt and tore it open. She was not wearing a bra and did not move as his eyes glanced over her breasts and stayed there.

"Who belongs to whom now?" she said without moving.

He came back to himself. "Where were you?"

"It's none of your business."

"You're my wife. It is my business. I locked the doors. How the hell did you get out?"

"I scratched my way out."

"Where were you?" He raised his eyebrows. "You went to your cousin, Melody. No one else would've taken you in."

"I didn't go to Melody."

He was not listening. "She's a witch and she always hated me. I saw some powder outside the door, the other day . . ."

"Powder?"

"Black powder. Your cousin, Melody, must've been visiting. How could I've not recognized it? And I stepped right over it. Black magic, of course!"

Black magic? He was even more primitive than she thought.

He grabbed her neck and squeezed it so that she could barely breathe.

"Black magic killed my father. Maman told me everything. She'd noticed the black powder. It was an old aunt who hated Maman—"

"Your father died from overdose of opium, you fool." She had to force the words out. "There is no such thing as black magic."

"Of course, you'd say that, because you're in it with her."

"With whom?"

"Melody."

"You're crazy!"

He laughed. "Thank you for reminding me about your big-headed cousin. I forgot all about her. It's time for her to join her daddy."

"No, it's not."

She drove her knee between his legs.

He fell back. She jumped on top of him but he finally shoved her off, grabbed her by the hair and flung her away.

"You're insane," she screamed. "You're mad."

"Shut up." Abruptly he walked out of the house, slamming the door shut.

She waited for a few minutes until he was gone, then pulled herself up, grabbed her purse, and ran after him.

★ ★ ★

Melody hung up the phone and felt cold to her bones. She already knew the reaction she would get.

"What?" Julia asked.

Arman had joined them a few hours ago. He held her hand. "Who was it?"

"Maryam." She looked back at him and knew he knew.

"What did she want again?" Nader threw an ace of hearts on the table for Julia to pick up. They had been playing cards for the last hour.

"Melody?" Arman said again.

"She said Ali's coming after me."

"What?" Nader threw all his cards on the table. "I told you, you shouldn't have helped her."

"He's only after me. I think the rest of you should get out of here as soon as possible."

Arman squeezed her arm. "What else?"

"She said he knows where I live so he'll be here any minute. She suggested going to the Karaj villa. He's never been there and that'll give me some time." Melody sighed. "She kept apologizing."

Nader stood up. "As if that's going to do any good."

"What should we do?" Julia's hand was on her mouth. She stared at Arman.

"I checked on your Karaj villa this morning, Melody. Nobody was there."

"I told you, Melody," Nader said. "I told you—"

"I'm sorry," Melody said. "Please, Arman, can you take the two of them somewhere safe? This is really not your problem."

"No, Melody," Arman said. "There is nowhere safe for them either. Besides, I'm not going to leave you here alone."

"I can try to go to the villa. I'd really appreciate it if you'd take them somewhere secure until this business is all finished. Please, Arman."

"I'm not leaving you alone," Nader said. "We'll figure this out together."

"All right, then," Arman said. "Let's head out to the villa. Whoever's coming, pack. Only essentials. Nothing fancy and hurry downstairs in five minutes."

Within minutes they were all downstairs. Arman had already pulled his jeep forward. Nader sat in the front and the women jumped in the back. Arman turned on the engine.

"Did you bring scarves, Melody?"

"Yes."

"Good. Help Julia put one on."

"And why should I do this?" Julia asked.

"Because, Julia darling, we don't want the pasdars to see your lovely blond hair, now do we?"

"Of course."

"This is going to be the longest drive of our lives," Nader said as Arman pulled out of the driveway. Melody turned back to take a last look at the house, disappearing from their view and wondered if this was how her father had felt when they had dragged him away to prison.

★ ★ ★

They reached the villa just before midnight. They had not stopped once during the two-hour drive.

"Turn right here, Arman," Melody said. "This is the back way. If anyone's parked in the driveway we'll see them before they see us."

Arman cut across the mountain road and drove down the steep narrow dirt driveway, which ended up in front of the villa. As he parked the car across from the villa, Melody pulled down her window to listen. She couldn't hear anything but the sound of the Karaj River beating against the rocks as it poured down the hills behind the house.

"Thank God we made it," Julia whispered.

"I'm still not sure about this," Nader said. "But at least we seem to be safe here for a bit."

"Not yet," Arman said.

"What?" Nader asked.

"I'm going in. It looks okay but I need to double-check. Melody?"

"Yes, Arman."

"If I'm not out in five minutes, I want you to back out of this driveway at top speed and get out of here. You hear me?"

"I can take care of that," Nader said. "You shouldn't put such a responsibility on Melody. She's had enough stress to deal with—"

"No." Arman pointed a finger at Nader. "I know Melody can handle this. I've seen her do it before."

"Oh now he's 007 or something?" Nader said with a smirk but as no one acknowledged him, he frowned and got quiet.

Arman opened the door and stepped out. They watched him turn Melody's key in the villa door and push it slightly ajar. Soon he disappeared from their view.

"Be careful, Arman," Julia murmured. "Come back. Please come back."

Melody's right hand rested on Nader's backseat. She glanced over the key, the gear, and the release on the brake. She looked at her watch.

One minute left.

If Arman did not come out in one minute, she would back out of the driveway at maximum speed. She had done it several times before for fun. Arman had seen her do it and that was the reason he trusted her with the car. Sure, this wasn't her father's Jaguar, but all she needed to do was handle it carefully.

"It's almost five minutes," Nader said.

But right then the door to the villa opened and Arman stepped out. She breathed and relaxed against the seat.

Arman put his pistol in his waistband and opened the car door. "Looks all right. We can move in."

A mixed feeling of relief and sorrow hit Melody as she entered the villa. The rooms were barren of life, but the furniture had remained intact. It was a shock to see it as it had always been.

"Time for a shower," Julia said.

"Up the stairs, third door to your right," Melody replied.

Julia did not look at her as she walked past her up the stairs. Melody knew Julia was upset with her but had the feeling that it wasn't just because she had helped Maryam. She knew that Julia had noticed the way Arman looked at her, with quiet observing eyes, so warm that they could melt a woman's heart. No woman would have missed those stares and why should Julia be any different?

Melody walked into the living room, which extended over the roaring river where not too long ago she had rafted almost every summer weekend. On the other side of the riverbank she could see the tall branches of the trees swaying in the wind.

It was almost as if she had stepped back in time. If she closed her eyes and waited patiently, her maman would walk into the room with her normal authority and warmth, instructing the servants in her sweet calm voice to clean up the rooms for the newly arrived guests, who must clearly be exhausted.

She picked up one of the pictures on top of the fireplace. Her parents stood in their wedding garments smiling into the camera. She put the picture back and walked to the record player. She turned it on. "The Blue Danube." Her father had played it the week before his arrest. He had been sitting on that cream couch, his back to the window, his head in the newspaper reading an article about the latest political unrest. Melody could still smell their scent in the room and hear her father's laughter, the way he used to throw back his head even after the revolution and laugh as if life was nothing but a simple joke.

"Melody?" Nader cried from the kitchen.

She did not answer. Instead, she walked to the back door and down the narrow staircase leading to the river. She didn't need to turn on the patio light for she knew her way quite well. She stood by the river, pulling her fleece jacket tight. She took a long deep breath.

"I thought I'd find you here."

She turned around and saw Arman leaning against a tree, behind her. "What are you doing here?"

"Same as you are. Trying to find a quiet moment, I guess."

She grinned and looked away. "Do you remember when Maman and I got in the raft that weekend you were here? She was so terrified but she couldn't stop laughing."

"I remember. You barely made it across and you were both soaked. It was freezing cold and it began to rain. I was proud of you. You didn't give up till you reached the bank."

"And you were there with a bottle of wine and a warm blanket. We went inside and changed and then you and I made a small fire and sat here all night talking."

"What did we talk about?"

"I don't remember—oh, yes, I do. You wanted me to read you a poem in French again."

He chuckled, remembering. "True."

"Seems like a lifetime ago," she said.

"'The Blue Danube'?" he asked, tilting his head to the side, listening to the music coming from the living room above them.

"Baba liked it."

He nodded. The river thrashed itself against the rocks. A bird sat on the rail of the stairs.

"Do you know how much I used to love you, Melody?" he asked.

He was standing by her now, their faces next to one another. She put a hand around his arm and rested her lips on his right cheek. She was about to say something but then suddenly, the patio light turned on and the door at the top of the stairs opened.

"Melody?"

Melody and Arman separated and Melody asked, "Yes, Nader?"

"Where are you?"

"By the river."

"It's freezing out there. You'll catch a cold. Come on up. I'm hungry. Do you know if there is anything to eat around here?"

"I'll be up in a minute, Nader."

Nader shut the door but left the patio light on. Melody looked back into Arman's eyes. "I have to go."

He let go of her hand. "I understand."

"You always have."

She turned and walked up the stairs.

★ ★ ★

The police officer quietly handed a plastic bag to Commander Shirazi. Hamid saw the contempt in the police officer's face. Tehran police detested the new Revolutionary Guard Corps—found them to be ruthless people who did not abide by laws.

For their part, the Revolutionary Guard Corps, who held the majority of power, made a point of openly degrading and ignoring the National Police Force.

And now although Hamid knew Commander Shirazi could see the irritated glance on the police officer's face, they both ignored it as customary.

"Thank you, Officer. You may leave now."

The police officer walked out of the room.

Hamid opened the bag and threw the contents of General Jalili's pockets on the desk. "A box of cards . . ." Hamid began.

"How becoming!" Commander Shirazi said.

Hamid grinned. "A cigar case. The general seems to have liked Cubans. His entire wardrobe smelled of it too. An ink pen—a Montblanc—a Porsche leather wallet—"

"The general seems to have had a taste for luxuries."

"Fifty tomans of cash and a few receipts. Oddly enough there is a picture here of some plant. What do you make of it?"

Commander Shirazi took it. "Odd. Maybe some exotic fruit you smoke, like hashish?" He threw the picture back on the table. "Well, anyway, there doesn't seem to be anything important here. Zip them back up, Hamid, and put them away."

"Yes, sir." Hamid put the items back in the bag.

"Afterward come to my office. We need to figure how to find Arman. What were the reports from Yazd?"

"The Yazd estate has been evacuated, sir. The farmers have taken over the land. Arman couldn't go back even if he wanted to."

"Any other property he may have?"

"He had a villa up north by the Caspian, in Chalous, right by the water, sir."

"Send someone up there then—"

"With due respect, sir, I already have. The place is empty and locked up. There was only a gardener who came by to feed the two German shepherds that used to belong to Arman."

"What did the gardener say?"

"He's deaf, sir, so not much."

Commander Shirazi sighed. "What about Arman's father?"

"We heard he's in the hospital, sir."

Commander Shirazi walked to the window and looked outside, his hands behind his back. "Did you talk to him?"

"We tried but he's very ill. It was useless."

"This is getting better by the minute."

"I left a guard in the lobby to watch over him for a few days. Just in case Arman goes there to visit." Hamid turned to walk around, the plastic bag in his hand.

"One more thing, Hamid."

"Yes, sir?"

His eyes narrowed. "Any news from Jamshid?"

"Yes, sir." Hamid kept his voice steady. "Last we heard he was driving to the Caspian. The pasdar who had stopped him didn't check his books. Again he got away."

Commander Shirazi shook his head and then frowned. "I wonder where he is now."

"I would think, sir, that he may have joined the Mujahedin-e Khalgh. He learned enough about them working here to know about their hideouts in the Caspian jungles. Our files also state that he had a close friend by the name of Firooz Jahani who joined the Mujahedin right after April of last year."

"And we didn't know about this friend till now?"

"No, sir. I'm afraid we hadn't checked."

"So he gave up on the Islamic regime to go in with the Islamic Marxists? What a bright young man."

★ ★ ★

A few minutes later Hamid closed his office door behind him and dumped the contents of the bag on his desk. He pulled out the picture of the plant.

Why would General Jalili have a picture of a plant with him on the night he was murdered?

It had been cut carefully from a magazine. The police officer had told them that they had found it in his outside jacket pocket while the rest of his belongings were in his inner jacket pocket, meaning that he probably wanted to be ready to pull it out at any time.

Hamid walked to his bookshelf and pulled out a plant encyclopedia. It was one of those books he'd inherited from the last official in this office who had been interested in gardening. He opened the book and looked through the pictures. For an hour, he searched. Then he made a few wild guesses, the last of which proved successful. In the poisonous herb section, his finger moved down the pictures of the plants and stopped on one. It was identical to the picture found on General Jalili. He began reading.

Nightshade is mostly found in central and southern Europe, as well as in parts of Asia and North Africa but will grow well most anywhere in the shade of trees and large bushes. The scientific name of Deadly Nightshade is Atropa Belladonna. The herb got its name from one of the three death goddesses, Atropos, the inevitable. She was the one who cut your life thread when your time was done.

The Deadly Nightshade has been used throughout history for various purposes, most of which were quite unsavory. The ancient Greeks used to drink it when they visited the Oracle of Delphi. Deadly Nightshade was used to poison the troops of Mark Anthony during the Parthian wars and was in a liquor Macbeth gave to a party of Danes during a truce.

Hamid closed the book with a frown. Why in the world would General Jalili be carrying the picture of a Deadly Nightshade to meet with his murderer? What was he trying to say?

He walked out and made a copy of the picture, put the original back into the bag and zipped it up. He dropped it off at the clerk's desk, walked back into his office, put the copy of the picture in his drawer, and locked it.

He was not sure he wanted to share his thoughts with Commander Shirazi. Commander Shirazi was a perfectionist. Hamid wanted to make sure this was an important discovery before presenting it to him.

★ ★ ★

On the other side of the town, Maryam walked out of her house and locked the door behind her. She wore a long black veil, covering her top to bottom, exposing only the right half of her face. She caught a taxi and, after forty-five minutes walked into the prosecutor's office building. The elevator was out of service, so she walked to the third floor. A pasdar stopped her at the counter. "Yes?"

"I'm here to meet Haj Agha Akbari," she said.

The pasdar did not look up. "Do you have an appointment?"

"Yes."

"Your name?"

"Maryam Alizadeh, sir."

"Take a seat, Khanum."

She turned around and for the first time noticed the group of people in the waiting room. They were here to meet Akbari, Chief Prosecutor of Iran's Islamic revolutionary court, to ask for freedom for their loved ones. A man stood to give his seat to her. She thanked him and sat down.

Fifteen minutes later, she was admitted to the judge's office. Akbari had been eating a dish of rice and now was picking his teeth. He looked up at Maryam. "Sit down, Mrs. Alizadeh."

"Thank you, Haj Agha Akbari."

He looked through his papers. "What can I do for you?"

"I'm here, Haj Agha Akbari, to give you some information."

He frowned. "This is not the usual place for this, Khanum. Have you tried the Revolutionary Guard Corps headquarters?"

"Yes, Haj Agha, but I've always felt you were someone I could confide in, especially with such important information—"

"What sort of information?" He picked up his toothpick and went at it again.

"Something evil has been occurring, Haj Agha, and I'm so scared. I've heard of your competence and high morals and decided to share my thoughts with you to ask for your advice."

"Are you the wife of my employee, Ali Alizadeh?"

"Yes, Haj Agha."

"We're very proud of your husband, Khanum. He's been a great supporter of the revolution. What can I do for you?"

She twisted her veil nervously in her hand. "I hate to do this to him, Haj Agha, especially after what you just said . . ."

"What is it you want to tell me, Khanum?" He put down his toothpick.

"It's so difficult for a weak woman like me. After all I'm only a simple woman. But I must . . . for Allah's sake, I must. I cannot live one more day knowing the truth and feeling this heartache inside of me . . ."

"What's troubling you Khanum?"

"Yes, I believe it's the right thing to do and if not, I believe in you, Haj Agha, and I know you will correct me—"

"Get to the point, Khanum."

"Yes, Haj Agha. I've seen things which I shouldn't have, which I know he wouldn't want me to see—"

"Who, Khanum?"

"My husband, your employee, Ali Alizadeh."

There was a thoughtful pause. "What about him?"

"We've had visitors, Haj Agha, big meetings with many people. I know it's not his fault. It's probably that of an old friend of his—"

"Meetings about what, Khanum?"

"I don't know much, Haj Agha. After all I'm not very political."

Haj Agha Akbari's nostrils opened irritably.

She quickly added, "But I read some of the pamphlets and then listened to them because I was curious." She leaned forward. "I believe my husband is a secret member of the Mujahedin-e Khalgh."

"What?" Akbari broke his toothpick. She had his attention now.

"Yes, sir," she said.

"An employee of the Islamic government and especially a pasdar of the highest esteem, a member of the Mujahedin-e Khalgh movement? You must be mistaken, Khanum."

"I wish, Haj Agha, but I'm afraid I'm not and I hate them, the Mujahedin. All the bombs they put in civilian places and besides that I always thought they were Marxists." She leaned forward, a hand to her cheek, her eyes wide open. "They don't believe in Allah, that's what a neighbor said. And that's a sin!"

She knew that was not quite accurate, but Akbari seemed to find it unnecessary to correct her. After all, she was merely an uneducated housewife. Instead he leaned forward. "Tell me all that you have seen, Khanum."

NINE

THE AMERICAN HOSTAGE RESCUE team, now code name *Eagle Claw*, had been practicing for more than five months, averaging 1,000 flying hours. They'd gone through a rough training mission in Arizona and six C-130s had departed Florida bound for Wadi Qena, Egypt where troops awaited orders. For days they had eaten nothing but C-rations but this morning a truck had rolled up and served them hot breakfast. Always a clear sign. The mission was a go.

Next stop had been Masirah, a small island off the coast of Oman, which was just a couple of tents and a blacktop strip. This would be their last stop before mission launch.

Colonel Wilson's lead MC-130's crew would be the first to land in Iran. Abroad, they had an air force combat control team and the commandos. The Delta task force commanders each had a satellite radio for direct communication with the command post, code name "Red Barn."

The plan was this: helicopters from the *Nimitz* were to take off from the flight deck and rendezvous with Air Force C-130s at Desert One. They would then refuel and take off to a second location, code name Desert Two. From there they would assault the American embassy in Tehran.

★ ★ ★

"Where have you been?"

Arman pulled the receiver back from his ear. "Don't shout, Zia. I'm worried enough as it is with seven days left to Desert One. I'm supposed to contact you every day at this hour. That's all you need to know."

"I'm afraid that won't do. I've been waiting for the list of names."

"List of names?"

"You were supposed to get the list of people involved in this. We've got to make sure we don't have any traitors. I have to do my background checks."

"I told you I can't. Most of them are staying anonymous, and I don't blame them. If that list falls into the wrong hands, all five hundred of them will be shot. We've given them the oath of privacy. We can't break that. I can't break that."

"Don't give me that bullshit excuse."

"I don't understand why you keep insisting—"

"Told you there is a leak somewhere—"

"That was General Jalili."

There was a pause. "You heard about that too?"

"Of course, I did. The whole city heard about it. What happened, do you know?"

"The guy was a gambler. Got into debt left and right. Probably borrowed money from a city shark and they finished him off."

"In a playground?"

"City sharks can finish you off anywhere they want."

Arman hesitated. "How do you know it was the city sharks?"

"Just a guess." Zia breathed deeply a moment and said in a softer voice, "Who are you staying with now?"

"Not your business."

"Stop playing this game with me. Give me the list of names—"

"You can't do anything with the names anyway. What are you going to do, check all five hundred of them? If there is a traitor, we'll find out as we go along."

"I can try to figure it out—"

"You won't be able to find anything. There's no time. Besides I'm doing my own investigation."

"What investigation?"

"There's a man I want you to check out for me. His name is Taji and I believe he's currently a member of the revolutionary council. He may also be our leak."

"Why him? He doesn't know anything about our plans—"

"He used to be a close friend of General Jalili's, so he probably knows through him."

Zia was listening now. His voice came across as more excited this time. Arman guessed that the CIA would award Zia if the conspirator were found. "Tell me more."

"I don't know more. I was hoping you could figure it out. Dig a little bit deeper, do your dirty tricks, you know that thing you're so good at . . ."

Arman smiled, but there was complete silence over the phone.

"You're not trying to trick me, are you, Arman?"

"I swear to God, I'm not. We have a real reason to believe this guy is Nightshade."

"Who?"

"A double agent, code-named Nightshade."

"Who is that?"

"He or she may have killed David and we think that he may also be the traitor we're looking for."

"Interesting." There was a slight pause. "All right, I'll check Taji out, but that doesn't change my mind about the list of names, Arman. You don't understand. I have to have that list."

"Why in the world—"

"Because the people above me want it. They want to know who they're dealing with."

"They're dealing with us. They know the main people, what does it matter—"

"I need that list Arman. Or else!"

"Or else what?"

"Your father—"

Arman squeezed the pay phone in his sweaty hand. "Keep Baba out of this—"

Zia chuckled over the line. "Tomorrow at the park, same place, same time, and bring the list of names. Otherwise you'll hear the bad news—"

"God damn it, leave him alone!"

"Sorry, my friend, but I got to do what I've got to do."

"You fucking piece of—"

The line went dead. Arman knocked his fist twice into the pay phone, opened the door of the yellow telephone booth and stepped out.

★ ★ ★

At the villa, Julia was sleeping and Arman, who had left in the morning, had not yet returned. Melody made sandwiches while Nader sat on the sofa watching *Casablanca*. She looked through the kitchen window and saw a jeep pull into the driveway. First she thought it was Arman, but then she looked closer and saw the jeep's green and white stripes. She immediately put the plate down and walked into the living room. "Turn that off, Nader. They're here."

Nader snapped the set off. "Who is?"

She rushed up the wooden steps to Gilda's old room. Julia was sleeping on her side, her back to the door. Melody shook her by the shoulder.

Julia woke up with a gasp. "What?"

"They're here."

"Who is?"

"The pasdars! Move!"

Julia didn't even stop to put on her shoes. She ran out in Arman's tee shirt in which she had slept, her blond hair in disarray. She was trembling all over. Nader was frozen, his eyes and mouth wide, watching the jeep park and the doors open. Four pasdars stepped out.

"It's over," Nader said.

"No," Melody said. "The back door."

She opened the back door to the stairs that led to the river, then closed it behind them and locked it from the outside. She put the key in her pocket and ran down after Julia and Nader. A cool wind blew against her face. The river dashed against the riverbank.

Melody signaled them to turn right, under the living room extension over the shore. Nader rested a hand on her back and she grabbed on to Julia's arm, feeling her shiver. "A few meters down we can cross the river and get into the woods."

They began to run.

★ ★ ★

One of the pasdars walked around the villa and stepped down the stone pathway leading to the bank, his AK-47 on his shoulder. The other three were inside, but he had already guessed that the fugitives had fled. He thought he heard a movement and walked faster down the path until he saw blond hair from a distance.

He picked up his rifle, aimed, and pulled the trigger.

★ ★ ★

The shot passed above their heads and Julia screamed. They still had a few meters to a ford. But in her frenzy, Julia turned left and jumped into the river, then screamed again as her body hit its ice-cold water. The current swept her under for a moment, then she surfaced to grab a branch hanging over the river. Her hand slipped, and the battering current drove her downstream. Her left leg hit a rock and she screamed again. She choked and tried to swim, her body numb, the river sweeping over her.

★ ★ ★

Another shot passed over their heads. The pasdar pulled down his rifle and charged after them down the pathway.

Melody paused, turned around and caught sight of Julia's long blond hair disappearing down the dark river. There was no time to think. She ran to the edge and dove in.

★ ★ ★

As soon as Melody hit the frigid water she felt a pain in her chest but she'd expected that. She had swum this river twice before when her raft had collapsed and she had to find her way out. She swam vigorously to the center of the river, and then let go, allowing the current to do the rest of the work for her while she kept her body off the rocks.

She saw Julia hanging on to a rock, horrified, her blond wet hair in her face. Melody swam to her but before she could reach her, a bullet passed over their heads and Julia screamed and dove under water.

Melody dove down after her. When she looked up, she saw Julia a few meters farther down the river. She was not struggling and her head had fallen back, the rough water dragging her away.

Melody swam toward her and grabbed her by the shoulder, but the current was strong and pinned them against a rock. She moaned from the pain of the rock in her back, but that did not stop her. She braced her legs against the rock and managed to shove off hard enough to reach the main current, where she was swept down. She could see Julia's head lolling about, above and below the water.

Melody snatched Julia's hair, then took a hold of her right arm. She managed to hook the other arm around a rock, but the river pounded her. Her hand slipped and she almost lost Julia again, but she grabbed on to her arm harder. This time she snatched a branch extending over the river. They were already half a mile from the villa. With a last pull she fell onto the shore and dragged Julia with her.

She put her ear against Julia's mouth but could not feel her breathing.

She turned her over and slapped her on the back.

Julia coughed and spat out water. Melody then turned her around and lay next to her to warm her. A cold wind blew over their wet bodies and they waited.

A few moments later, Melody heard a movement and looked up. On the other side of the bank, by their villa, a pasdar walked, a rifle in his hand.

She put a finger to her lips and Julia nodded and closed her eyes. They both lay on the ground and Melody watched the pasdar. It was very dark and she knew he would have a hard time locating them from this distance. Then again, if Melody had spotted him, he could see them.

★ ★ ★

The pasdar knew that they must be somewhere close. He looked at the river thrashing itself against the pointed rocks. He knew if he crossed the river he would find them, but he was not quite sure where to pass. It had snowed quite a bit last winter causing the Karaj River to run higher than usual.

He stopped and looked across the river. It was pitch dark and the branches of the trees moved in the cold wind. The pasdar turned his flashlight on and threw the beam across the river.

A colleague came up behind him. "Found them?"

"There were two of them. Two women. One blond, I think, but it could've been the light. They disappeared down the river with the current."

"Did you see where they went?"

"They went far down for a while. One of them seemed to be trying to grab the other. Then they both went under for some time and I lost them."

"Forget it. They're dead. Let's go back in."

"What about the guy?"

"I don't know but it doesn't matter. Besides we really only needed to confiscate the villa. It's freezing out here and I'm starved. There's some sandwiches on the bar upstairs that look very inviting. Are you coming?"

The pasdar turned off his flashlight. "Guess so. No man could beat this river the way it is this year, never mind a woman."

★ ★ ★

Melody watched the pasdars walk toward the house and began to breathe again. "They're gone. Julia, we need to get up and run into the woods as fast as our legs can carry us. Are you up for it?"

"I'm barefoot." Julia's eyes met Melody's. "I'll try."

"Good. Let's count to five. I'll help pull you up. One. Two." She watched the pasdars walk into the villa. "Three. Four. Five!"

She pulled Julia up by the hand and they ran into the woods. When they were far enough inside, they sat behind a tree, breathless.

"Now. Let's try to find Nader," Melody said.

Julia nodded, her teeth chattering.

They could barely find their way through the woods. Melody walked in front with Julia right behind.

"I can't see anything," Julia said, her voice steadier now.

"Keep close to me and keep low. If it's any comfort I've done this many times in the dark."

They made their way back upstream, past the shore across from the villa to the narrow riverbank. Melody kneeled on the ground and Julia followed her, breathing heavily. Melody's eyes looked around her speedily and then concentrated on one point. She knew the pasdars could still be in the woods looking for them, but she'd found the trail. Then she signed to Julia and they stood up.

She heard a gasp and turned around. Julia had fallen over a tree root. She helped her up. "You all right?"

"Yes," Julia said. "It's just a scratch. Hey!" She pointed at something behind Melody.

Melody turned around in alarm and saw Nader walking toward them.

"Arman is with him," Julia said and breathed in relief.

"Must have found him when he got back. Thank God they're safe. Let's go."

Arman pulled Julia close. His eyes met Melody's and she nodded assuring him that she was all right. Nader looked blank but then walked to Melody. "You shouldn't have dived in like that. It should've been me. I'm so sorry. Before I knew it—"

"No worries. I'm fine." Melody took him by the arm and pointed inside the forest. Arman nodded and they began to walk further into the woods.

A few minutes later they reached a small area covered with tangled branches of maple trees and large bushes and rocks.

"We can sleep inside here tonight," Melody said. "I hid here as a kid once when I ran away from home." She smiled at the memory. "It's pretty well hidden even if they decide to come looking for us."

"I think they may have given up anyway," Arman said, "but I think it's better to wait till early morning and then try to find our way out. Here Nader, take my jacket, and put it on Julia. She's freezing."

"Arman . . ."

"Yes, Julia?"

"Please come here. Hold me."

"I'm right here. I have some things I have to take care of. Let Nader warm you up."

The old Julia would have insisted but now, she leaned forward, her hand held out, staring at Melody.

Confused, Melody leaned over and took her hand.

Julia squeezed it, her face as pale as a ghost's. "Thank you, Melody."

Melody smiled and nodded while Arman put the jacket over Julia. Then Melody looked up, her dark eyes meeting Arman's in the night. "Where are you going?"

"Keeping an eye out for the killers."

"Can I help?"

"You can help by staying here. Here." He pulled a pistol from his pocket. "I fetched this for you. You know how to use it?"

"Not very well, but I took some shooting lessons, remember? Uncle Kia used to hunt."

"Good. I'll be back soon." His eyes glanced over her soaked body. "You okay?"

"A little cold, that's all." She forced a smile, holding firmly to the pistol, and then crawled into the shelter.

Julia's tee shirt hung on a branch and now she seemed warmer under Arman's jacket and had closed her eyes to the dark forest. Melody sat across from her and Nader, watching them, the pistol by her side, out of Nader's sight. She knew he would both disapprove of it and want to take it for himself. Although even he seemed exhausted.

The wind blowing against her wet clothes made her shiver and she crossed her arms.

★ ★ ★

Hours later, Arman came back. He held a flask of water to Julia's lips. She drank some and fell back asleep in Nader's arms. Arman crawled to Melody and passed the flask to her. Melody drank.

"Take your shirt off."

Melody raised her eyebrows.

"You have a bra on, don't you? Take your shirt off so it'll dry. It's wet."

Melody's eyes rested on Nader. Something else he would not approve of, but he was asleep now. She took off her shirt and handed it to Arman. He hung it over the branch next to Julia's tee shirt. He put an arm around her to warm her.

"Are they gone?"

"It looks dark in the villa but they may be sleeping there. It seems unlikely. Wonder why they gave up?"

"They may have thought we're dead when they saw us being swept away by the river."

"You could've been, you know."

"What else could I do? She would've drowned."

"Thank you for saving her life, Melody."

She smiled but did not respond.

"I sometimes worry about you," he said at last.

"You need to stop doing that, Arman. You've known me too long to worry about me."

"I guess it's just that I care, that's all."

"I know." She held his hand. "Thank you."

He looked around the shelter and smiled. "How do you know of this place anyway?"

Melody chuckled. "I was twelve years old and I . . . wasn't an easy child. Not like Gilda. Well, one day I felt I had enough. It was because of some silly argument with Gilda and Baba took her side. I decided I wasn't going to take it, so I'd live like an Indian in the forest. I packed some essentials and came to the woods. I found this shelter before it was dark and made it almost comfortable."

"And you stayed all night?"

"Hell, yes, I had something to prove. My parents first laughed it off and then they got worried. They looked everywhere for me. All night I was petrified by the noises in the forest, but I refused to give in. I finally fell asleep at dawn and father found me. I was grounded for a week."

"You deserved it."

"Yes, I did, but that taught me something."

"What?"

"To never leave my comfortable bed again, until I was old enough to afford a bed of my own."

He laughed and she grinned. Then his eyes rested on Julia. "She was so terrified," he said. "I could see it in her face when we found you. I asked her not to come but she wouldn't listen. This is not for her. She's having a hard time of it."

"She's holding up. And she has you, Arman, and that makes it easier for her."

"The bad thing is that I'm not sure she has me for that long either. I keep thinking of the rescue mission and the coup. There are so many risks involved. And I need to get Julia . . . and you all . . . out of Iran. I don't even know if I'll come out of this alive. You know, she saw a house she liked in San Diego. We even made an offer, but then we lost it, because I wasn't there. She's been wanting me to marry her for such a long time . . . "

"And why haven't you?"

"I don't remember anymore. Life was good. We got along. There was no reason to complicate it. But what's worse is that she doesn't know that, after all this is over, if anything goes wrong with the mission, she may never see me again."

"She will." She sat forward and looked in his eyes. "You will come out of this alive and you and Julia will have a wonderful life together. You must come out of this alive, Arman. We all will."

Arman winked at her. "That's what I like about you. You're a survivor. I bet if one of those pasdars came your way, you'd kill them and not feel a thing."

She smiled back. "You're probably right. Wouldn't you?"

"I would." He grinned. "Funny."

"What is?"

But he chose not to answer. Instead he looked at her as if he could see right through her. She sighed, knowing what he was thinking. "It was odd, the way we matched, but then Baba saw things differently. Nader was the best man for me. He was older sure, wasn't as exciting, but Baba thought I needed the stability. So, I accepted. I loved Baba very dearly, Arman."

"I know you did. The question is do you love Nader?"

She looked at Nader in the dark. She could see the silver in his hair, his normally soft face frazzled and weak. He looked so old and lost next to Julia's fresh and young body. "Nader has been so destroyed by the revolution. I can't hurt him more than he's already hurting." She was quiet for a few seconds. Finally, she looked up. "I want to apologize to you, Arman, for the way I treated you after Nader proposed. The way I completely ignored you no matter how many times you called. I was spoiled. Life was easy. Looking back I'm ashamed of the way I treated some who were poorer than me. I was so oblivious to other people's pain and struggles. I want you to know that I'm truly sorry if I ever hurt you."

He squeezed her hand. "I'm sorry too. I think there's enough blame to go around." He pulled her hair back from her face. "You look beautiful even now."

"I don't believe you," she said with a quick laughter. She pulled herself away. "What's your plan?"

"I'll drive you all to the border. I know a man who can help get you to Turkey. He's a friend of Kami's. They can drive you across the border in trucks."

"And that'll work?"

"If it's done right, yes. This guy is one of the best. I'll be speaking to him once we get to Khoy."

"And until we get to Khoy?"

"The fake papers I just got for you should work."

"So Zia knows about this?"

"Oh God, no! I got the name of the guy who does the fake papers the first time we got Colonel Moradi out. He took care of it and with a nice bribe said he'll keep his mouth shut. Hopefully he can keep it shut for a couple of days until we get you out of Iran."

"You'll be coming back then to finish off the mission?"

"I can't leave Baba and the other officers are relying on me. I have to finish what I started."

"I understand."

Suddenly she heard the cries rising all around them. *"Allah-o akbar!"* the voices cried. *"Allah-o akbar!"*

It was then that it hit her. The pasdars had seized the other villas by the Karaj River as well. Now they stood on rooftops hailing Allah for the victory He had granted them. The great victory of taking over empty houses.

Her head still on his shoulder, her hand holding his, she felt the muscles of his arm become tense. She closed her eyes and felt a terrifying pang of grief, regret, and terror pass through her body.

★ ★ ★

Melody had found that many of the problems she had magnified during the night would unravel in the morning. But not this morning. She woke up hungry, exhausted, and more terrified than she had ever been in her entire life. She was not alone—she could see it on the faces around her as they made their way back toward the villa. Arman had already checked the villa, confirmed that the pasdars had left and returned with scarves and clothes for Julia.

They climbed east down the riverbank until they saw Arman's car parked on the road. They climbed the steep hill until they reached the mountain road.

"Where in the world can we go?" Nader finally asked. It was the first he'd said since last night's adventure.

"To Turkey," Arman said simply and handed a box of chocolate to Julia.

"Turkey? Are we leaving the country? Maybe we should talk about this—"

"We don't have time to talk. You don't have to come if you don't want to." Arman slammed the door shut.

Nader glared at him for a few long seconds. Melody cringed.

"How long of a drive is it going to be?" Julia asked.

"If we drive fast we can probably make it to Tabriz in less than five hours and spend the night in Khoy."
"Why Khoy?"
"I've got a friend there who can help us."
His eyes caught Julia in the rearview mirror pushing the chocolates in her mouth while she held the box open for Melody. He turned on the engine. "On the way we'll stop for food."

★ ★ ★

The doorbell rang. Maryam took a hurried look around. Everything was clean and tidy in the living room, and the papers were all in places where they were sure to be found.

She checked that her dark veil covered all parts of her body, except her face, then opened the door to the three men in green Islamic uniforms and military boots. The two in the back were holding rifles. The man standing in front only had a pistol in his waistband. He was a thin long-bearded man and was looking at her feet rather than her face. It was now considered religiously impertinent to look at a woman's face, unless she was your wife, sister, or mother.

"Yes, Agha?" she asked.

The pasdar's words were formal but his tone sounded as though he spoke to a child. "We're here at the request of the court, Khanum. We have an order to search your house."

She pulled back modestly, her head also down looking at the rug beneath her feet. "My husband is not home, Agha. Can this wait?"

"Unfortunately not. It's urgent."

"All right then, Agha, if you have to. Please come in."

The men entered and each walked to a different room. The head pasdar began searching the living room.

"Tea, Agha?"

"No thank you, Khanum. We won't be long."

She walked into the kitchen anyway to make some tea. It was customary to do so even if the men didn't want any. As she busied herself, she heard them turning over the carpets and sofa cushions, pulling pictures out of albums, rifling cupboards, opening boxes in the storage room. And at last they turned the bed mattress over. She had thought that would be one of the first places they would have looked. A moment later, the lead pasdar let out a cry. The other two joined him. Almost immediately they walked back into the living room where Maryam stood dutifully with a tray in her hand, ready to serve them fresh hot Persian tea. The lead pasdar had a gray folder in his hand.

"Every evidence we need is here, Khanum."

The tray in her hand began to shake and she had to put it down on the table. When she looked up she knew her little act had worked. The men appeared uncomfortable, fidgeting. Most pasdars either knew Ali personally or had heard others praise him. She could feel their devastation in finding evidence of treason in what they considered to be an Islamic house.

She tried to look agitated. "What evidence, Agha?"

"We're not at a liberty to say. We're not really aware of the complete story either. It's been given top confidentiality."

"*Vallah!*" Maryam put a hand to her face. "What has he done?"

"Again we're not at a liberty to say, Khanum, but I must ask of you that for the sake of Islam and the Ayatollah not to give any hints to your husband as to what we have found today. Let Allah and religion take its own course. He will be contacted shortly by the Revolutionary Guard Corps."

"He told me he's taking the day off today, but Haj Mammad a few blocks down should know where he is . . . "

"Thanks for the tip. We appreciate your help."

"For Allah no help is enough, brother. If he's done anything against Islam, he should be punished. He'll be at work tomorrow starting at eight in the morning."

"Thank you, Khanum."

"Allah bless you, brother."

They rushed to their green and white jeep. She closed the door behind them, rested her cheek on it, and chuckled.

★ ★ ★

Hamid knocked on the door and upon hearing Commander Shirazi's voice walked inside. Commander Shirazi sat at his desk, updating a file. He didn't look up. "Yes, Hamid?"

"Commander Habibi was just here, Commander."

"What did he want?"

"To let us know about the Mujahedin case. There have been new developments."

"That's not my area, Hamid."

"Yes, but I thought it may still interest you. It seems that Ali Alizadeh has been working for the Mujahedin all along."

Commander Shirazi dropped his pen and looked up. "What?"

"It's all in this folder. I'd bet that's the reason it's been so difficult to get information about the Mujahedin from him. All along he's been telling us that he's interrogating political prisoners and hasn't found any new data. Because all along he, himself, has been involved with the Mujahedin and could've given us the information himself."

"Are you sure about this?"

"Here, read this." Hamid threw a gray folder on Commander Shirazi's desk. "Commander Habibi and his men searched Ali's house today and they found this."

Commander Shirazi read through the papers. If there was one group he hated with a passion, it was the Mujahedin. He read out loud, "A meeting held in the house of Firooz Jahani a few months ago . . . Who is Firooz Jahani?"

"A mujahid, Commander. They were friends in college. So was Jamshid. Firooz was one of our better men. Certainly not the best and had too hot a temper, but he was still all right."

"Where did he work?"

"The Revolutionary Guard Corps. He became disillusioned a few months after the revolution and last year joined the Mujahedin. We haven't heard of him since. Rumor has it that Jamshid used him as a contact to join the Mujahedin."

"I remember you telling me that. Here it says that Ali and his wife went on a trip to the Caspian in June of last year. They stayed at a hotel in Chalous for a few days. What's wrong with that?"

"That's the Hotel Javan that got closed down a few months back. The owner fled and was arrested at the border. He was also a mujahid and hosted Mujahedin meetings."

Commander Shirazi paused. "How sure are you Ali was there?"

"His wife confirmed. We found a hotel receipt from a couple of years back in that folder, but nothing recent . . ."

"Can we trust the wife?"

Hamid sat down, leaned back, and crossed his arms and legs. "We have no reason to doubt her word. She's very devoted to him. He says so himself."

"*Ey vay.* This is unbelievable." Commander Shirazi rolled his pen aimlessly between his fingers. "One of our best men has been a double agent? Allah knows how much damage he's done so far."

"I always thought something was deadly wrong with him." Hamid did not care to disclose that he felt mostly this way because Ali was so incredibly brutal with prisoners.

"Tell Commander Habibi to keep digging a bit longer but I think he's got enough proof here to get this guy in jail. If all the facts check out, we'd want him eliminated immediately. If the commander needs any help, ask him to contact me."

"Yes, sir."

Hamid stood, walked out, and closed the door behind him.

★ ★ ★

A few hours later Arman pulled over to the side of the mountain road by Marand for a bathroom break. He walked down the hill with Julia. Melody rested one foot against a tree and stretched. Nader leaned against the car door and pulled out a cigarette and lit it. "I think we need to talk, Melody. I'm furious with you."

She stopped stretching.

"You should've never let Maryam in." He looked her straight in the eyes. "If you had listened to me, this wouldn't have happened. Sometimes, you should take the advice of someone older than you; someone who's done more than taking care of her hair."

A year ago when her father had patted her on the shoulder, when fame and wealth were hers, and her mother was there to morally support her, marrying a man who she did not love had seemed trivial. After all, as her father had said, if respect was there, love would surely blossom. Now, everything she had once relied on, anyone she had ever loved, had disappeared. It felt as if all along she had been standing on a flying carpet and the carpet had suddenly been pulled from under her and she was thrown onto the hard floor. Now, how she and Nader thought of one another, how he held her hand, how he spoke to her, meant everything to her, because there was nothing else left.

"Don't look at me like that, young lady!" he said, the cigarette shaking in his sweaty hand.

She looked away. She hadn't realized she'd been staring at him.

"You owe me a big one, Melody. I'll put your past behavior down to your stubbornness. Next time you should respect my opinion. After all, your father did."

"Nader, I—"

"I know you're sorry, Melody. I know you didn't mean any harm. But it's because of your obstinacy we're in this mess. Poor Julia has to suffer too because of you. She is so . . . different . . . " He looked away, inhaling the cigarette smoke and then exhaling it, his thumb pressed against his forehead. "But you've changed so much. You've become harsh, Melody. I hardly recognize you."

She could not bear to look at him. She had no energy left to argue. She turned to look behind her and was glad to see Arman and Julia walk toward them. Julia was holding on to Arman's arm, tears gathered in her eyes. Melody began to walk.

"You should go with Melody, Arman," Julia said. "I don't think it's safe for her to walk alone."

Arman took a quick look at his watch. "All right. We've got about three minutes while Julia stretches. You want to go, Melody?"

Melody looked at the horizon, her right hand extended to shield her eyes from the sun. "Yes, please." And once they were a few meters away, she whispered, "Thank you for that. Nader was lecturing me again."

Arman threw back his head and laughed. "Maybe he's trying to make up for the fact that he wasn't brave enough to jump in after Julia and you were."

She laughed as they walked down the hill and behind the trees. "Are we stopping again before we reach Amir Khan's house in Khoy?"

"One more time. I have to make a quick phone call to Zia."

"Any more developments on the mission?"

"Not much since I last spoke with Kami. He is on top of it. I'm not sure what I would've done without him. I do need to get back though to help however I can. We haven't got much time left." He sat on a rock and made room for her to sit by him. They could hear the sound of the freeway in the background.

"I have to find a way to tell Julia that I'm not going with her to Turkey. It'll break her heart."

Melody nodded. "When are you going to do it?"

"At Amir Khan's house, I think. Just before you leave."

"Maybe you should give her a bit more time to get used to the idea?"

"I'm thinking it's actually best if she doesn't have any time to think about it. She already has enough to worry about. She has to get out of Iran and while she thinks I'm going with her, she'll be more willing to go. Will you take care of her for me, Melody?"

"Of course, I'll do what I can."

"Thank you."

She squeezed her eyes shut. She could feel a bad headache coming on. "Any news from your father?"

"Last I heard he was doing fine. Kami visited him. I think his days are limited."

There was a coldness to his tone that surprised her, but she sensed the anguish underneath. "I'm sorry, Arman." Her hand gently touched his cheek. He turned to look at her.

Suddenly, she knew they were both thinking the same thing.

She pulled herself back. He stood up and looked down at her and suddenly his face opened into a wide pleasant grin that turned him into a boy again. He pulled her up after him, holding on to her hand longer than necessary.

"Let's get going," he said.

She realized her headache was gone.

★ ★ ★

Arman pulled open the door to the telephone booth and picked up the phone. He threw a few coins in the slot. Zia's phone rang several times but no one picked up. Arman saw a green and white jeep pull forward. He hung up, turned around, and walked to his car.

He'd make his next call from Amir Khan's house. After all, what could Zia really do? He still needed Arman until the mission was finalized. He wouldn't do anything to jeopardize the mission.

Would he?

★ ★ ★

A man with thick black hair waved and walked into room 212. Leila, the on-call nurse of the intensive care unit, wondered why so many men wore wigs nowadays. She shrugged and returned to her paperwork.

Her phone rang.

"Hello?"

"Leila Khanum?"

"Yes?"

"You're needed in radiology. One of your patients passed out during x-ray. We have to move him back to his room as soon as possible."

"Oh dear! What's his name?"

"Vahidi."

"Vahidi?" Leila flipped through the pages of her files. She didn't recognize the name, but it was only her second day on the job. "Are you sure that's his name?"

"Yes, I am. Can't you find his file?"

She knew what the doctor was thinking: these unorganized new nurses. She pulled herself together. "I'm looking for it—"

"That's not necessary. Just come by. I need to get him out of here soon. I've got patients waiting."

"Where is he now?"

"I told you, radiology, on the other side of the building."

"Yes, Doctor. I'll come by immediately—"

"And, Nurse?"

"Yes, Doctor?"

"Don't send somebody else, please. The patient just woke up and the nurse here tells me he's adamant about you helping him. He doesn't want anybody else."

Leila hesitated. She was surprised to find any patient so stubborn about having only her attend him. A pang of guilt passed through her body when she realized once more that she did not even recognize the patient's name. "Of course, Doctor. I'll be there in a few minutes."

She picked up a notebook and a pen, pushed back her chair, and walked down the hallway. She did not notice the door of room 212 open and the black-haired man walk out, pushing the unconscious General Pakran in a wheelchair down the hallway.

★ ★ ★

Zia pushed the invalid past the attendant clerk on the first floor, who turned to look at them. He was sure that with his new disguise nobody would recognize him, especially since the pasdar responsible for guarding the hospital had also received an anonymous phone call causing him to leave immediately.

Zia laid General Pakran in the backseat of his blue BMW and slammed the door shut. He sat in the driver's seat and started the engine. In a few seconds he had driven off.

★ ★ ★

Leila returned to her station. The doctor had claimed he'd never summoned her and there was no patient named Vahidi in radiology, passed out or otherwise. She opened her drawer and looked through her files. There had been a Vahidi hospitalized here a few months back but he was no longer here. She shut the drawer and looked around with a frown. Who had made that phone call?

Then she noticed that the door to room 212 was slightly ajar. The general's son had entered his room. Something about the man had disturbed her, but at the moment she couldn't remember what it was. She pushed the door open and walked in.

The bed was empty and IV and heart monitoring needles hung loose. She gasped and pressed the red emergency button.

★ ★ ★

Twenty minutes later, Commander Shirazi and Hamid stepped into the intensive care unit and walked to the desk where a short slim woman wearing a white scarf rose to greet them. She looked worried.

Commander Shirazi showed his badge. "We're here to investigate the disappearance of General Pakran. We received a call saying that he had disappeared. They said you were the nurse in charge of this area. Is this correct?"

"Yes, sir."

"What's your name, Khanum?"

"Leila Kamali, sir."

"How long have you been working here?"

Leila's hand shivered as she adjusted her scarf. "In this division, only two days, sir."

"Phone number and address, please."

She told them and Hamid wrote it down.

"What happened this morning?"

Leila repeated what she had noticed when General Pakran had disappeared.

"A man with black hair? Was he young?"

"I would say mid to late thirties."

"What else did you notice, Khanum?"

"He had a wide grin on his face that looked awkward, like a child's. He gave a very positive impression. I heard him call the general 'baba' when he entered the room."

Commander Shirazi threw a quick glance at Hamid, who was frowning but did not look up as he took notes.

"What else did you hear?"

"Nothing. He closed the door behind him."

"Is that it then?"

"Well, yes, except that there was something . . ."

Hamid looked up. "What?"

"Something that seemed odd, but for some reason I can't recall now . . ."

"Please think, Khanum. This is very important."

She frowned, then shook her head. "Sorry. I see so many people during the day. If it comes to me, I'll let you know."

"Here." Commander Shirazi pulled out a business card and handed it to Leila. Hamid did the same. "Give me a call if you remember. In the meantime we'll interview the rest of the staff. Goodbye, Khanum."

As they walked away, Commander Shirazi turned to Hamid. "Arman Pakran. It had to be. Sounds like the boy knows he's in trouble and is trying to protect his father. Maybe he's afraid he'll talk and give him away."

"All of this appears very strange, Commander."

"Why, Hamid?"

"What about the anonymous phone call our man received? It was clearly to get him out of the picture while our thug takes out the general. How did Arman know who our guard was?"

Commander Shirazi bit his lower lip and nodded. "What exactly happened?"

"Someone gave Pasdar Taheri a call, asking him to contact our man, saying his wife was giving birth. By the time his replacement got here, it was all over."

"Was she having a baby?"

"No, sir, though she is eight months pregnant."

"I see what you mean." He nodded. "Arman could have heard the guard talking with someone, but . . . it is very convenient. Yes, I can see your point. Let's talk to the guard when we get back."

"And also . . . "

Commander Shirazi was looking at General Pakran's hospital files. "Yes?"

Hamid made up his mind. "Remember the picture of the plant we found in General Jalili's jacket?"

"What about it?"

"I did some research. It was actually the picture of a plant called the Deadly Nightshade."

Commander Shirazi turned a page. "What's that?"

"It's a poisonous herb with some history behind it."

"So are you trying to tell me General Jalili poisoned somebody?"

"Unlikely."

Commander Shirazi finally looked up from the files. "I'm not following you."

"I was confused too at the beginning, so I went over the SAVAK files. I found a document, which seemed to explain some things. It seems that there was a CIA agent at the time of the Shah—"

"There were quite a few agents during the Shah's time, Hamid."

"I know, but this agent's name was Nightshade."

"Really?" Commander Shirazi closed the file. "Interesting. I'm impressed, Hamid." Then he frowned. "I wonder if Arman is Nightshade . . . "

A police officer glanced around the doorway. "Commander Shirazi?"

"Yes?"

"The first-floor clerk thinks he may have useful information to pass on to you, if you'd like to speak to him."

"Bring him here at once."

A moment later a man in his early twenties approached them.

"What is it you want to tell me, kid?"

The young man glared. "My name is Sayeed Daftari, sir, and I am twenty-four years old. You can hardly call me a kid."

Commander Shirazi raised an eyebrow and Hamid hid an amused smile. It was not every day that an ordinary civilian stood up to a pasdar. Commander Shirazi gestured the clerk to go on. The young man cleared his throat. "I figured you wanted information about some patient who's disappeared?"

"Yes. Phone and address."

The clerk recited his phone and address. Hamid copied them down.

"Go on."

"I saw something that grabbed my attention and I think may have something to do with this case. An hour ago a black-haired man with a mustache walked by pushing an old man in a wheelchair."

"What's so odd about that?"

"The old man's arm had a bandage wrapped around it that was hanging loose. It looked like someone, probably the man pushing him, carelessly pulled out the needles of an IV and forgot to cover the wounds. Seemed odd to me that a nurse would allow the patient to go out like that. On top of it the patient appeared unconscious."

"Why didn't you try to stop him then?"

"It's not my area of responsibility, sir. I mentioned it to the security guard but by then he'd received the phone call from the second floor that a patient had been kidnapped."

Commander Shirazi sighed. "I see."

"But I did notice that the man had a BMW and I happened to jot down the license plate number just in case." The clerk passed a piece of paper to Hamid.

"Good job, young man. I can see you're going places."

The clerk who did not seem to be very fond of revolutionary guards smiled coldly and walked away. Hamid's amused glance met Commander Shirazi's.

But Commander Shirazi didn't look amused. "Let's go. I don't like this one bit. We have a mad man on the loose and God knows what he's going to do next."

TEN

"OUT! GET OUT OF this car at once!"

The rifle barrel poking Nader's cheek emphasized the words even more. Nader's hand shook, searching for the car door handle. He pulled it and fell out of the car.

Melody suppressed a sigh.

Arman opened the car door for Julia and her. Julia was completely pale and Melody squeezed her hand. The closer they got to the Turkish border, the more revolutionary guards they encountered. At the border to Tabriz they searched all cars and checked identification papers.

"Men to the right, woman to the left!" a pasdar barked. "Hurry up! We haven't got all day!"

Melody pulled Julia after her. Julia's fake papers said that she was deaf-mute. This was done to ensure she would not have to speak. They had already discussed their fake identities several times.

Across the mountain road, they walked to a curve where not too long ago lovers had no doubt parked to watch the sun set behind the breathtaking Zagros Mountains. The cliffs stood high and grand, shaggy with trees. It was chilly though the sun hadn't set, and Julia and Melody held on to each other's arms. In a corner on a few chairs sat flocks of black-veiled women. These were the female version of the Islamic militants.

Arman and Nader stood in the men's line. Melody could see Nader's hand shaking as he held on to his identification papers.

"I think I'm going to pass out," Julia whispered.

"Sh! It'll be fine. Just keep cool."

Julia raised an eyebrow but did not respond. If Julia were discovered to be an American, she would be thrown in with the hostages until the negotiations concluded. Her Iranian friends who had harbored her could be shot for treason.

"Those planning to go to Turkey, hand out your passports," the same pasdar shouted. A few passengers pulled out their passports. A young pasdar rushed between the lines to retrieve them. The women were body searched. When Melody's turn came, the woman did not even look at her as she rubbed her hands across her body, searching between her legs, around her waist, under her breasts and arms, meanwhile proving Melody's inferiority in front of the Islamic regime.

"Where are you going, sister?" the woman asked.

"To Khoy."

"What for?"

"To visit. My cousin and I," she pointed to Julia, "have relatives there."

The woman's glance passed over Julia's white face and turned to Melody again. "Crossing the border?"

"No."

The woman studied her quietly. Melody knew that though she was dressed properly, her tone of voice and bearing still labeled her as upper class. Those were things she could not easily change. Instead she tried to appear timid, insecure, and afraid—qualities the Islamic government encouraged in women. Her behavior seemed to slightly ease the woman's suspicion as her eyes turned to rest on Julia's fair skin. "Your cousin?"

"Yes."

She held out a hand.

Julia understood the gesture and handed over her papers.

"What's your name, sister?"

"She's deaf-mute," Melody said.

The woman looked at the birth certificate and handed it back. "All right. Is she going with you?"

"Yes. We're both going to Khoy."

"Come here! I said come here!" She signed to Julia. Julia went forward and the woman searched her body. "Take off your shoes."

Julia looked up in confusion.

"Tell her to take off her shoes."

Melody squatted and untied Julia's shoelaces. Julia nodded and took her shoes off. The woman turned each shoe upside down and threw them to the side. "All right. You're done. Next in line."

Melody helped Julia put her shoes back on. They walked to the car where Nader and Arman waited for them.

"Is everything all right, Julia?" Arman asked as he turned on the engine.

"You mean aside from the fact that I'm terrified and humiliated? No, everything's fine."

Arman turned the wheel and pulled back onto the road.

"In less than an hour we'll be in Khoy. After that things will get easier."

But Julia was looking out of the window with a strong silence that was hard to ignore.

★ ★ ★

Half an hour later Arman stopped to call Kami.

"Hello."

"Kami?"

"Arman! Where in the world are you? I've been worried sick—"

"I'm sorry. I'll explain later. How is everything going with the mission? I've been doing nothing but worry about it every second of the day—"

"Everything is in order. Only five days left—"

"I know." Five days before the Americans would head for Desert One. The thought made Arman's heart skip a beat.

"Zia called. He's gone mad," Kami said. "He's taken your father from the hospital."

"What?"

"He said he's been waiting for your phone call and hasn't received it. He said he thought something was suspicious yesterday when you spoke with him. I tried to convince him otherwise, but he wouldn't listen. Why didn't you call him?"

"I did. He wasn't there. Where has he taken Baba? I swear if he's hurt him—"

"I'm not sure. I'm sorry, Arman. He's wasn't doing well and this may . . ."

Finish him off! Arman knew Kami could not complete the sentence. After all, Kami had known General Pakran since he was a teenager.

"Did you give Zia the list of names he asked for?" Kami asked.

"No. That's what pissed him off yesterday. He said to give him a call this morning to tell him where he can pick it up. I wasn't going to give it to him though, not until I know what the hell he wants to do with it. That list is worth a lot of cash and I still don't know whose side he's on."

"You may be right. I've more news though. An insider told me they found a picture of a plant inside General Jalili's pocket when he was killed."

"What has that got to do anything?"

"It was Deadly Nightshade."

Arman did not answer. Instead, he looked at the bakery across the street, where the baker threw the dough inside the wall oven.

"It's kind of ironic," Kami said, "but I was doing some research a few days ago. One of the definitions of the Deadly Nightshade is Atropos, the inevitable—the fate who cuts your life thread when your time is done."

Arman eyes froze on the last flat bread the baker threw on the pile.

Kami laughed. "It's also what Macbeth gave to a party of Danes after a truce. Given that he may have picked his own code name, sounds like we've got someone with a real dramatic flair."

"Or a real sick sense of humor."

Kami stopped laughing. An old woman, wrapped in a long veil, holding a child's hand, paid the baker. Arman was thinking fast, something was wrong, very wrong. He had known it all along, but now he was certain.

Deadly Nightshade . . . Macbeth gave it to a party of Danes after a truce . . . Atropos, the inevitable, the one who cut your life thread when your time was done . . .

It was starting to make sense.

"When are you coming back to Tehran?" Kami asked.

"I'll be there to pick you up as planned. It probably won't be until a day or two before the mission. I have some things to take care of."

"Take care of yourself, Arman. We want you in one piece."

"Don't worry. I'll be there." Arman hung up, slid the door to the telephone booth open and walked out.

This mission would be larger, greater, than any coup attempted in Iran since Prime Minister Mossadegh's overthrow in 1953 and even though Arman tried to ignore how anxious he was, he knew how seriously he was putting his life in danger.

The woman in the long black veil paused to offer him a piece of the bread she had just bought. An old custom still practiced across the country. He mumbled a few words of thanks but suddenly he had trouble standing.

Deadly Nightshade. Of course.

★ ★ ★

They pulled into a narrow road leading to Amir Khan's estate. They stepped out in awe of the scenery. The mountains stood tall and proud in the distance. Closer in, a river cut through the valley and cattle grazed on the hills beyond. Small red tulips covered the area around the gate of the estate. It seemed as though the world had been left unchanged here.

The ancient wooden door squeaked as it opened, and an old man in slippers and a village cap looked out. He smiled warmly and without further questioning opened the door. They all bent their heads to walk inside and into a short covered hall with a red-tiled walkway that led to a round green courtyard surrounded by rooms. Many trees, most of which bore oranges, berries, and apples, gave color to the yard. A stream passing through the garden provided a refreshing burble that added to the peaceful, dreamlike atmosphere.

An old woman, a thin white veil wrapped around her waist, washed dishes in the running water. She looked up and smiled. Two children, one of whom was already halfway up a tree, laughed at them. While the guests looked about them in awe and tried to grasp the simple beauty of Iran as it once had been, a tall man with warm eyes, a large mustache and belly, came forward and grasped Arman by the hand.

"Good to see you again," he said. "It's such an honor. How is your father doing?"

"Thank you, Amir Khan. He's not doing well. Heart attack. It's left him paralyzed."

Amir Khan's expression became genuinely sad. "I'm very sorry to hear that, Arman." Then he looked around. "You all look extremely exhausted."

"I'm afraid we are," Nader whined.

Apparently, Nader's peevish stare seemed amusing to the old gentleman. He laughed, his belly shaking heartily. "Come on in. Take those awful scarves off of your heads and relax. We've prepared warm baths for you and rooms for you to sleep in. Dinner will be served shortly."

"Thank you, Amir Khan," Melody said.

"No trouble at all, Khanum." And he bent his head sideways to whisper to Arman, "I've prepared everything. It'll be difficult and it's risky. The borders are checked thoroughly but I think we can still manage."

Arman nodded but before he could respond Amir Khan's eyes rested on Julia's fair skin and hair. "As beautiful as *mah-e shab-e chardah*!" He bent funnily to kiss her hand. "It's an honor to have such a goddess as one's guest."

Julia blushed when the words were translated for her, and for the first time in days she openly laughed.

★ ★ ★

Shortly afterward Melody stepped out of the bathtub and rubbed her hair with a towel. The water drops fell onto the blue-tiled floors of the ancient bathroom. She wrapped another towel around her slim body. The hot bath gave her new life. She opened the door to walk to her own room, hearing Julia's laughter from the living room and deciding that she did not feel as lively as her girlfriend, who had found the men's attentiveness to her beauty so charming. Melody was merely exhausted. Still being here made her think that, perhaps somewhere again, she would find the peace within herself that she had thought so drastically destroyed.

She turned the corner to the bedrooms and hesitated. Arman stood next to an oil lamp with a map in his hand. He looked up and his stare turned from surprise into amusement as his glance passed over her body wrapped in a towel. And then their eyes met.

In another world, another time, when her parents were alive and she was to marry Nader, she would have behaved like a true medieval maiden and walked away from him. But now, under the oil lamp, in their solitude it did not seem to matter anymore.

He turned and walked into his bedroom as if he could not endure seeing her like this. She stopped in the doorway and then followed him inside. He was looking out the window into the green yard, his back toward her, deep in thought. She knew what he was thinking.

She closed the door behind her. He turned at the sound and looked at her in sheer astonishment.

"Melody..."

She dropped the towel and walked toward him.

His eyes rested on her face for a few seconds. "You know what this means?"

She did. If Nader ever found out, he would not marry her, and if her father were alive he might even disinherit her. Since it was probable that no other Iranian man would ever marry her, making love now could mean her ruin.

"I don't care," she said.

"What about Nader—"

"I've never loved him. You know that."

"I can't do this to you—"

She put a finger to his lips. "I think I'm allowed a moment of happiness in a world that has gone mad. Make love to me, Arman."

Without further hesitation, he swept her up, and lay her on the bed. The fresh breeze coming through the open window made the drawn curtains sway slightly. He looked into her eyes and pulled her wet hair back from her face, breathing in that mixture of innocence and wildness. It was as though he could lie there forever simply watching her and feeling her naked body next to his.

She moved her hand and turned off the oil lamp.

In complete darkness, there were no secrets anymore. His lips touched her face and hungrily descended to her neck and breasts. She felt his warmth against her, pulling off his shirt, touching the muscles on his chest and arms. He opened her legs and found her softness in between, his body on top of hers, and she allowed him to slide inside of her. It was a moment of completeness they had both longed for keenly and which society had held back from them for far too long.

★ ★ ★

Arman had watched Melody sleep for as long as he could. He reached over and shook her shoulder gently. She woke, and he saw her knowledge of last night's thoughtless action, which their entire society would condemn, flood into her face. Her hand drew back from his chest slowly. But she did not look sorry.

He kissed her and stood up. "It's ten to three." He pulled up his pants. "The truck will leave in forty minutes. You have to get ready."

She pushed aside the covers and stood up. He wrapped the towel around her body, still a bit in awe of the courageous decision she had made. He walked her to the door and kissed her hand.

"No regrets?" he asked.

"No."

He saw the momentary sorrow in her face as she turned to walk out. He put a hand on her shoulder. "Melody . . ."

She turned to look at him.

"Don't ever doubt that I love you," he said, then seeing the confusion in her expression added, "This doesn't make any difference. What we did last night won't change how I feel about you. It only makes me love you even more. Do you believe me, Melody?"

"Yes."

"When I'm done with this business, I'll call you and we'll meet again. Unless . . . you want to still stay with Nader?" He hadn't thought of this. A 'yes' would once more break his heart.

She laughed quietly. "Call me and I'll be there."

"I'll walk you to your room."

"No, Nader may be waiting."

He nodded.

She paused, then looked up. "Julia?"

"I'll let her know later. She has enough troubling her now."

"I understand if you want to stay with her. I didn't mean to hurt her—"

"Julia's a smart girl, Melody. She's already guessed. It's always been you anyway. She would've been blind not to see it."

Her eyes filled with tears.

He pushed back a strand of hair that had fallen onto her face. "What are you thinking?"

"That it's all very ironic."

"What is?"

"The day I finally feel free is the day when everyone and everything I've held dear in my life has vanished."

She walked away. He watched her disappear down the hallway and then closed the door behind her.

★ ★ ★

They stood by the large flatbed truck carrying a huge stack of bricks. In the center of the stack, visible through a narrow passage through the bricks, was a small steel shelter. Two large aluminum oxygen tanks with a regulator were placed inside. A few steel bars ran through the bricks at strategically placed points. It was three thirty-five. They would have to leave in five minutes.

"What are those tanks?" Nader asked with a suspicious frown.

"Haven't you ever seen a scuba tank, my good man?" the truck driver, a broad-shouldered short man named Haj Mammad, asked.

"No. What's it for?"

"What's it for?" Haj Mammad laughed. "Have you ever left home before, Haji, or have you lain on your couch being pampered all day? It's for oxygen. You've got to breathe somehow."

"Just two?" Nader asked again, sweat running down his forehead.

"You'll have to share them. Couldn't fit more in that hole and the three of you on top of it. Now get in."

"How do we share it?" Julia asked.

"You pass the regulator back and forth," Arman said. "It'll last you until you get there."

"And if it doesn't?" Nader's face was pale and he was clinging to the side of the truck.

Haj Mammad laughed. "Then you'd better get the hell out of that hole and fast."

"This is insane!" Nader jumped back from the truck as if it were evil. "Forget it! I'm not going."

"If it takes longer than three hours, Haj Mammad here," Arman put a hand on Haj Mammad's shoulder, "will stop the truck and get you guys out no matter what. Besides he has another tank in the front with him."

Julia held on to Arman. "Why didn't you tell me you're not coming with us, Arman? It's insane. It's not worth it, whatever you're involved in."

"Julia." Arman pulled her aside. "Listen to me. Where I'm going, you can't come. You must get out of Iran. The situation is very dangerous right now, especially for you. The negotiations are taking forever."

Julia threw a quick glance at Melody and then turned to look at Arman. "Will I ever hear from you again?"

"Of course you will. Now, you must be strong. It'll be over before you know it."

"You really think you're going to get away with this?" Nader said louder than necessary.

Melody put a hand to his arm. "It's all right, Nader. It's been done before. This is better than going in a pile of carpet or fruit, which they'd be expecting—"

"You and your ideas!" Nader grabbed Melody by the shoulders. "You got us into this mess in the first place. Don't even let me start with that again—"

Without thinking about it, Arman pinned Nader against the truck. "Enough!" Arman slowly let Nader go. "Either go away or get in. It's your choice."

A line of sweat covered Nader's upper lip and he was shivering. In his pale blue shirt and black pants he seemed a misplaced image in the night. He pulled himself away, a hand to his mouth and looked around. They were in a narrow street of a construction zone where a pharmaceutical company was once being built. Since the owners had fled, it was left to slowly decay.

Julia leaned over and gently kissed Arman on the cheek. Arman pulled her to him and caressed her long blond hair under her scarf. He whispered some vague words of encouragement. He hated misleading her like this, but she was his responsibility, and he had to get her out of the country.

She took his hand and climbed into the truck, the first person to get in. She trembled as she sat in the back. Arman passed her a blanket. "It'll be a few hours until the border. It might get cold."

"Do you think this is safe, Arman?" Melody asked. The scuba oxygen tanks were placed in the center of the hole.

"They've done it several times, Melody. Each time has been successful."

"Who came up with the scuba tank idea?" Melody smiled.

"Some navy officer. Makes sense and it works, the Hezbollahies wouldn't even think about it. Too intelligent for them."

She laughed despite herself.

He took her hand. "You have the pistol I gave you?"

She touched her pocket.

"Good. You never know what may happen—"

"Believe me, I won't let them take us in. Either way."

"I wish I could come with you, but in three days the U.S. Marines will be landing in Desert One." He frowned, a feeling of anxiety passing through his body. "Kami and the other officers are counting on me being there."

"We'll be all right. Any news from your father?"

"Not since Zia took him. I . . . I've been assuming he's gone." His voice trembled. "There's no way he could've survived the kidnapping."

"I'm very sorry, Arman." She caressed his cheek. "Take care. I don't want to lose you now that we finally have each other."

"I'll be back for you, Melody. I promise."

"I hope all this is worth it. I wish you could come with us. We need you."

"And you? Do you need me?"

"You know I do."

He smiled. "Maybe it's *ghesmat*."

"I didn't think you were one to believe in fate."

"I don't. That's why I want to fight it one more time. I want to fight what we so fondly claim has been written."

"Some would say that you can't change what's written no matter how hard you try."

"Nothing is written. It's the actions we take that make an impact."

"If all Iranians thought this way, Iran would be a different place."

"So you agree with me?"

"Oh, yes. But somehow suddenly only one thing seems to matter to me."

"What?"

"To live with you in peace." She looked away. "I guess I'm just tired of it all, of all the violence and hate. I want it to simply end so we can start our lives again."

"I know what you mean."

"Do what you have to do. I hope you'll succeed, I truly do. But come back to me, Arman, or I know I'll never learn to live again."

He kissed her and helped her into the truck. By then, Nader had also gotten onto the truck on his own. Haj Mammad and two helpers jumped up and began putting the bricks in front of their hole. Their eyes locked as the last brick was placed and complete darkness took over.

"*Allah-o akbar!*" Nader said.

★ ★ ★

"Hold my hand, Nader," Julia said. "I'm scared out of my mind."

"It'll be all right, Julia." Nader's voice was trembling in the dark. He then leaned back and put his other arm around Melody. "We'll be fine."

Melody could feel the ice-cold wind of the Zagros Mountains blowing down the valley and through the cracks of their shelter. The howling echoed through the darkness as the truck drove on the mountain road. While Julia breathed in the oxygen and passed the regulator to Melody, Nader murmured prayers under his breath. Melody could not help but feel a deep resentment toward those religious words. These expressions of love and trust in God had begun to represent to her the very things that had destroyed her life. They frightened her more than reassured her.

"What the . . . " Nader said out loud. Melody squeezed his arm and he froze.

The truck had stopped.

★ ★ ★

Haj Mammad jumped down onto the road. A cold wind blew through the valley, ruffling his short hair and he pulled his jacket tighter around him. He had seen the police station from afar and from the signs on the road knew he had to stop to have the cargo checked. He was relieved to see not a revolutionary guard but a police officer covered with a white rainproof jacket.

"What have you got?" the officer cried over the wind.

"Bricks." A few drops of rain began to fall on his head.

The police officer frowned, looking through a list of refugee names in his hand. Haj Mammad decided it was time to interrupt. "You seem well prepared, Officer. Did you know it would be raining tonight?"

"I checked the weather channel." The police officer turned to his sergeant. "Go check out the cargo. Let me know what you find. Your papers, please."

Haj Mammad passed him his work papers.

"You're exporting a lot of bricks to Turkey, Haj Agha." The police officer frowned. "This is your third time going through, isn't it?"

Haj Mammad laughed and shrugged. "We sell it if they want it."

The police officer sneezed.

"Bless you. Do you have a cold?"

"How can I be healthy in these conditions? This isn't my station anyway. The Revolutionary Guard Corps built it to spy on passengers. Now, they've abandoned it to us."

"Why's that?"

"They opened up several more sophisticated ones right by the border. They figured it's useless checking all the cargo here and that it's best to check the ones that could be going across the border."

Haj Mammad caught the contempt in the police officer's voice. "You'd think that would've been pretty obvious in the first place."

"Of course, my good man. But would they listen? They're a bunch of useless kids and suddenly they think they understand the entire police operation. They think they can rule the country just because they've got better guns and learned how to shoot more or less at a target. Oh well, let them play their games. I have my pension to worry about. Here." He passed the papers back to him. "It looks clean. You can go."

He turned to the sergeant who was looking around the truck. "Come here, Sergeant. It's fine. Let the gentleman through."

"Thank you, Officer," Haj Mammad said and walked to the truck. As he started the engine he rolled down his driver's window and winked at the police officer. "Long live the Ayatollah!"

The police officer unwillingly looked up. "Yes, yes, long live. Now good day." And he put his hand to his mouth to cough, which did little to hide his disagreement.

Haj Mammad chuckled, waved, and drove on.

★ ★ ★

In Tehran, Commander Shirazi and Hamid sat at Farid's, the filing clerk's desk with cups of tea in their hands while the latter went through the files.

"We shouldn't be wasting time," Commander Shirazi said. "Arman is our man. We just need to figure out where he is."

Hamid's left foot tapped against the desk, ignoring the revolutionary songs coming from the radio in the background.

The Arman he knew could not possibly have become such a professional killer. So somebody else must be behind all this. He could hardly voice his doubts to his commander though—Commander Shirazi would immediately conclude Hamid was not suitable for this case. Still, Hamid was determined to get to the bottom of this.

"All right!" Commander Shirazi stood and put a copy of Arman's birth certificate in his inside jacket pocket. "It's been forty minutes we've been looking. We don't have any more time to waste. Have you received any information on the whereabouts of Arman, Hamid?"

"No, unfortunately—"

"Here." Farid put a folder on the desk. "The license number matches an old SAVAK agent's BMW. I have it belonging to Zia Mohseni. His address is Yaser Three-way, Nahid Avenue, number 54. I have a phone number for him as well."

"Zia Mohseni?" Commander Shirazi said. "I thought we got rid of him at the beginning."

"You knew him?"

"Who didn't?"

"Well, must've fallen through the cracks," Farid said. "Anyway, the BMW belonged to him."

Hamid stood. "Should we check it out, Commander?"

"No more than a day. Now, I've a quick meeting scheduled with Commander Habibi to discuss Ali Alizadeh's situation. After that we can go. It shouldn't take more than half an hour."

"Give me a call when you're ready, Commander."

"Will do."

Commander Shirazi walked out.

★ ★ ★

Hamid had barely sat at his desk when his phone rang. "Hello?"

"Lieutenant Rahimi?" a woman's voice said.

"Yes. Who's speaking?"

"This is Leila Kamali. General Pakran's nurse. Do you remember me?"

"Of course. How are you doing, Khanum?"

"Fine, thank you. I tried calling Commander Shirazi a few minutes ago, but he wasn't there. So I called you. I hope it's okay."

"Definitely. How can I help you?"

"I wanted to tell you I remembered what had struck me as odd with the man who kidnapped the general."

"Yes?"

"It may not seem important but—"

"Everything in this case is important, believe me."

"Well, there were two things actually. It's odd, you know, as a man you may not notice—I mean men can't see beyond their noses. I'm sorry. I don't mean to be rude but . . . "

Hamid took a deep breath. "I understand."

"The odd thing was that his hair looked strange. It was unnatural, but then many men have unnatural-looking hair. Anyway, if you ask me that was not his real hair."

"You mean he wore a wig?"

"At least that's what I thought . . . "

"And the second thing, Khanum?"

"Now, this sounds really bizarre and I completely understand if you think I'm imagining things. But you know how it is, as a mother you always notice things like this. You have to. Your husband isn't normally home and it's up to you to figure out if your children are doing things they shouldn't be doing—"

Hamid breathed in again. "Such as?"

"You see, in my family it's not really encouraged to put makeup on until you enter college, sometimes even until you get married. Worst of all is seeing your sons do it. That's when you know you're in real trouble."

Hamid had a choice. He could be frustrated by this prattling woman or amused. Since he needed to know what she knew, he chose to be amused. "Go on, Khanum."

"Well, I assume that's why I noticed really . . ."

"Noticed what?"

"That he wore makeup, too."

"What was that?"

"He had powder on his face, Lieutenant. He had as much as I do when I try to cover a zit or some scar. When he passed me I thought he had tried too hard to cover the scar on his right cheek . . . or was it left? No, right cheek. But at the time I just thought it strange and nothing more. He was a bit farther away and it's possible I could be mistaken."

"I see. Anything else?"

"No, that was it. It may have been all wrong and silly. I'm just telling you what I thought at the time. I hope it was useful. I feel very sorry for the poor old general. I really don't think he'll make it."

"Yes, it is unfortunate. Thank you for the information, Khanum." He hung up and called Farid. "Farid, check something for me, will you?"

"Anything, Hamid."

Now that Commander Shirazi was not there they could be informal again. "Can you pull up Zia's picture?"

"Just a minute."

He could barely remember the man. Zia had harassed the Pakrans in their Tehran house for the most part, but once he had stopped at their estate in Yazd and Hamid had seen him. He had been a child then, hiding in the bushes, and Zia had been younger. Perhaps he looked different now.

But he thought there had been a scar.

Two minutes later, Farid said. "Got it. What are you looking for?"

"Has he got a scar on one of his cheeks?"

"Long scar, right cheek."

Hamid paused for a moment, then said, "Can you bring the picture by immediately please, Farid?"

"Sure."

★ ★ ★

It was an hour and half later when Haj Mammad took the exit that led to the station at the border. The station was packed. People sat on their luggage drooping and listless as if they'd been there for hours. The area smelled of perspiration and garbage. A few tourist buses had pulled over and their baggage was tossed about.

Haj Mammad walked to the line above which hung a banner "Cargo Truck Drivers." He waited patiently with the papers in his hand. Thankfully, there weren't many truck drivers in line. An hour later he reached the counter. His papers were checked and four revolutionary guards were called to inspect the truck.

Before they'd arrived, the heavens opened and rain pounded down. The passengers, who had been harassed by the mosquitoes during the day, scattered for shelter. A few people were arguing near his truck. The head pasdar, no older than thirty, said, "Get on with it." He looked as if he'd worked all night and even his zealotry was beginning to fade at this early hour of the morning.

The others began to pull back the truck's cover.

"There isn't anything under there but my cargo, sir," Haj Mammad said. "Please. It'll be a pain putting everything back on again."

"We have to check everything." The lead pasdar pressed his red eyes with his soiled fingers. "Too many people try to escape on the back of trucks just like yours."

"Makes me furious that people abuse our system so much. It makes the lives of simple truck drivers like me so much more difficult."

"I don't like it anymore than you do, Haj Agha, believe me. But I've got to do what I've got to do. Unload the truck."

Haj Mammad no longer protested. The pasdars began to toss down bricks as the wind blew hard against them and the rain began to beat on their bodies.

Haj Mammad quietly waited for fate to take its course.

★ ★ ★

Through the light, which found its way from the station into their shelter, Melody could see Julia sitting with her legs pulled to her, her face in the palm of her hands, deadly still. Time seemed eternal, as they felt absolutely nothing but pointed sharp terror.

They heard the bricks hit the ground. Light began to shine clearer through the openings created by the removal of the bricks.

"It's over!" Nader said without as much as a tremor in his voice.

★ ★ ★

A few bricks fell to the ground and hit one of the pasdars on his left foot. He yelled.

"What the hell is going on?" the lead pasdar shouted.

"We've hit a wall of something, sir."

Haj Mammad caught his breath.

"A wall of what?"

"Steel pieces, sir. They look like steel bars. We'd need a crane to move them."

The lead pasdar turned to Haj Mammad. "I thought you were carrying bricks. What are the steel bars for?"

"Construction. We sell those too. I reported it in the papers. It's all there."

The pasdar looked at the papers and frowned.

"Strange to combine the two, Haj Agha."

"Not really. Sometimes we don't have the appropriate trucks for the steel bars, and if we balance the load right we can take a few of them along with the bricks. The police officer before your time was used to the practice. Besides half an hour ago this whole thing was checked by your comrade at the station outside of Khoy."

The pasdar at the truck ran back to his boss. "What should we do, sir?"

The lead pasdar looked at the sky. His hair and uniform were soaked. "We don't have the right equipment to move the steel bars. Do you see anything so far?"

"No sir. The load is larger than it seems. We'd have to unload a lot more to see if there is anything in the center, but frankly nothing would have stayed alive with that amount of steel and brick around it."

The lead pasdar hesitated and then looked up. "Put the bricks back on the truck, Sergeant." He signed Haj Mammad's papers and passed them on to him. "Allah be with you, Haj Agha. I wish you a safe trip."

"Thank you, sir. Allah blesses you for your hard work. Good night."

"Good night."

★ ★ ★

The truck began to move and Julia glanced at Melody as Nader squeezed her hand reassuringly. Julia understood and smiled suddenly in relief. They were passing the border into Turkey. Alive.

ELEVEN

THE NEXT MORNING MARYAM received an envelope from the postman. It had the look and feel of an official letter. She tore it open.

> *"In the name of Allah—the good and the merciful;*
> *We hereby request the presence of Mrs. Ali Alizadeh at Qasr Prison. Please provide this letter upon your admission . . ."*

What did they want from her?

It must have something to do with Ali. She knew he had been arrested and put to trial. Perhaps he had been able to convince them of his innocence and had learned that she had been behind the allegations. But Ali's revenge would be harsh and speedy. He would show up at her door and beat her, perhaps this time to death, not mess about with formal letters. So, this could not be it.

Maybe they wanted her to testify against him?

There was no way of second-guessing them. Besides when you received an official command like this, you had to abide by it. She picked up her veil and covered herself.

The traffic was worse than ever in Abbas Abad. A few policemen stood idly on the corners, trying to balance out the abnormal harshness of the revolutionary guards with overwhelming negligence.

At Qasr Prison she handed the guard her letter. They guided her through a gate into the prison grounds. She was led through a dark hallway. She imagined her father caged in this humid hell, behind these tall walls, and she trembled.

She walked into a large conference room with a few chairs clustered forlornly in the center and around a wooden table.

"Sit down," the guard said. "Mr. Najabi will be with you shortly."

"Who is Mr. Najabi?"

"A lawyer."

The guard walked out shutting the door behind him. One of the walls had a large glass window looking out to the prison courtyard.

A few minutes later the door opened and a tall thin stoop-shouldered man, stumbled inside without a smile. "Greetings. My name is Najabi."

"Good day, Agha."

He nodded, without looking at her. His face was so pale he looked like he had never left this building. Something in his look caused a chill of terror to pass through her body. This was what good people looked like when the system was through with them. When she spoke, her voice trembled, "May I ask what this is concerning?"

He put a large folder on the table. "Legal issues, that's all." He pulled out a stapled booklet from the folder, sat down, and turned a page. Every move seemed like a great effort.

"What is this for?" Maryam leaned forward.

"You may read here." His bony finger moved over a paragraph. "All we are asking is that you sign that you agree all charges made against your husband are true and that you will support those accusations in court if necessary."

"I thought the trial was over. Besides I didn't make any accusations. The revolutionary guards did their own investigation."

"It was you who brought it to their attention. And, it was your evidence that corroborated the allegations."

He looked up after stating these facts and his eyes were an ice-cold gray. Maryam looked down, avoiding eye contact.

"I see . . . I guess," she said.

"Sign here. Yes. Thank you. No need to worry, Khanum. The judges nowadays want something to come back to later on, something to fall back on, that's all. Used to be that right after the revolution we didn't need lawyers but now we're back to the same legal issues. The judges can be held accountable for their decisions. Well, decisions concerning someone as important as Ali Alizadeh anyway. Ah yes! And sign here too. Very good."

He closed the folder, pushed back his chair, and winced as he stood up.

"Are you all right?" Maryam finally asked. "You look rather ill."

He walked to the door. "Allah will heal everything."

"Can I leave now too, Agha?"

"No, not yet." He shifted his weight from one foot to another. "They said you should stay here for a few more minutes."

"What for?" she asked.

"I'm not sure. But if I were you I wouldn't leave."

He closed the door behind him, looking oddly guarded. She looked away, the last thing she saw was his awkwardly bent back.

★ ★ ★

A pasdar spun Ali around and mashed his face into the cement prison wall. Ali felt the heat in the corner of his mouth and a splash of warm liquid on his broken teeth. He moaned.

This brutal treatment had gone on for days. The worst had been his interrogation in the red room. For once he had seen the events in the red room from the receiving point of view. He had sworn he did not know anything about the Mujahedin movement, but no one had believed him. They seemed to think they had enough evidence to nail him and were only delaying it to get the details from him.

"I want a lawyer," he moaned for the thousandth time. "I have a right to a lawyer."

"Shut up." The pasdar pulled him away from the wall and he closed his eyes awaiting another blow. Instead he was turned around and leaned against the wall.

"I told you I don't know anything," Ali said. "I support the Ayatollah. I'm an honorable—"

A hard punch landed in his stomach.

He bent forward and groaned, spitting out blood. "Oh God! Please stop! Just tell me who made these accusations? Please. They're lying. I'll take care of it. I'll explain to the judge once I know who—"

"Shut up."

"I'm innocent, God damn it!"

"The judge decided you're guilty."

"But how can I defend myself if I don't know the truth?"

"It's over, brother."

"Oh God! No!" He shivered as he tried to free his hands. A hand pushed him forward and he stumbled.

The pasdar pulled him up by the collar. "It's time for you to die, brother."

★ ★ ★

Maryam heard the sound of a steel door open and shut and looked up. A man was pushed to the center of the courtyard. She could see him clearly from the window of the conference room where she waited. But who was it? The figure was so bruised, so beaten that—

It was Ali.

She could see him, struggling, his eyes blindfolded. She put the palm of her hands against the window and waited.

He was shoved against the wall and she saw the gold chain around his neck with Allah's name imprinted on it. It was the one he always wore. The one she had touched and held in her hand the first night of their lovemaking, when fires were burning in Tehran's streets, and the scent of revolution had filled their tiny room. Her eyes passed over the line of his broad shoulders, the hair on his chest, pronounced jaw, the strong nose, and those ruthless lips.

They took off his blindfold. The normal primitive fury in his eyes was replaced by open terror.

She was vaguely aware she should have felt gratification, should have gloated to see the suffering of the man who had done so much damage to her life as well as to so many others. It should have given her pleasure to see him feel the horror and pain of his own acts. Yet, it did not. It was simply horrible.

She could see his eyes glancing at the window. He knew someone was watching him. He knew the ritual.

He was shaking his head.

The firing squad picked up their rifles.

He was shot in the shoulder. Another bullet hit him in his leg. The firing squad was enjoying torturing a mujahid to death. Bullies, mad boys like he, they had no sympathy. She wanted to scream to them to stop but she did not move.

Finally a shot hit him between his eyes.

She pulled herself back from the window. She had achieved the revenge she had wanted for so long. He was dead and she had killed him. A cold appalled feeling swept over her body as she realized that, now that the goal was achieved, she was still not satisfied.

She pulled her veil to herself, shivered, and walked out of the room.

★ ★ ★

Maryam walked into the bathroom of her house to wash her hands. Her eyes caught her own image in the mirror. She had been back for hours but it still seemed as if she was in that small room, watching Ali die. She stared back into her eyes. They were the eyes of a deranged and mentally disturbed woman—a stranger. It was a phantom, a human who was merely physically there. Her fingers rested on the mirror, on her own reflection, on her eyes, her nose, and lips, trying to recognize, or comprehend. No. Her mind had snapped. She would have thought it would have disturbed her more.

Where was that girl who had once laughed, the wind blowing through her uncovered hair, lying by the pool in her bikini after a large family meal? Where was she?

She was dead.

She strolled to the basement, opened a door to her left and pulled out a few boxes. She threw some of Ali's old junk—a cigarette case, an old yellow tie, a law book—to the floor. Then she found what she was looking for, grabbed it, and walked back upstairs.

She climbed a chair to reach the fan on the living room ceiling and wrapped the rope around it. She put her neck through the opening of the rope, closed her eyes, and kicked the chair aside.

She only struggled for a moment before she hung motionless and at last in eternal peace.

★ ★ ★

An old woman dressed in a long white frock, her white hair showing from underneath her short scarf, opened the door. She looked out with a frown first at Hamid and then Commander Shirazi. It was obvious from her look that, like most citizens, she was not pleased to find revolutionary guards at her door. Even Hamid had to admit that they rarely brought good news.

"And what do you want?" she said, her hands on her hips.

Commander Shirazi cleared his throat. "We believe there is a Mr. Zia Mohseni who lives here. Is this correct?"

"Who's asking?"

Hamid bent his head to hide an amused smile.

"Revolutionary guards," Commander Shirazi said. "Please, Khanum. We need to speak to him."

She looked over their shoulder at the two jeeps parked across the street. One of them had four men waiting inside. She pulled open the door and stepped aside. "Number two, upstairs, the flat to your left and be quiet, my grandchildren are sleeping."

Commander Shirazi and Hamid walked up the winding staircase to the second floor. It was an old building but well kept. They could smell food from the apartment to the right, which had a large floor mat in front of it saying *welcome*.

Commander Shirazi knocked on the door. No one responded. Hamid put his ear against the door. He could hear music—western orchestral music. He focused on the sound. It was *Das Rheingold*. General Pakran's favorite piece. He had played it regularly since his wife had died. He gestured the landlady to open the door for them. They stepped in and pulled out their guns. The room was empty. Commander Shirazi signed to Hamid to search the living room and kitchen. He turned left into the hallway leading to the bathroom and bedrooms.

Hamid saw a glass of cognac on the table. He picked it up and smelled it. Remy Martin. General Pakran's favorite drink.

Hamid walked into the kitchen. Nothing was in the sink. He pulled open the refrigerator and then heard Commander Shirazi walking down the hallway.

"I found something."

"What is it?"

Hamid followed. In the master bedroom, there was a desk in the corner and a chair that faced the window overlooking the street. The record player playing *Das Rheingold* was on the bureau. Hamid impatiently turned it off. Commander Shirazi looked up in surprise and turned the chair around.

A man dressed in a bathrobe lay on the chair. His white hair fell to one side. Two thirds of his face was battered and only a small portion of the scar could still be seen on his right cheek.

"Zia Mohseni!" Commander Shirazi said and then turned the face around. "The hair, figure, and scar match the picture and the description—"

Hamid rushed to the kitchen and threw up in the sink. Images of the past blew through his mind. The Pakrans, the Yazd estate, that land in the dry desert where he was raised. The nights when General Pakran would read to them by the fire and now this . . . this monstrosity . . . this murder . . .

What had happened? Who had Arman become?

Commander Shirazi stood behind him with a towel, a sympathetic hand on his shoulder. "Are you all right?"

Breathing heavily, his face chalk white, his hands on either side of the sink, Hamid nodded.

"When you're done, get our guys to move his body. Meanwhile, I'll have a chat with the landlady. Maybe she knows something."

Commander Shirazi turned and walked out of the room. But Hamid stood there awhile longer, looking at himself in the reflection of the window but not seeing anything.

Pieces of a puzzle were slowly coming together.

★ ★ ★

Arman pulled over on the dirt road and rushed past the old garage and gas station. He slid open the door to the telephone booth and looked at the paper in his hand. He dialed a number.

"The Azad Cement Factory. May I help you?"

The Azad Cement Factory was a front for the Mujahedin base in Azerbaijan.

"I'm trying to get a hold of one of your employees. It's urgent."

"Who are you looking for?" the woman asked.

"Jamshid Mahmoudi."

"Let me look through the books. A moment please."

For a moment he was on hold and then a voice responded carefully, "Jamshid speaking."

"Jamshid? Arman."

"Where are you calling from?"

"A phone booth outside of Tabriz. I'm on my way back to Tehran."

"And how are you, my friend?"

"Everything is great. This whole place looks like *pardees*."

"Great. When do you want to get together then? I haven't seen you in a long time."

"It might be tonight or early tomorrow morning. Where can I get a hold of you?"

"Write down this address." Jamshid dictated it to him. It was at a town called Bahar outside of Tabriz. "What time do you think you'll make it?"

"Sometime late in the night. If I change my mind I'll let you know."

"All right. I'll be around. See you then."

Aman hung up. Now that he'd gotten the Mujahedin's help, he had to figure out how to get out from under their membership clause. He chuckled as he turned the car down the mountain road. He would have asked Amir Khan for help, but then the CIA, who was in close contact with Amir Khan's group, would hear about it and that meant Zia would know. And after this whole business was over, the last thing he needed was Zia knocking on his door again.

Was Zia even worth worrying about? After all, if the mission failed, Arman would not only be wanted by the revolutionary guards and the Mujahedin—and the CIA—but also by almost all of the extremist terrorist groups who would want to kill him for degrading the greatest Islamic movement ever known in the Middle East. It was quite a change from his marketing position in California and his leisurely hours by the beach, when his only concern had been to meet target revenue for the next quarter.

But now was not a time to think about these things. He had to get back to Tehran, pick up Kami, and head for Desert One.

Today the U.S. Marines would arrive.

5:50 PM

General Kramer sent a message to all units.

"Execute mission as planned. Godspeed."

The crew cheered, their fists jammed into the air. They had been waiting for this for too long. At exactly 6:05 the lead C-130 rose toward the sunset Oman sky, heading to Desert One. They flew a northeasterly course at 1,000 feet between the two radar sites along the southern Iranian shoreline.

The cockpit temperature was rising. Sweat rolled down Colonel Wilson's cheeks. He looked up and saw John Degg, who was performing safety pilot duties, staring at him. Wilson knew what he was thinking. They were in enemy territory and the pucker factor was high.

★ ★ ★

Captain Blinov read the report on board the Russian warship, Krivak. An American C-130 had been detected flying over the Strait of Hormuz, heading toward the Iranian border. He walked to the radio transmission area where Lieutenant Lev Vagin sat. Blinov put a hand on Vagin's shoulder.

Vagin looked up. "Yes, sir?"

"Report this to Kremlin." He leaned over. "We were just notified that an American C-130 flew off heading north toward Iran. We can't tell where they are now. It could be a routine exercise. I don't think the Americans would be stupid enough to start World War III, but we still have to report it."

6:20 PM

Arman pulled over by the Jamshidieh Park. A crowd of people was leaving—young girls covered from top to bottom with black Islamic uniforms, women with children, and men who were no longer allowed short sleeves. His car door opened and he looked up. Kami climbed in with an easy smile and then slammed the door shut. Kami zipped up his khaki jacket. "Head two blocks down to the right."

Arman started the car and drove in the direction he was pointing. "Why?"

"We need to change cars. Zia called. He said they've been looking for a car like yours and that they may tie you to me. Seems they're blaming you for General Jalili's death. Were you in on it, Arman?"

"You know me better than that, Kami. Where did you hear that?"

"Zia said he got some info from the Revolutionary Guard Corps—turn to the right here. We're switching to that car parked over there. I have the keys."

Arman stepped out and slammed the door. Kami took the wheel of the BMW and Arman climbed into the passenger seat.

"I've seen this car before," he said as Kami turned on the engine.

"You probably have. It's Zia's. He's letting us borrow it."

Kami pulled out from the side street and headed for the freeway. "Desert One has kicked off. My men reported the lead C-130 crossing the border."

"The satellite dishes?"

"Taken care of. No one saw anything."

"The men?"

"They're ready. The plan is to first meet up with the marines and attack the embassy. Then we'll help them get the hostages out, then we'll finish up the regime."

"I have a bad feeling about this, Kami."

"Why?"

"I don't know, but something doesn't feel right."

"Can't you pin it down more than that?"

"Well, the list of names Zia keeps asking for. Why does he want it so badly?"

"I thought that was to find the traitor."

"That's another thing. We never recruited General Jalili. How did he know what he knew and how much did he know? Also, where does Zia get all his information? What about Nightshade? Who is Nightshade and why did he kill General Jalili?"

"Sounds like you're being paranoid."

"Maybe you're right."

"I don't blame you, but either way it's late for this. It's showtime."

Kami entered the freeway heading east toward Posht-e Badam. Code name Desert One.

6:30 PM

Commander Shirazi walked into the hallway, a report in his hand, his glasses resting on the tip of his nose. "This is ridiculous, Hamid. The investigation has been a complete failure. Where can Arman be hiding?"

"All the Tehran police are on guard. If they see anything they'll let us know. He may have already fled the country."

"No, he won't be going anywhere until we see some action. With the coup I mean. Any news about the lost BMW?"

"Not yet, sir. I'm sure—"

His phone rang. Hamid picked it up, listened a moment, then hung up.

"What was that, Hamid?"

"They found the BMW, sir."

"Great!" Commander Shirazi looked openly astonished. "Where was it?"

"It's on the road, heading east on the freeway. Two men in it. They were too far away to be recognized."

"You're sure it's the correct car?"

"The license plate matches," Hamid frowned, "which seems odd. You'd think they would know to at least switch a suspect car."

"They don't know it's a suspect car."

"True."

"Besides, you'll be surprised how stupid some criminals can be. In one of my past investigations, a thief used the same method every time he robbed a bank. He would walk in, light a lady's cigarette, grab her by the wrist, put a gun to her head, and say if the bank didn't hand over all the money, he'd shoot the woman. All it took was narrowing it down to the few banks he hadn't robbed and putting a good-looking woman officer in each one. Before long, he approached one, lit her cigarette, grabbed her, and she broke his arm. You would've thought he'd know better. But," he waved a careless hand, "they seldom do."

Hamid smiled but did not respond.

"Have the guards follow that BMW at a reasonable distance. Have all forces keep an eye on them. Don't make any arrests. Let's see what they're up to."

"With due respect, sir, I'd like to catch up with the police to keep an eye on them as well. I want to make sure we finish this up."

Commander Shirazi chuckled. "You bet we want to see this end. Let's go."

Hamid picked up his hat and followed.

7:05 PM

The *Nimitz* had been brought up to 30 knots. Within minutes, eight choppers flew off, heading toward Iran in total darkness. The helicopters flew at about 100 feet above the sea, avoiding radar detection.

"Bluebeard 1. Eight helicopters airborne."

8:30 PM

"Colonel, I'm seeing some high clouds," John Degg reported.

Colonel Wilson rushed forward to look. He could see the desert surface clearly. Their weather experts had reported a chance of encountering a high layer of clouds along the route. "What is that?"

"Not sure. Something's screwing up our slant-range visibility . . ."

Colonel Wilson leaned forward to take a better look. Now he could see what John Degg was talking about. There was something out there, which he'd never seen before and could best describe as a milky condition. He walked to the back and asked the navigator to scan the desert surface. The monitor lit up but Colonel Wilson still couldn't see what was hindering visibility.

Then suddenly they were in the clear. It was as though the haze had never been there. "It doesn't look that bad, John," Colonel Wilson said. "I sure don't want to have to break radio silence for this. I think the choppers will be just fine."

This would be a decision he would regret later.

9:00 PM

"Look here, Colonel. Here it is again," John Degg yelled back.

Colonel Wilson gazed out and saw the same milky condition. "What in the world is this?"

"I don't know, sir. But visibility with these night vision goggles has been reduced to about a mile."

Colonel Wilson looked behind him at Robert Shaw, one of the CIA operatives. "What do you make of this, Rob?"

Rob looked out of the copilot window. "Iranians call it a *haboob*."

"What's a *haboob*?"

"Suspended dust. It's caused by a down rush of air after a thunderstorm. The air pressures force the sand to rise and hang in the air for hours."

"Why in the world weren't we told about this?"

"They're hard to predict, that's why."

Colonel Wilson turned to one of his men. "Alert the choppers, immediately. They're flying much lower than us and may have a hard time at it."

"Yes, sir."

9:00 PM

"Double fuck! The BIM is on," Major Rodney Rosenthal, the Bluebeard 6 pilot, growled. The Blade Inspection Method usually warned of a leak of the pressurized nitrogen in the Sea Stallion's hollow rotors. The BIM indicator could also suggest a crack in one of the massive blades, which in the past had resulted in rotor failures and a few fatal crashes. This meant that the Marine H-53 pilots were trained to land immediately once they received a BIM warning.

Major Rosenthal only hesitated for a second. He knew that to make the mission work, they really needed only six choppers. They could still spare two.

He decreased speed and eased his bird down.

9:45 PM

"I wasn't able to notify the choppers, Colonel."

Colonel Wilson looked behind him at Jones who he'd asked to contact the choppers about the *haboob*. "Why not?"

"It was too dark back there and I couldn't make out the code-word message. The flashlight and the matrix were worthless."

Colonel Wilson cringed. They had been told to use the code-word instructions to communicate but hadn't been trained properly on how to use them. They really were making this up as they went.

"Damn it!" Colonel Wilson said. "It's too late now. They must've already hit the dust."

9:45 PM

The cockpit of Bluebeard 5 shook. It was a gentle shudder and nothing more. Colonel Pede bent over the pilot seat. Vince Gardiosa was staring ahead of him.

"What's going on, Vince?"

Vince was about to respond when a huge dust cloud hit the chopper causing them to lose balance.

"Son of a bitch," Vince cried.

"Vince," Colonel Pede said. "Can you fly us?"

"Not with these God damned night vision goggles on. Now sit tight, Colonel. I've been in Vietnam, for God's sake. I can do this."

10:00 PM

Kami spoke over his walkie-talkie as he drove down the dusty freeway heading to Desert One. They had only ten minutes to reach their destination.

"What's going on?" Arman asked.

"One of the helicopters is having technical difficulties. They landed right by the Baluchi military station."

"Shit."

But Kami was already back on his walkie-talkie. "Bluebeard 6 just landed by Station 32."

"Yes, I heard," a voice responded. "We've made arrangements. Station 32 has been informed that Bluebeard 6 is a friend of the regime and they are our soldiers."

"And I assume Bluebeard 6 is getting fixed?"

"Yes, sir. Our engineers are working on it. Bluebeard 8 is picking up the crew."

Kami hung up.

"That was close," Arman said.

"Yes, it was. Good thing they picked commandos who look like us and trained them in Farsi. Otherwise, we'd be in deep shit. We've got ten men in Desert One. Thirty located a few miles east of here. We'll be heading that way once the marines land. Now we've got only seven choppers left." Kami put his walk-talkie down. "One of the pilots mentioned a milky condition. Have you ever heard of anything like that?"

Arman nodded. "Exactly what I warned Zia about."

"What?"

"*Haboobs*. They're storm clouds. They come at you like a wall of dust."

"But the CIA weather forecast said it would be clear today."

"Zia may insist they can do magic but the desert is unpredictable, even for the CIA."

10:00 PM

The seven helicopters struggled in the dust cloud. The visibility had dropped to yards and the cockpit temperature soared. Vince wiped the sweat and dust off of his forehead. In the last few minutes, his most essential flight and navigation instruments had failed due to electrical problems.

Colonel Pede had remained with him, leaning forward, his teeth covered with dust, watching them fail and now he had begun to lose hope. "Vince?"

"Goddamn partial panel, needle-ball, wet compass—a real vertigo inducer," Vince said. "Hold on tight, we're having fun now."

"I think we're turning," Colonel Pede said.

"No we're not. It sure feels like it though," Vince said. "That's the trick of vertigo. Your inner ear tells you the aircraft is turning while your eyes tell you it's not. Fun, isn't it?"

Well, no. Especially because they had lost all contact with the outside world.

10:00 PM

Captain Blinov continued to stare at the clear image of a helicopter on the radar screen flying toward northern Iran, getting closer to the Afghani border. They hadn't been able to see the eight choppers that had flown off, but finally one of them had been detected by the radar, if only sporadically.

"A report from Kremlin, sir." Vagin broke his train of thought.

"What does it say, Vagin?"

"They say that per our 1921 agreement with Iran, USSR has the permission to defend Iran if threatened by any outside force."

"The Iranians broke that agreement years ago."

"Should I report that to Kremlin, sir?"

Blinov paused. He knew it would do little good to disagree with his superiors. "What else does it say?"

"They want us to be ready," Vagin said. "Kremlin was not aware of an American mission in Iran. They think they may be targeting Afghanistan. The report says also, sir, that they have contacted the missile station by the Iranian border in Turkmenistan. We're told that the orders are to shoot on command."

"In other words, prepare for World War III."

10:00 PM

The lead C-130 landed on Desert One. The commandos raced out to block the dirt road that traversed the site with the help of the Iranian soldiers. Kami parked the car and rushed out, followed by Arman.

They found Robert Shaw standing by combat engineers who were installing a portable navigation system and runway lights to guide the other mission aircraft to Desert One. Rob told them of the difficulty of the flight.

"When will the choppers arrive?" Arman asked.

"From the latest radio transmission," Rob said, "they should be here in about twenty minutes."

"My men are ready," Kami said. "One command from me and they know what to do."

"Perfect." Rob lowered his voice and when Kami looked up he seemed disturbed. He shook his head. A moment later Rob walked away.

"What was that?" Arman asked.

"He asked if I thought Nightshade was a good name for a chopper."

Arman frowned. "Interesting. He wanted to see if you're Nightshade, which confirms . . ."

"That he's one of us."

10:20 PM

Hamid honked. They were trapped behind a passenger bus.

Commander Shirazi was frowning. "I've never seen a passenger bus here at this time of night."

"I don't normally come here," Hamid said. "But last I heard they were trying to set up a minor transportation system between Tabas and Tehran. During the Shah's time nobody did anything about it and those poor people had to somehow manage to catch a ride to one of the bigger cities and catch a bus there. Now, we've put in one line that goes there once a week. It started a month ago."

"I didn't know about it."

"It wasn't a big deal. Just saw it in the internal reports one day in the office. They said it wasn't even worth investigating for runaway refugees. The bus turns around at Tabas."

"See if you can pass him."

Hamid swung the car to the left to look at the oncoming traffic from behind the bus. Then he pushed on the accelerator and swerved to the left of the bus. It was right before a curve when he made it around the bus. The bus driver put his hand on the horn and a few of the passengers screamed out of the windows.

Five minutes later they saw the lead C-130 on the runway and the American commandos standing in various corners.

"*Besmellah-e Rahman-e Rahim!*" Commander Shirazi said.

"You can say that again." Hamid pulled over and snapped his headlights off. "We're on the verge of an American takeover. What do we do now?"

"Stay put." Commander Shirazi's voice trembled. "I want to make sure we get all of them."

Hamid's eyes scanned the men standing by the runway. He thought he recognized Arman, standing with his back to him, next to a truck, a pistol in his right hand.

10:55 PM

"What the fuck . . . " Colonel Wilson growled. "Down. Everybody down."

While the commandos pulled out their weapons and lay on the ground, Arman and Kami turned around. They saw headlights coming at them.

"I thought this godforsaken place was empty," Colonel Wilson said. "What's this?"

The vehicle headlights were getting closer.

"Looks like a passenger bus," Arman said.

"What in the world is a passenger bus doing here?"

Arman turned to an anxious Kami. "Let the Americans take care of this. We don't need the passengers remembering the faces of our officers. The Americans are getting out, our men will want to come back."

Kami nodded. "You're right. Colonel Wilson?"

"Yes, Lieutenant. What are we going to do with a fucking bus?"

"You have a few Farsi-speaking commandos, yes?"

"Several."

"Good. Tell them to take the passengers hostage until we're done. They'll never know they're Americans and your commandos don't need to live in this country. After the mission we can release them."

Colonel Wilson walked over to his men.

★ ★ ★

The troops blocked the Mercedes bus and fired a few warning shots. Colonel Wilson squinted in the sandstorm and ran toward the bus. The lights were on inside and he could see several frightened faces staring back at him. One of the passengers, a young man, leaned his head out and said in perfect English, "It's about time you came, Yanks."

Within a few minutes, the protesting bus passengers and the driver were herded a few hundred meters away, where two commandos watched over them.

Major Jason Finley, one of the linguists, recited Omar Khayyám poetry for the hostages, to put them at ease.

10:55 PM

"We've been in this hellhole for way too long. We're behind schedule," Colonel Pede said.

"It'll fly, Sergeant," Vince said. "The real question is whether we'll get to land it."

Colonel Pede watched a drop of sweat run down Vince's forehead and cheek onto his chest. "All right, Vince," he said, "turn this baby around. We're heading home."

Vince didn't argue. He turned the chopper around. "Let's hope we'll find our way to *Nimitz*. We've still got some while to go to get out of this dust wall."

Because of the abrupt turn, the chopper shook, and they held on to the sides to keep their balance. What they didn't know was that they were only twenty-five minutes from clear air, which prevailed all the way to Desert One.

1:05 AM

"I wonder what they're going to do with the bus passengers," Hamid said. "Should we contact headquarters?"

"Not yet. I still want to wait. Let's see what they're really . . . Look there!"

Hamid looked up. A fleet of helicopters lumbered out of the dark, coming in ones and twos, and from different directions. Hamid began to count under his breath as six helicopters landed on Desert One.

2:00 AM.

As the helicopters struggled through unexpected deep sand to get into position behind the tankers, one shut down its engines. Bluebeard 2 had suffered a secondary hydraulic system failure and now had minimal pressure for its flight controls.

Colonel Wilson and Rob walked up to the Bluebeard 2 pilot, who said, "I'll try to take my sick bird on to the hideout in Desert Two."

"No, you won't." Eric Davis, who was now the commander of the helicopters since Colonel Pede had to turn back, shook his head. "Flying with one system with this much weight and at high temperature . . . you'll have a control lockup. Then you'll have a crash that'll kill not only the crew but also the commandos on board. Let's not do that." He then turned to Colonel Wilson. "I'm afraid we have to abort the mission, Colonel."

"Shit!" Colonel Wilson ran a hand through his hair and threw an irritated glance at Rob who cringed.

"What about using five helicopters?" Arman asked, watching Kami standing by one of the choppers speaking to a controller examining Bluebeard 2. Kami and the controller began to walk to a tanker provided by an Iranian officer for extra fuel.

"We can't. We're running out of time and we won't have enough—"

Colonel Wilson stopped as they heard a noise and looked back to see the commandos staring into the horizon. A red line of fire appeared in the sky, coming from the north, and heading toward them. Colonel Wilson had hardly enough time to give out a cry when a missile hit.

The ground shook and Arman fell, his face in the desert sand.

When Arman looked up, the fuel tanker where Kami and the American commando had stood was a burning hell. He pulled himself up and ran to the fire. Another explosion threw him on his back.

Colonel Wilson shouted something Arman couldn't hear as he began to run toward the choppers. Colonel Wilson jumped in the lead C-130 while the remaining C-130s lifted off, leaving a cloud of dust, feeding the fire even more.

The passengers who had been held hostage ran back toward the bus. The driver had already started the engine.

Arman ran closer to the fire. He had to find Kami. The heat beat against his body and face. Body parts were everywhere. "Kami?" he cried.

An Iranian officer grabbed him by the arm and pulled him away. "Pakran. Lieutenant Pakran."

He didn't move and only stared at the glowing fire in the dark where eight Americans and his friend had burned to ashes.

"Run. The mission's aborted."

"Kami—"

The officer pulled him and he fell to the ground. Another tanker exploded. He stood and began to run. He got in the BMW parked a few meters away. The American birds were heading south back into the *haboob*. It was a nightmare of flames and burned bodies. One of them Kami's. Arman started the engine. He saw the rest of the officers jump into their vehicles and drive away. He turned on the desert sand, leaving a trail of dust behind him.

3:00 AM

Hamid found his way around the car to Commander Shirazi, who was stretched out on the sand. He pulled him up as the latter began to cough. Covered with dust from head to toe, they looked at the fires burning in all directions. A few bits and pieces of the exploded tankers and planes had flown about and one had made a hole in the back passenger seat window.

"What was that?" Commander Shirazi stood.

"Looked like a missile from the Russian border. From the way it was headed here, I'd say it came from Turkmenistan."

Commander Shirazi sat back in the car, breathing heavily. His face was pale, he was trembling all over. "Would make sense," he said in a voice hardly above a whisper. "There is a USSR missile station there. They probably got alarmed with Americans so close and didn't know what was going on. They overreacted."

Hamid turned the car around.

"Wait!" Commander Shirazi said. "Is Arman dead?"

"No, he drove west in his BMW. Meanwhile," he pulled out his radio and handed it to Commander Shirazi, "let's let the bosses know what's happened here so they can do something about it."

Commander Shirazi's hand shook while he pushed the talk button. He cleared his throat and gave the report.

TWELVE

"**YOU'VE KILLED EIGHT OF** our soldiers," President Carter screamed into the hotline to Moscow. "Without any warning you destroyed our choppers, and killed eight of our men. Do you know what this means? Do you understand the grave responsibility you've placed on all of our shoulders?"

"You, Mr. President," Brezhnev shouted back, "you have a larger responsibility. You and your military and all the decadent capitalists want to take the responsibility of the entire world on your own shoulders."

President Carter was standing at his desk in the Oval Office. Vice President Mondale paced the floors while Defense Minister Harold Brown sat thoughtfully. Brzezinski and the CIA Chief were staring at the speakerphone mesmerized, it seemed, by the furious voice reaching them over the secure line to Kremlin.

"You want war," Brezhnev said. "If this is so, we are fully ready and capable. Your choppers landed so close to our borders. Why I ask you? Maybe it was a friendly gesture, Mr. President? We want to be friends again, Mr. President?" There was a pause after which Brezhnev added, "The Soviet Union and all the socialist democratic and communist nations of the world are willing to stand up to your imperialism, which you thrust down our throats. We are ready to fight you."

Carter realized he was in a losing position. He couldn't deny that the proximity of the C-130s and RH-53s only 137 miles from the Russian border would have alarmed the Soviets. He was also disturbed that he had not thought this out better in advance.

"Obviously," Carter said, "we couldn't have any military plans against your country. You must understand that our troops were there on a legitimate mission to save American lives."

There was a heavy silence.

"What mission?" Brezhnev said. "Maybe Afghanistan? Who could doubt that this action was against our very own regime in Afghanistan?"

"No. No. This had nothing to do with Afghanistan—"

"Oh really? I see. So maybe this was for Iran itself? Is that so, Mr. President? Was this to occupy Iran?"

"Not at all! We had no intention to occupy Iran."

Carter stopped. He was feeling numb to his bones. He knew for a fact that the Russian president suspected an invasion of Iran, but it was too late to do anything about that now. "We have nothing, I repeat, nothing against the Iranian Islamic regime, but we can't stand still when our nation is humiliated and our diplomats are held hostage for more than 170 days. We had to do something. If you must know, Mr. President, we were sending in our choppers to rescue our hostages. If your diplomats were taken hostage by a foreign country, wouldn't you do the same?"

The silence stretched on and on. Carter looked back at the glaring eyes of his staff. Some of them were staring at the phone as if too shocked to speak and the rest looked back at him blankly.

"Mr. President?" Carter said.

"You must admit," Brezhnev said, his voice calmer, "that our reaction to your military proximity was quite natural. In our opinion, when enemy planes come close to our borders, we have the right to react and in this case we did. Even if this was a mistake, it was not our mistake. I also need to tell you that we will do anything to defend our borders. Our entire military is on the ready and with one signal will react. I must openly state that we will not allow the repetition of such an act again. Do you understand me, Mr. President?"

The blunt words from Brezhnev caused a wave of anger to spread through the Oval Office, but Carter held up a hand.

"After detailed investigation," Brezhnev said, "we will discover what actually happened. But I must warn you that the world media must not know the truth. They must know nothing of the reason behind the explosion. Obviously we do not want to be portrayed as an aggressor to the world. In the past we have both agreed that our countries will not be responsible for triggering a nuclear war. We have to ensure that such a war will not happen. You understand, Mr. President, I'm sure."

★ ★ ★

Two hours later, President Carter stood in front of his nation to regretfully announce the death of eight American soldiers during the *Eagle Claw* mission, without revealing the Soviet connection. The ninth body, belonging to Kami, was never mentioned.

★ ★ ★

Arman ran up the stairs of Zia's apartment building. The door was locked. He rang, but no one answered. He was standing there when he heard the sound of slippers gliding up the stairs. He stepped back and waited.

An old woman appeared and eyed him curiously. "Who are you?"

"A friend of Mr. Zia Mohseni."

"I'm the landlady. My eyes don't see that well, anymore. I thought you were one of those pasdars coming back for more information. I've had enough of them."

Arman was not quite sure what she was talking about but he had no time for this. "Do you know where Zia is?"

"Oh you don't know? I'm sorry to tell you that he passed away." The old lady shook her head. "He was found dead a couple of days ago. Shot."

"Shot?"

"They say a Pakran did it. Lieutenant Arman Pakran. Do you know him? His name is all over the news. Seems like such a nice young man too."

Arman began walking down the stairs. "I'm so sorry to hear about Zia. He was a good friend of my uncle's. We went way back."

"Strange then that you hadn't heard the news."

"I just got back from Europe. I haven't looked at the papers. You know how it is, visiting relatives and all. It's been busy. Anyway, sounds like the police are investigating it?"

The lady nodded, walking down with him. "They've been here several times. It's been like a crime scene. Well, I guess it really is." She laughed. "He used to work for the SAVAK. Never led a very peaceful life. I guess some people like it that way. Anyway, the door is locked. You can't get in. They took my key too. They said they'd bring it back tomorrow, but you never know with the pasdars. I may have to change the locks."

They reached the ground floor. The lady didn't seem to have recognized him, so that encouraged Arman. "Did you see another man, by any chance? A little older and paralyzed? He was very sick. He was also an old friend and Zia brought him over at times."

The lady slowed down, looking up at him, and finally shrugged. "Well . . . thinking of it, one night I heard a noise and came out and Zia was helping this poor old man up the stairs, but I never saw him again. He looked really bad though. I don't think he would've survived whatever happened up there, God bless his soul. What is your name, my son?"

"Ali. Ali Alizadeh."

He walked to the car and turned on the engine. His father was dead. He hesitated for a second, trying to grasp the fact. Then his mind wandered to the other information he had received. Zia was dead. Of course it could all be a fabricated lie, although Arman was not sure why. But if Zia was really dead, who had killed him? The only name that came to Arman's mind was Nightshade.

He pressed on the accelerator. He'd had enough of the intrigue around him. He wanted some peace of mind.

It was time to head to the border.

★ ★ ★

On the way, he picked up Kami's Porsche. He had driven only a few kilometers when he noticed a black Mercedes, two curves behind him. Through his rearview mirror, he could see outlines of two men sitting in the front seat. He saw them make the last turn and was sure the license plate was yellow, which indicated a government car. He turned on the radio. On every station they spoke about the explosion in the Iranian desert. But he had other matters on his mind. He had to get to Jamshid, and with his help, out of the country. Afterward, he would think of world problems.

He felt the heat of blood on his upper lip. He'd been chewing it. He pressed on the accelerator, watching the black Mercedes behind him, noticing that they too gradually increased speed. Yes, he had a tail.

★ ★ ★

Hamid watched the Porsche in front of him closely. He had switched seats with Commander Shirazi, who was now driving. They had been looking for a BMW, then Arman's own jeep, but at the end figured that Arman must have switched to some other car. They had finally received a call from a motorcycle police officer about a black Porsche speeding on the freeway to Azerbaijan. With that car, Arman could move more than fast enough to get to the border on time. The Mercedes had a hard time keeping up.

Hamid put his walkie-talkie on the seat between his thighs, his eyes never leaving the Porsche in front of him. How much could Arman have possibly changed to be responsible for all these murders? When had he joined the CIA? There were so many questions Hamid would have liked to ask, but he had a feeling he would not get to. Hamid knew Commander Shirazi would shoot first and then ask questions.

"What did they say?" Commander Shirazi asked, keeping a watchful distance from the Porsche.

"The guards are waiting for him at the border. Five more kilometers and we'll have three squads of revolutionary guards waiting for him as well. They've blocked the road."

"Perfect."

"But I've got even better news, sir. I just got a call from Commander Habibi who took over the Mujahedin case—"

"Oh yes. He was trying to find the hideout of the Mujahedin by the border. Did he find it?"

Hamid nodded. "They've found a company with the pseudonym Azad Cement Factory. They seem to think that it's the place the Mujahedin work out of."

"How did they figure that out?"

"By having one of our own pretend to be a refugee. The Mujahedin helped him to get out of the country. He reported the details to us."

"When was this?" Commander Shirazi turned another curve, staring with deadly aggression at the car in front of him.

"This morning, sir. Also, one of the prisoners Ali had been investigating finally cracked. He even gave more detail on the Azad Cement Factory operation. It seems this week they have another mujahedin team joining them for training. So, Commander Habibi thinks he may kill two birds with one stone."

"So Ali wasn't that useless, after all."

"That was another thing, Commander. The mujahid who confessed swore he didn't think Ali was a mujahid. He said Ali'd been real brutal with him in the red room."

Commander Shirazi made another turn. "He could be lying."

"Or maybe Ali was innocent."

But Commander Shirazi did not seem interested in Ali's innocence. "You said you think Jamshid joined the Mujahedin?"

"That's what I heard."

"When are they planning to assault the factory?"

Hamid picked up his walkie-talkie. "Not sure. Should we make it tonight?"

"Yes. I've got a feeling that our friend here will be giving his buddy, Jamshid, a call. We may be able to kill three birds with one stone, Hamid."

Hamid put through the call.

Commander Shirazi swore and Hamid looked up. "What—"

Three revolutionary guard jeeps blocked the road ahead, but the Porsche had increased its speed.

"Where the hell does he think he's going?"

"Straight at it, it seems," Hamid said with a faint smile. So Arman hadn't changed so much after all.

★ ★ ★

Arman pushed on the gas pedal. The green jeeps were parked across the road, but they had left a small gap on the side, barely the width of the Porsche. For maybe two seconds he would have one tire right on edge of the cliff. One pasdar stood in front of the jeeps, his hands to his sides. Only one had pulled out his rifle. The third was on his walkie-talkie talking to the black Mercedes behind him. No time to think. He went straight at the jeeps.

The pasdar in the front pulled out his pistol and aimed at his windshield but before he could fire, Arman cut the wheel to the left and went for the tiny gap. The pasdar standing in the gap gave out a cry and jumped onto the jeep.

A bullet cracked the windshield.

And then Arman was past the revolutionary guards. He grinned as he looked at his rearview mirror. The black Mercedes braked in front of the blocking jeeps and the driver jumped out and began shouting.

★ ★ ★

"Get the hell out of my way!"

Hamid had never seen Commander Shirazi this furious. Hamid did not get out of the car. If he had, he could not have suppressed his laughter. He may be on the side of the Islamic regime but he had no problem seeing a good old friend giving Commander Shirazi's men a hard time. As Commander Shirazi got back behind the wheel, he missed Hamid's amused glance.

"The idiots, sons of dogs. They just stand there, watching! Finally, one of them pulls the trigger and he doesn't even manage to hit the car! What morons. Never seen anything like it. In the old days, you'd get reprimanded for this." He started the engine.

"In the old days, sir?"

Commander Shirazi turned around and threw a quick glace at Hamid. "Gah, I don't know what I'm talking about anymore."

One of the pasdars was attempting a tight U-turn. Commander Shirazi pulled down his window and yelled, "If you don't get the hell out of my way fast enough Sergeant, I swear to God, I'll have your neck!"

The jeep almost fell over the edge as it made room. The black Mercedes zoomed through the open gap. Commander Shirazi pressed madly on the accelerator trying to catch up with the Porsche, which was already far ahead of them.

★ ★ ★

Ten minutes later, Arman made a right turn into a long narrow dirt road that curved through an olive farm. There was still no sign of the Mercedes and he felt certain he wasn't followed.

He had only a second to glance at the sunrise. In that moment, he wished he could live here, farm, and get away from all the turmoil of the world.

He didn't have time for such romantic thoughts. When he turned left, he found an old shack, with a door loose, swinging in the wind. The place looked empty. He parked the car behind a few tall bushes and stepped out. He hesitated for a second and then walked into the shack.

Immediately, two rifles pointed at him and a voice from the shadows said, "Hello Arman. Glad you made it alive."

Jamshid walked into the light. He had a Mujahedin guerrilla uniform on and a rifle on his back. He smiled widely and shook Arman's hand. The two other mujahideen lowered their rifles and relaxed.

"You weren't followed, were you?" Jamshid said.

"A black Mercedes followed me up to a couple of kilometers ago but I lost him."

Jamshid frowned. "Well, then, we'd better get out of here as soon as possible."

"My car is parked outside."

"We'll take care of it." Jamshid signaled to one of the mujahideen, who seemed hardly over twenty. The mujahid grinned and held out a hand. Arman tossed him the keys. A few seconds later, Arman heard Kami's toy car head off in the opposite direction.

Jamshid looked through the window. "Sorry you had to lose it, Arman. Unfortunately, we're past worrying about worldly matters—"

"It wasn't mine anyway and its owner is dead."

"I see." Jamshid studied him for a moment. "A friend of yours?"

"A good friend, yes."

"I'm sorry about your loss. Let's go." Jamshid walked out the back door. "Otherwise our friends in the Mercedes may find us."

Arman followed. "Where are we going?"

"To our headquarters. It'll be a short drive and a walk and then we'll be there."

From behind the few bushes, Arman caught the sight of a white Peykan. Jamshid opened the backseat for him. "Lay low. We'll be covering you with a blanket. No need to get alarmed. Unfortunately, as you're not yet one of us we need to make sure you don't see much. Jafar."

"Yes, sir?" one of the mujahideen said.

"Cover our friend's eyes with a black cloth." He saw the suspicion in Arman's eyes. "Don't worry, Arman. This is routine. We'll be there in no time."

Last thing Arman saw was Jamshid sitting on the passenger seat, turning to grin at him, and then the cloth wrapped around his eyes.

"At least tell me where we're going?" he said when the engine started.

"To the Azad Cement Factory. Now hold tight. You're in safe hands."

★ ★ ★

In a café outside the Sofia mosque in Istanbul, Melody drank her Turkish coffee. They were still exhausted from their long journey. Melody and Nader had requested visas from any western country that would take them. Julia's uncle had arranged for both to get accepted to the United States. Although Julia would get to leave immediately, Melody and Nader had to wait two months before they could enter the country. A small price to pay, they both agreed, for freedom.

Melody glanced at the kebab on a stick, grilling in the fire. She remembered her last night's conversation with Julia while they had sat by the warm Mediterranean Sea in a fish restaurant. While Nader talked in Turkish with the owner of the restaurant, she and Julia had quietly looked at the reflection of the Istanbul lights on the ocean. Istanbul was a beautiful city and at sunset the seagulls flew around the dome of the ancient mosques. Melody had been thinking of Arman and what he was going through at the moment. She wished she could have stayed with him.

Julia finally broke the silence. "You know, Melody, I want to tell you that I don't . . . " She took a breath. "I want you to know that I do understand."

Melody looked up. Had Julia found out about Arman and her lovemaking? "Understand?"

"I mean about your cousin, Maryam. I understand why you helped her. God, if I had seen anyone dear to me looking like that, it would've broken my heart. I would've tried to help her too. I . . . behaved badly about it. I'm sorry."

Melody waved it aside. "I understand, Julia. It was a difficult time. I'm sorry too for some of my outbursts."

"Aren't you going to ask me why I was such a pain?"

Melody looked up, surprised. "You want me to?"

"Yes. I think it'll make me feel better, but . . . a lot of my anger has been because I've been jealous of you."

"Jealous of *me?*"

Julia nodded. "You had it all, you know. I didn't know you before all this insanity started, but I'd heard of you. God! It must be a nightmare losing everything the way you have. It would've crushed me, but somehow you'd survived it and I want you to know I really admire that." She stared out at the sea for a moment. "Nader is destroyed, isn't he? Is that why you stay with him?"

Melody's voice came softly. "Maybe."

"Arman told me long ago about you. It stayed with me. I decided then that I didn't like you because I knew he'd once been in love with you. No, that's not true. It was more than that. You were the one. He should've asked me long ago to marry him, but something held him back. The moment I met you, I knew it was you. It had always been you."

Melody looked away. "I'm sorry Julia. I—"

"Let me finish, Melody. I tried to get him back, but you know when it's over, don't you?"

Melody did not answer.

"I know this is uncomfortable. It's nobody's fault really. You and Arman have something very special, which I could never have with him. It's more than love. It's a sort of friendship you've had I assume since you were very young. I understood that the day I fell in the river and you saved me. I guess I understood then why Arman liked you so much. So I made peace with it, and now I feel a great deal better. I hope we can be friends and I want to let you know that you can count on me."

"Count on you?"

"In the States. I know how it feels being in another country, knowing that your chances of going back are slim. I really do understand now what it feels like to be a refugee. The world may think we're enemies, but we know, Melody, don't we? We know that an Iranian and an American can be friends, the best of friends and they can love each other very dearly. I'll be there for you when we're home—my home—because it's not your home. Not yet anyway."

"Thank you, Julia."

The next morning Julia caught a flight to San Diego. Now, Nader and Melody sat at this old café listening to news of the failed mission on the radio, wondering if Arman had made it out alive.

"Are you still upset with me?" Melody finally asked Nader, now that they were alone.

He looked up and then switched to lecture mode. "There are some things I believe in, some things that will never change. One of them is the type of woman I want. I want someone accepting, who trusts me and believes in me, and listens to me. Lately you haven't done any of these things, have you Melody?"

"I'm sorry, Nader."

"I liked you when I met you because you appeared so childish. Sure, you were wild and beautiful, but you seemed so artless and naïve. There were times we haven't agreed, but even now I think it's because you're a true pure Persian woman, who's been too kindhearted about matters where logic would've been more appropriate. But I accept that as the characteristic of a fragile sensitive woman and even that I'm willing to forgive."

A fragile sensitive woman? A pure Persian woman? Forgive her kindheartedness?

"I want someone who not only understands my culture but embraces it. You're stubborn at times and don't listen to me as much as I'd want you to. You don't seem to realize that I know better because I'm . . . well . . . twice your age and wiser. But I'm willing to accept it as your youth and believe that you'll change."

"And this is why you want to marry me?" She was actually a little surprised that she wasn't surprised. None of this was news to her.

He nodded.

An underdressed tourist—American, from the flag scarf wrapped around her neck—walked by. She wore a tight revealing dress, and a Turkish man whistled when she passed him. The American woman appeared confused as to why her attire was causing such a reaction.

Melody looked away from the woman. "What if I don't change?"

"Oh, but you will. You're still very young and you'll change." He smiled warmly at her. "Trust me."

"What if I don't want to change?"

He pulled back. "What do you mean?"

"What if this is how I am and I'm happy the way I am. Are you going to be able to live with me?"

"Well of course. I think . . . well, anyway, what is all this about?"

"You started it. Tell me, Nader, if I told you I'd sinned, what would you say?"

He frowned. "Sinned? What do you mean by that?"

"Had sex? Would you still call me a pure Persian flower then, Nader?"

"Well, in that case . . . I mean that is different. Well . . . have you . . . or haven't you?"

The smell of Turkish kebab reached her nostrils. Her eyes followed a man who threw a napkin on the already filthy street, not caring to throw it into the trash can just a few meters away.

"What are you trying to say, Melody?"

"I've wanted this, you know. I wanted us to be happy. I wanted Baba, yes, I wanted Baba even more than myself to be happy. But I just can't. I simply can't."

"Can't what?"

"Love you."

His first reaction was to pull back his head, his eyes wide. "What do you mean?"

"I agreed to marry you because of Baba but I never loved you."

"Oh, I see." He appeared calmer. "I understood that. He told me love would come later. What makes you bring it up now? Is it the way I look or because I've lost everything? I still have money you know. I have a bank account in Switzerland and I'm a millionaire. If that's—"

"No. That's not it. I'm sorry, Nader, but I'm not—"

"It's Arman, isn't it? I always knew there was something between you two. I still remember when he came to the house the week we met, how you changed. Suddenly you were all lively and excited. You two were utterly childish and I thought with your horseback riding you'd break your neck—"

"That's called fun, Nader. We were having fun and maybe it was childish, but we were friends and I laughed a lot."

"Now I wish he had fallen off the horse and killed himself."

She stroked his hand. "It's not about him. It's about you and me, and this . . . " she gestured with her hand, " . . . is not working."

"But I thought we had a connection. How can you do this to me . . . like this?"

"You're right. I should've done it long ago. I should've stood up to Baba. But . . . things that didn't matter then, matter now. Things that mattered then don't matter anymore. Can't you see, Nader? I can't live with you knowing I don't love you. I can't keep deceiving us both like this."

"But you're my pure Persian flower," he said. "You'll learn to love me. You will—"

"Stop Nader. Please stop!" She looked away. She had no idea she would cause him so much pain. But she had no choice. "I am not a pure Persian flower. I'm a woman and this woman has the right to her body and to her mind. This woman has the right to tell you that she does not love you."

"What are you talking about? It's a compliment. How can you have changed so much, so fast? It's a compliment to be pure, to be clean—"

"To be a virgin?" She sighed. "I'm not."

"Not, what?"

"I'm not a virgin. I'm like you, Nader. I've had sex."

"What?"

"I should've told you before, I know. I'm sorry."

Nader leaned forward, his voice hoarse. "When?"

"Before I knew you." She did not want to hurt him any more.

"I don't believe it. You never told me before . . ."

"It's true, Nader. Baba didn't know. Surely, you wouldn't want a woman who's not a virgin, who's not pure, would you?"

He was openly shivering in disappointment and disgust. He stood and paused, looking down on her. Then he walked away.

Melody leaned back watching him disappear into the crowd, knowing well that she would never see him again and somehow feeling very little regret. They had all changed one way or another, but Nader's opinion would never change.

★ ★ ★

It was close to midnight when five green and white striped jeeps pulled up, their headlights already off. Twenty pasdars stepped out, dressed in their formal green uniforms with rifles on their backs. One man stepped forward, the only one wearing a military green cap. The rest were wearing military helmets.

"This is the location, sir," he said to Commander Shirazi.

Hamid looked in the direction Commander Shirazi was staring. It was a tall, dilapidated building, a cement factory that had been abandoned by its owner when a group of factory workers had set it on fire. Now the west wing of the building, looking out to the river was gutted.

"So it was a cement factory," Hamid said.

"And a perfect place for the Mujahedin hideout," the lieutenant replied. "We found the plans for the building. There are five doors, two of which have been blocked and bolted. Two more have direct connections to the building's top floor and one in the back, which we're not quite sure about but believe leads to the burned side of the building and was meant to be a way out toward the river."

"What's the plan?" Commander Shirazi said. "I'll leave you in charge as you've had time to plan this out."

"Yes, sir." He picked up his helmet and pointed to his men. "You six divide up and guard the two doors. You four head for the north side to guard any entrances leading toward the river. When you hear gunfire, come up and join us, so we can ambush them from all sides. The rest of you follow me."

"What about us?" Hamid asked.

"You can stay with the jeeps as backup with the rest of my men. Give us about fifteen minutes and then either we're done or it's time for you to do something."

"All right."

"I'll come with you, Lieutenant," Commander Shirazi said.

"Whatever you wish, Commander." He pulled out his revolver. "Let's get moving."

The ground floor of the factory was quiet. Commander Shirazi had a pistol in his shoulder holster but no rifle. The lieutenant signaled to two of his men to ascend the staircase leading to the second floor.

★ ★ ★

"So, when are you leaving?" Jamshid asked Zari while he bounced a tennis ball on the factory floor. Across from them and behind a column, Arman lay on a sleeping bag, facing the lake. Jamshid's eyes turned from Arman to rest on Zari who said, "Early tomorrow morning. I should start packing."

It would be a sad departure. He had grown fond of Zari who was from Babul, a city by the Caspian Sea. Her eyes were hazel, her skin white, and hair the color of auburn. He had watched her for a long time from across the hall. Finally tonight they were both assigned to guard the building. They sat next to the large opening caused by fire damage that provided a breathtaking view to the river. It had only been then that they'd finally spoken. She had just finished telling him where she was from.

"How did you end up here?" he asked.

She had a serious face, not one who laughed easily. "My father had a clothing store in Babul. He carried midpriced brands but he did well. After the revolution a bunch of Hezbollahies showed up at his shop and beat him up."

"Why?"

"We're not sure. Someone told us some druggie who owed father money set them on him. We never figured out who it was, but I don't think it matters. You've got druggies all over the world, but they can't tell a simple lie and get someone like father beaten up by government people."

"What did they want?"

"We didn't find out. Father had real high blood pressure. He had a stroke and just fell down on the shop floor and died."

"So they took him to the hospital?"

"No. They must've figured they screwed up, so they fled. They left him there to spend his last moments alone. We didn't know until close of business that day. Maman and I got worried and we went to find him and then . . ." Her eyes filled with tears.

"And that's what caused you to join?"

"You don't think that's enough? I'm taking revenge on the men who killed my father. I enjoy it every time I put a bullet in one of those jerks. I think my father may be feeling just a bit better."

"Where's your mother?"

"Still in Babul."

"Does she approve?"

"She'd join herself if she could. Will you stop bouncing that ball?"

"Sorry. Nervous habit." Jamshid put down the ball.

"That's fine, but you may wake him up." She pointed at Arman. "Whatever his name is."

"Arman. Nice guy."

"He looked worn out, almost lost, when he got here. When are you taking him out?"

"Tomorrow morning right after your group returns to the Caspian headquarters." Jamshid bounced the ball again. "I'll take him personally."

★ ★ ★

Three pasdars on each side of the door held up their pistols. One knelt forward, looking through the keyhole. Commander Shirazi stood at the bottom of the stairs, behind everyone else.

"*Allah-o akbar!*" one of the pasdars murmured in a breathless voice and shoved the door open. The door flung to one side and hit the wall with a bang that echoed through the darkness. The pasdars charged through into their pre-assigned positions. Commander Shirazi followed.

The entire factory room was empty. For a moment, they thought they had made a mistake. They had believed this was the last accessible floor, but then the lieutenant held up a hand and they kept quiet. A sound—a bouncing ball?—echoed through the building. Commander Shirazi and the rest of the men looked up at the ceiling.

★ ★ ★

Jamshid threw the ball up one more time. A hand grabbed it in midair.

Jamshid froze, looking back in alarm. One of the mujahideen held on to the ball, his dark brown eyes larger than normal. He pointed at something in the field. Jamshid stared outside.

Some meters below in the woods a shadow moved. It stooped while it ran through the bushes. They could clearly make out the outline of a rifle on his back.

Jamshid grabbed his gun. The mujahid made a few signs with his hands and all others took their positions behind columns. Jamshid knelt on one knee. A mujahid shoved Arman with his boot. Arman woke up and his eyes caught Jamshid, who put a finger to his lips. Arman pulled himself back and sat in the shadows, his eyes red from lack of sleep. He pulled out his pistol and waited.

★ ★ ★

The pasdars found the last staircase on the other side of the fourth floor leading to the top from where they had heard the noise. One pasdar leaned his ear against the door. It was quiet. He turned the handle. It opened.

A blizzard of bullets battered the door. Two of the pasdars fell backwards and the others rushed in.

★ ★ ★

"Allah-o akbar!" a voice screamed. Other voices echoed, *"Allah-o akbar! Allah-o akbar!"*

Across from Jamshid, Zari hid behind a column. She shot at the crowd that rapidly ganged up on them, their numbers increasing. Two more pasdars fell to the ground. A mujahid standing next to Jamshid yelled obscenities and fired at the moving green phantoms. Smoke of gunfire thickened, making it harder to see. Another mujahid, hit in the back, looked up in surprise, and fell on his face.

The back door opened and four more pasdars rushed in.

The mujahideen were pinned and were being butchered like animals. Bodies fell in green uniforms, in their own blood and the blood of their brothers.

Zari charged forward through the smoke, screaming her father's name, and shot two of the pasdars. One pasdar jumped up in the thick smoke of gunfire, shot her, and disappeared. Zari screamed and fell down. Jamshid rushed to grab her. She was already dead.

Five of the mujahideen fought their way to the back door, only to meet the pasdars waiting for them downstairs. They shrieked while they were slaughtered.

One pasdar beat a mujahid in the face with the butt of his gun. Jamshid rushed forward and emptied his clip frantically at the pasdar. The latter fell down but Jamshid would not stop. Bullet after bullet he fired as he shouted meaningless words, even tearing at the corpses of the already fallen men, his eyes blind with hate.

"*Stop!*" Arman cried.

Men had fallen about him, in blood, all young. One of the last mujahideen sprang to his feet. A pasdar grabbed him from the back and clung to his left leg. The mujahid turned on his stomach, pulled back his right leg, and kicked the pasdar in the face. The pasdar cried, hanging on to his broken nose. The mujahid rushed for the door. The pasdar scooped up his pistol and fired. The bullet hit the mujahid in his spine and he dropped with a moan.

Jamshid pointed at the pasdar and pulled the trigger. The pasdar fell motionless, blood spilling from his neck.

Another pasdar stepped out from behind a column, a rifle in his hand, turned around, and pulled the trigger. The bullet hit Jamshid right in his stomach. Arman shot his last two bullets at the pasdar and the soldier fell down, dead.

Jamshid stepped back in astonishment, hand to his stomach.

"Jamshid?" Arman said.

Jamshid looked at his stomach and the blood that covered his hands. He fell to his knees. Arman dragged Jamshid to the shadows and laid him on his back.

Jamshid whispered something.

Arman leaned forward. "What?"

"Why? Why do we do this, Arman?"

His head fell to one side.

Arman shut Jamshid's eyes. With the back of his right hand, he wiped the sweat off his eyes to better see Jamshid but his vision was blurred and vague as if Jamshid was a phantom disappearing into nothingness. For long moments he sat by his friend, motionless, careless of the fighting still going on in the center of the room. Blood splashed on his shirt, pants, hands, and face. He thought of Kami, his laughter, his enthusiasm, his love for Iran, and at the end his body torn to pieces by an explosion. He remembered his father, so proud, so solid in his beliefs and in his trust in Iran and Iranians. And yet his son now was not at all sure what he believed in anymore. When he looked up, the room was oddly quiet and he realized in agony that masses of dead bodies surrounded him. One pasdar turned to his side and moaned. He thought he could hear sounds of barbaric laughter in the road below. A group of them were beating somebody up. A mujahid? A pasdar? An ordinary Iranian?

A human being. Somehow he didn't think it mattered anymore.

"Freeze!"

He came to himself. His back had been to the front door and he had paid no attention. There was no excuse in a battle for that. He waited for his aggressor to pull the trigger.

"Put your hands over your head, stand up, and turn around."

As if in a dream or a hallucination, he let go of Jamshid's head, gently resting it on the floor. His hand moved to Jamshid's pocket. He pulled out the pistol and slipped it under his shirt. Then he put his hands over his head and pushed himself up with his legs. He tried to pull himself together but somehow he had lost all capability to care. It did not matter at all anymore.

When he turned around, he saw a bald man with a long beard, wearing a pasdar uniform, pointing his gun at him.

"Well, well, Arman, we finally meet."

Arman tried to look closer through the smoke. It was hard to see. He stepped forward.

The man made a nervous gesture. "Uh-uh. No bravado now."

"Who are you?"

"Commander Shirazi. I've been in charge of arresting you and delivering you to the authorities. I must say you haven't made it very easy for me."

"Why don't you shoot me then?"

"Because my friend, you've got something I need."

"What?"

"A list of names of the officers involved with the coup."

"How do you—" He stopped and then all became clear. He stepped forward. "I still don't have it. Zia?"

"I don't know what you're talking about."

"The white wig's gone and the long beard covers your scar, but I wouldn't mistake those sick eyes of yours for anyone else's."

"Listen here, Arman. I don't have time for this nonsense—"

And to his own surprise, Arman laughed. "Tell me, how did you pull it off? Oh, but let me guess. Code name Nightshade is asked to help with mission *Eagle Claw*. Well, you'd be more than happy to, in order to keep the CIA's trust and make a profit, so you say okay. But you can't do it, can you? Because you're actually working for the Islamic regime, under . . . what's your title, Zia?"

"I don't know what you're talking about. I'm Commander Shirazi—"

"Perfect. Nightshade. I knew it when I heard it."

Zia did not respond.

"That's what triggered the thought at first. You'd poison your own friends for your own needs, just like Macbeth did to the Danes. It just matched your sick sense of humor, that code name. It was something you'd do. When you're done with someone, you'd cut the life out of him, without pity."

"I don't—"

"You were afraid someone might figure you out so you had me do your job for you. I get all the people together and pull your every dirty trick. Meanwhile, you give your bosses in the Islamic regime enough evidence to come after me, but not until I get it all done for you. Now, you collect twice. You were playing both sides for fools, weren't you, Zia?"

"I don't understand what you're talking about. Now hand me the list of names of people associated with the coup. I need this information to help safeguard the regime."

"Good Lord, Zia, you never fail to amaze me. I'd rather die than give you the names, you son of a bitch."

"You're a fucking idiot, Arman. I can save you if you tell me where that list is."

"It's here." Arman pointed to his head. "And unfortunately you won't be getting it."

"Well then, I'm afraid it's time for us to say farewell, Arman."

"You killed them all, didn't you? My father, General Jalili, and David. It must have been a great surprise to David to learn that his colleague was a double agent. You covered that well, just not well enough. How many friends have you got in the system? Quite a few I would imagine. A gang, a mafia, running this country into the ground! Efficient and resourceful, in some sick way almost admirable . . . "

They could hear running footsteps outside. A few mujahideen were missing and the pasdars were searching for them. Zia thumbed the hammer. Arman shut his eyes. Zia pulled the trigger but then there was just a click that echoed in the silence.

"Shit!" Zia had run out of bullets.

Arman promptly pulled out his pistol and aimed it at Zia's head. "Seems like you wasted a lot of good bullets on the wrong people."

Zia's eyes widened and he held up his arms. "No, listen to me, Arman—"

"You killed all those people—"

"Don't do this. I'll help you—"

"You son of a bitch, you killed my father—"

"Don't even think of it, Arman." A figure walked out of the shadows, pointing his gun at Arman.

Zia turned around and then sagged. "Hamid! Thank God you're here."

Arman's jaw fell open. Here was the boy who had once known everything about him, had shared all his dreams and thoughts. And now they were on different sides.

Zia grinned, not taking his eyes off of Arman's face. "Arman and I've had a nice little chat, but now it seems we're done."

Arman continued to aim at Zia's amused face, watching Hamid from the corner of his eye. Hamid steadily pointed his gun at Arman's head.

"Seems like you're at a dead end, Arman," Zia said. "Hamid and I have been on your trail since the very beginning. We've been watching your every move. Hamid has been particularly dedicated to following this investigation. He's been obsessed with capturing you. We've done a good job, haven't we Hamid?"

"I'd say so, Commander," Hamid said.

Zia smiled and then waved a bored hand. "Shoot the bastard, Hamid."

"As you wish!"

Hamid thumbed the hammer on his gun. Arman closed his eyes. Zia laughed. Hamid smiled and turned around, pointed at Zia's neck and pulled the trigger.

Zia gave a stunned cry and fell back, choking, and died.

It took a moment for Arman to realize the bullet was not directed at him. He turned to stare at Hamid who walked to Zia and grabbed Zia's beard and pulled it off. Underneath they could see the wide scar on his right cheek.

"How did you know?" Arman asked.

"I put two and two together. Some things didn't make sense and then I heard your conversation and it all came together. I knew you were telling the truth."

"And here I was thinking you'd do it for friendship."

Hamid chuckled. "It's been a long time, Arman."

"I know. I've tried walking away from Iran, but something kept pulling me right back. Now, meeting you like this, you'd think someone was playing a cruel joke on us." He glanced around at the carnage. "Except that, somehow, I don't think it's very funny."

A door slammed downstairs.

"They'll be here any minute," Hamid said.

"You have to arrest me."

Hamid did not respond.

"I'd rather die," Arman said in a voice slightly above a whisper. "Do your friend a favor. Pull the trigger, Hamid."

Hamid hesitated, then took off his jacket and helmet. "Take these. Wear them. Use the back door leading to the river. Now get out! Otherwise we'll both get killed."

"Why are you doing this?" Arman asked as he threw on the jacket and helmet.

"For everything I owe your father."

Arman looked at him for a second and then said, "Thank you." He turned on his heels and began to run.

★ ★ ★

As Arman's shadow disappeared in the darkness and his hurried footsteps faded, Hamid looked at Zia's face. He had to decide fast. He would have to explain how a past SAVAK agent could be part of the Revolutionary Guard Corps. Why was the bullet within his body fired from a pistol belonging to a pasdar? What was the case that he had been working on? Where had Arman disappeared to? Questions would be asked that Hamid would have to answer without condemning Arman or himself.

He made his decision. He pulled Zia by his feet between the corpses, down the back stairs. He waited a short while to make sure no one was around, then dragged him through the woods and a few meters to the riverbank. The river was roaring and the wind blew harshly across it.

He threw the corpse in the river and watched it float away with the current, under the moonlight. An owl cried loudly.

He stood there for a few minutes, then walked back to the road surrounding the factory. There were corpses everywhere and in every corner. It was already midnight and the song of *azan*, the Islamic call to prayer, echoed through the city. He stood to watch Jamshid's body dragged down from the building and tossed into the back of one of the jeeps, on top of the other corpses. He watched his friend's dead face until the tailgate closed.

He watched the victorious glow on the faces of the pasdars and felt . . . weary. He sank into the front seat of one of the jeeps and listened to the distant roar of the river. The radio played the *azan*. He snapped it off, his mind pounded with millions of thoughts, one of which was louder than all. One could struggle for earthly materialistic things or crave the other world where finally all martyrs will be rewarded for earthly sufferings. It made no difference.

The pasdar started the jeep and they began to move. The words of Koran coming from the mosque made him tremble slightly. He opened his eyes and saw the complete pointlessness of the hateful intolerance and bigotry encircling him and his sheer helplessness to stop it. He saw Iran and Iranians floating in the malevolent shadows surrounding them, feeble and misplaced, and devoured by darkness.

BACK TO THE PRESENT

THIRTEEN

DOCTOR REZA KETABI WALKED down the steps of the court, holding trial papers in a folder under his left arm. Next to him walked a fragile but an obviously content Hamid. Journalists took pictures. A woman in her midthirties, an unruly curl of highlighted hair slipping out of her headscarf onto her forehead, shoved the recorder under Reza's mouth. "Did the trial go as you had planned, Doctor?"

"Absolutely. The judiciary accepted our explanation for the case and we are pleased to announce that General Rahimi will be back in the parliament to serve a second term to the interest of his party."

A man in his late sixties asked, "General Rahimi, is it true that Commander Shirazi was actually a CIA agent?"

"The case is closed and confidential," Reza said quickly. "We can make no further comments. We're just glad to have the general back with us."

Hamid held out a hand. The woman immediately put the recorder close to his face.

"As Doctor Ketabi pointed out the case is closed," Hamid said. "However, it is important that the public knows the truth. Commander Shirazi was a CIA agent. He was in fact a double agent."

"Is it true that you shot Commander Shirazi in April of 1980, General Rahimi?"

"Yes I shot him, but only after I discovered he was a double agent."

Another young reporter came forward. "You're being very blunt, General. Do you think the authorities will have a problem if we publish the entire story?"

A heavy silence fell upon the crowd. Only a week ago two journalists who had asked "un-Islamic" (i.e., anti-regime) questions were thrown into jail, and three days ago another reformist newspaper was shut down. The young man was openly smiling. Hamid looked at him for a short while and then chuckled. "I don't think they will have a problem with you publishing the entire truth."

"Why is that, sir?" the young woman asked.

"Because our officials are smart enough to realize that without freedom of press there will be no democracy. Therefore I ask of you—no I demand of you, all of you—that you publish the entire truth and continue doing so without compromise."

The crowd cheered.

Reza took Hamid by the arm and rushed him down the stairs. The driver opened the back door of a BMW. Reza sat next to Hamid and shut the door. The crowd of journalists moved to the side as the car drove off.

"You know, General, if you go on like this, I don't know if I can get you out of jail a second time. You know what you said will get published, don't you?"

"Of course. If journalists do as their superiors tell them, they may as well go and find another job. Journalism is all about free press."

Reza laughed. "Are you planning on changing the entire system, General?"

"Only the part that abuses national freedom. And it's not just me; it's the entire country that wants it changed, Doctor. Now, if you drop me off at my flat, I'd greatly appreciate it."

"Pull over," Reza told the driver. "How is your daughter doing?"

"It's been hard for her since her mother passed away. She's doing okay now. Thank you."

Reza heard the tremble in Hamid's voice. His wife had died of cancer.

"I'd ask you upstairs, but right now . . . " Hamid gestured the rest of the sentence.

"I understand."

Hamid opened the car door, but before he could leave, Reza rested a hand on his arm. "General?"

"Yes?"

He lowered his voice so that the driver would not hear him. "I'd like to know the rest of the story."

"I'm sorry?"

"You told me as much as I needed to know and that should be enough, but it's not. I would really be interested, just out of curiosity, to hear how it all ended."

"I don't understand . . . "

"Please, General, don't be afraid of me. We've been through a great deal together and I admire your courage. But . . . while you were gone, a certain man took care of your daughter. He stayed with her throughout the nights and left your house only after he heard you were acquitted. He was dressed in old clothes and—"

"He's a kind servant we used to have some while ago."

Hamid tried to get out but Reza pulled him back. "Please, General. I'm not trying to cause trouble. It's simple curiosity. What do you say? Meet me tonight around seven at the teahouse down the street. Let's talk."

Hamid hesitated then looked into Reza's face and smiled. "All right, Doctor, if it's so important to you. Let's meet and talk."

Hamid walked out and slammed the door shut. Reza watched him walk into the apartment complex. He leaned back as the car drove off.

★ ★ ★

At precisely seven o'clock—Reza looked at his watch—the curtain between his table and the next pulled aside and Hamid stepped in. In the background, soft traditional Persian music played.

"I can't stay long. My daughter is alone, you understand."

"I understand. Thank you for coming, General."

Hamid sat on the floor. A waiter pulled the curtain aside, knelt down, and poured them tea. A few moments later he left and they were alone.

"What is it you want to know, Doctor?" Hamid said.

"I want to know what happened to Arman and Melody."

"Why?"

"Because you've got me interested in their story. I tried to forget it, telling myself it's none of my business, but it doesn't help when at nights I stay awake thinking whether they met again or not. I know it's odd, but ever since I've been a child, I've been fascinated with stories of romance and this is a good one."

Hamid laughed. "What is it you want to know?"

"Where are they? How are they doing? They feel like family now."

"I trust you Doctor, but I need to make sure that the people I care about are safe."

"I promise."

"In this government a promise is not enough . . ."

"Please, General. I deserve to be trusted."

Hamid sipped his tea and then sighed. "All right. But if this story ever gets out, I'll find you Doctor and make your life a living hell. Do you understand me?"

Reza laughed even though he knew Hamid was serious. "I understand."

"All right. You noticed the man visiting my house while I've been in jail?"

"The pasdars brought him to my attention. They couldn't identify him. He had a long beard and a French cap on. None of your relatives are in Tehran, General, so obviously we wondered . . ."

Hamid frowned. "Are they still investigating it?"

"No, I asked them to drop it. Since your case was resolved, they don't care anymore. They have more important things to attend to."

Hamid seemed to be relieved. He sipped his hot tea.

"I promise this will be confidential. They won't be bothered and no one will ever know about it."

Hamid put down his cup and sighed. "I assume it's all right now. It was such a long time ago, and now that I've been acquitted it's put Arman in the clear also. Well here it goes, Doctor. Are you ready?"

Reza leaned forward.

"After Arman disappeared and I disposed of Zia's body, I didn't expect to hear from Arman again. A couple of years later, I had a visitor. I'd moved to the Mayor's office and begun to work on cleaning up Tehran. When she walked into the office, I couldn't take my eyes off of her. That was a face that would get etched in your memory—not exotically beautiful, but she had a presence about her. It was a face, a character, you'd never forget."

"Melody."

Hamid nodded. "Like no other woman would, she returned to Iran after fleeing it like a refugee. Apparently, she had checked and her name had been cleared. The Islamic Republic started to go easier on women and children after a few years, so she could get a passport. It didn't matter to her that I still worked for the government. For her, a friend would always be a friend."

"What did she want?"

"She wanted to find him."

"But you didn't know where he was."

Hamid glanced at him for a second, but then seemed to make up his mind. "I had my suspicions. I knew Arman quite well and I knew the things he wanted out of life. By nature he was a peaceful man, and after all that he would find a peaceful place to live."

"So he got out of Iran?"

"That is what she wanted to know. At first I didn't trust her, so I said he was dead. She looked back at me without blinking and . . . I still remember those words, coming at me as cold as ice. "Don't lie to me like that, Hamid. I've known you for too long. I've been receiving orchids on the anniversary of the day we met for the last two years. An old man delivers them to my flat in San Francisco. It's an Iranian agency and they don't know who requests it."

"All the way from Iran?" I asked.

"Yes," she said. "And what's more he's the only one alive who knows when we met. Except you, and I think I can count on you not sending me flowers. Am I right Hamid?"

Reza sipped his tea, a thrill overtaking him. This was an even better romance than he'd imagined. "What did you say, General?"

"How could you lie to a woman like that? She was so blunt, it completely put you off balance. There was no slyness, no deceit. She never tried to be anything. She didn't need to."

"So what else did she say?"

"That she'd come all the way from America to find him because she couldn't live without him. And that she suspected I knew where he was."

"Did you?"

"I had a friend in the Iranian Agricultural News Agency and by chance he had once mentioned a new olive farm in Zanjan, which had become quite a success in the last year. They said the owner of the farm worked very hard and he appeared to come from an 'upper' background as far as the Zanjan farmers were concerned, but he was a nice man and they respected him. I'd already guessed that Arman would not want to leave Iran because he'd be afraid that one of the opposition groups may hear of his whereabouts and he'd be pulled into something he didn't want to be involved in. So, I'd assumed that was where he'd ended up and I told her so."

"What did she say?"

"She wanted to go there immediately. So we drove to Zanjan that weekend. I still remember the scenery. It was magnificent—the olive trees against the mountains. It was spring so there was still snow on the mountain peaks but the weather was warm. The flowers had blossomed. We followed my map and reached a dirt road, then ended up having to walk several kilometers because there were no roads that led to the farm. You had to use horses or walk, so we walked. When we got there, we saw a beautiful house. Not large. Not a mansion. It was old but renovated, probably single-handedly—Arman was a good craftsman. Nobody was home. An old lady said that the owner might be in the field. She gave us some name we didn't recognize."

"Was it Arman?"

"We walked in the direction the old lady had pointed. Melody was walking ahead of me. She was in turmoil. You couldn't see it on her face, but she felt it all right. She saw him first. He was looking at an olive tree intensely. He looked up and saw her. She ran to him and he to her. She fell into his arms."

"Why hadn't he contacted her before?"

"Fear of getting her into trouble. For months, she told me later, some man used to follow her. She had called the San

Francisco police and the man disappeared but returned again. Finally, whoever it was seemed to have figured Arman was not going to her, so they left her alone. Who was he? CIA, Hezbollah, Mujahedin-e Khalgh, some other fanatic group. God knows. And she didn't care. 'It's the symbols that separate us,' she told me once. She said that was the trouble with Iranians. We couldn't live and let live."

"I see." Reza smiled. "And Julia's father was freed."

"Yes, after the Shah died, and after Khomeini finished Carter's political career, the hostages were sent home. Julia's father was one of them. They all reunited in America. He was healthy but angry."

"Who could blame him."

"So are you satisfied now, Doctor?" Hamid put down his glass of tea.

"One more thing. When did you figure out it was Commander Shirazi?"

"I don't think I really figured out it was him until the end, but I had a feeling that he was somehow involved."

"When?"

"When General Jalili was killed. As I told you, in his pocket there was a picture of this herb, Nightshade. I had a hunch that it had been blackmail, and it had apparently only started recently. I realized General Jalili must have recognized Commander Shirazi as Zia the first time we went there to investigate him. Also when I told Commander Shirazi about Nightshade he seemed disturbed. I guess he must not have expected me to figure it out. What really tipped me off, though, was when we found Zia's so-called dead body in his house. The music and the drinks were right, but the body was not. Commander Shirazi didn't know that I in fact knew the Pakrans very well. One look at the face of the murdered man, no matter how badly it had been battered, and I knew that it was not Zia Mohseni. The man lying on that couch was General Abdullah Pakran, the man who had helped raise me as a child. I knew then something was terribly wrong.

"It was obvious that someone connected with Arman was also connected with us. Every time we suspected something, Arman would end up with it. For example, how could Arman have known that the hospital guard's wife was pregnant? Why was he driving Zia's BMW, when that was the car that he had used for the kidnapping? It was too neat—far too neat to be real."

"How long do you think Zia was a double agent?"

"Probably from before the revolution. I think he decided to sell Arman to the government when Taji met with him to promise that they would reward him for Arman's death. So he thought he could pull both things off and get rewards from both parties. I think he just got in over his head."

"So when did all of it fall into place?"

"When Arman was talking to Zia in the cement factory, I was standing in the shadows listening. I knew Commander Shirazi or Zia had run out of bullets because I'd seen him use them all up, so I was ready to take over. It must've caught Zia really by surprise though, when I shot him. I'm sure he wasn't expecting it."

"Incredible story. It should be published someday."

"Someday." Hamid smiled. "But hopefully you'll wait until I'm dead. The last thing I need is the publicity of this whole thing coming up again. I already have reporters standing at my apartment door. One of them has put out a carpet and is waiting for me to come back."

Reza grinned. "I thought you said that's their job, General."

Hamid laughed. "Touché!"

Reza poured more tea. "And the man who took care of your daughter while you were gone. Arman Pakran?"

"Arman is a good man and one who keeps his friendship and word. He's also very good at disguises."

Reza smiled as Hamid stood up. "I have to go now, Doctor. Thank you for all your help. I didn't think I'd make it out alive from that rat hole, but you made a promise and you kept it. I'm very grateful."

He shook him by the hand warmly, turned, and walked away. The curtain swayed momentarily and then stayed still.

★ ★ ★

The next morning Reza took the highway to Zanjan, the city that long ago had rested on the Silk Road. He found the dirt path leading to the olive farm Hamid had mentioned and began to walk. After a few kilometers he could see a man and a woman in the field in the distance. The woman was laughing and she had a tiny scarf on. When she pulled up her head to put an olive into her mouth, Reza thought he could see a glimmer of that wild beauty. By her a man stood, his back toward him, his sleeves rolled up. He couldn't see his face. The man pulled the woman to him and she threw back her head and laughed.

Reza turned and walked back down the road.

AUTHOR'S NOTE

CEMETERY OF DREAMS is a work of fiction, which has been inspired by true events from personal experience and years of research. I haven't kept a record of all the historical and political books and articles I have read to complete this novel. As always the inspiration came first and the idea of documenting references occurred much later.

The following are some of the books I have read in order to make *Cemetery of Dreams* as accurate as possible:

Mazandi, Yusef. *Iran, abargodrat-I qarn?* Tehran, Alborz, 1373.

Lohbeck, Kurt. *Holy War, Unholy Victory: Eyewitness to the CIA's Secret War in Afghanistan.* Washington, D.C.: Regnery Gateway, 1993.

Kyle, Col. James. *The Guts to Try: The Untold Story of the Iran Hostage Rescue Mission by the On-Scene Desert Commander.* New York: Ballantine Books, 1995.

Shawcross, Williams. *The Shah's Last Ride.* New York: Touchstone, 1989.

Kinzer, Stephen. *All the Shah's Men: An American Coup and the Roots of Middle East Terror.* Hoboken, NJ: John Wiley & Sons Inc., 2003.

Dorril, Stephen. *MI6: Inside the Covert World of Her Majesty's Secret Intelligence Service.* New York: Touchstone, 2000.

Milani, Abbas. *The Persian Sphinx: Amir Abbas Hoveyda and the Riddle of the Iranian Revolution.* Washington, D.C.: Mage Publishers, 2001.

Pahlavi, Mohammad Reza. *Answer to History.* New York: Stein & Day Pub, 1982.

Pakravan, Fatemah. *Memoirs of Fatemah Pakravan.* The Center for Middle Eastern Studies of Harvard University, 1998.

Zabih, Sepehr. *The Mossadegh Era: Roots of the Irainian Revolution.* Lake View Press, 1982.

Farmanfarma, Manuchehr. *Blood & Oil: A Prince's Memoir of Iran, from the Shah to the Ayatollah.* New York: Random House, 2005.

Ghahramani, Zarah & Hillman, Robert. *My Life as a Traitor.* New York: Ferrar, Straus and Giroux, 2008.

AUTHOR'S NOTE

I WOULD LIKE TO thank the many people who have been with me on this journey; my mother, whose determination and hard work allowed me to come to America and pursue my dreams; my father, whose knowledge and love for Iran have filled me with endless stories; my editor for his invaluable insights; and my friends, who took the time to read the manuscript and offer feedback. You know who you are.

I'd also like to thank my agents, Jeff Homes (The Holmes Literary Agency) and William E. Brown (Waterside Productions, Inc.), who were the first to believe in the potential of this book. Though we went our separate ways, I'm grateful for their encouragement.

My late uncle, a well-known Iranian writer, told me long ago that if I remember only one thing, it is to never sacrifice my creativity or passion for money. A day doesn't go by that I do not miss you.

And last but definitely not least, I'd like to thank my husband, James, whose love and support have helped me survive the madness. I love you.